I0586697

WINDRUNNER

Natli VanDerWerken

Zenith Star Publishing

Aurora, Colorado

Published by Zenith Star Publishing
1505 S Norfolk St
Aurora, CO 80017
303 755-5404 (Office)
natli@natlivanderwerken.com

Cover Design © 2019 Natli VanDerWerken.com
Book Layout © 2019 Natli VanDerWerken via BookDesignTemplates.com
Books may be purchased for sales promotion by contacting the publisher.

WindRunner/Natli VanDerWerken -- 1st ed.
ISBN   978-0-9991750-3-3 (paperback)
ISBN   978-0-9991750-4-0 (ePub)
ISBN   978-0-9991750-5-7 (audiobook)

Library of Congress Control Number

Dedication

To my grandchildren:
Thomas, Owen, Breanna, Cameron, and Evan.

Inspiration comes in many forms. You are mine.

And Forever

To my husband Dan, who always, always, had my back.

Review

I couldn't put it down!

"Wow. Just Wow. What can I say but WOW. What a wonderful story. So amazing. Owen grows up in front of our eyes. Where the heck is Cameron? That darn Dragon!

Love the Elf King. The variety of characters you have written is well done. All of them are consistent in their motivations and actions from one book to the next – even as they grow-up.

I also like the number of strong women you have written. None are weaklings. They all have strengths and weaknesses at the same time.

Don't you get a foreboding feeling about the amulets? If the amulets were separated to stop anyone using them to control the dragons – it is gonna be scary once they are all in one place. Oh man – get to writing girlfriend!

Can't wait to order and get my copy! *Ann Hicks*

Contents

Dedication ....

Review ....

Map of Ard An Tir ....

Map of Ard Ri ....

Map of Red Dragon's Keep ....

Map of Fasach ....

Map of Aos Si ....

Prologue ....

Second Son 1

WindWalkers 9

Dragon in the Garden 19

Mission Assigned 31

WindRunner...35

North Meall Escape 41

Owen's Quest 53

Red Dragon's Keep 71

The Glen 79

Danger Close 91

Traders Road 101

Sir Mathin's Trail..115

Pack Attack 123

The Tolling of the Bell 137

Neulach's Search 153

The King's Messenger.. 159

The Forest King's Choice 165

The FairyFly... 171

Sir Mathin's Men.. 185

Running Battle 191

The Search for Cameron... 205

Prophecy Fulfilled... 217

A Dream of Dragons 229

Amulet.. 243

Tapestry 261

Hell's Spawn 275

WindRunners and Demons 291

Aos Si.. 305

Acknowledgements 321

Characters 322

Dictionary 327

About the Author.. 331

Other Titles by Natli VanDerWerken............................ 332

Connect with Natli VanDerWerken............................. 333

Map of Ard An Tir

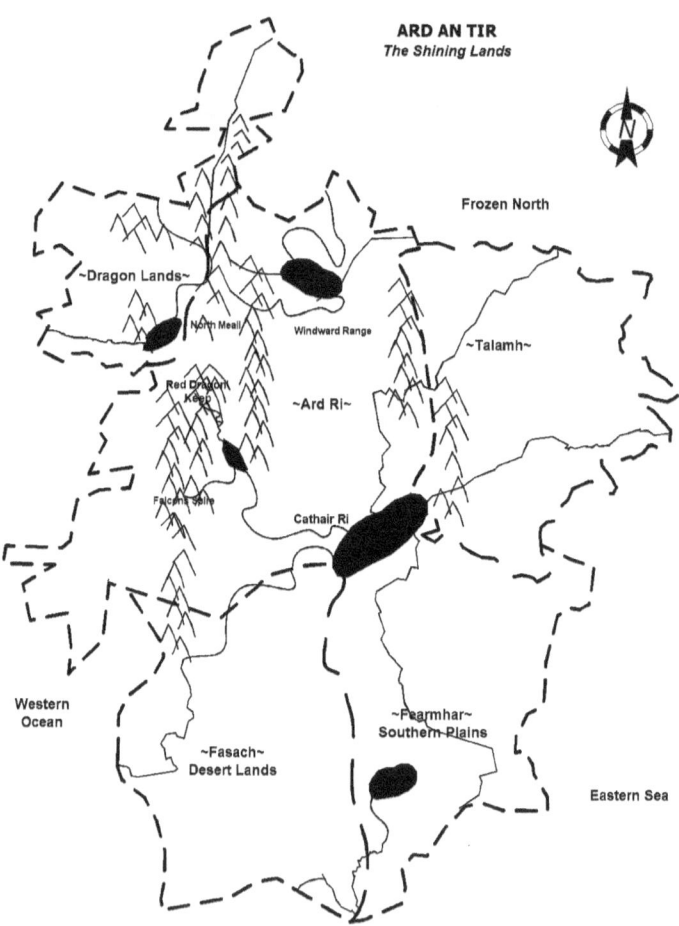

Map of Ard Ri

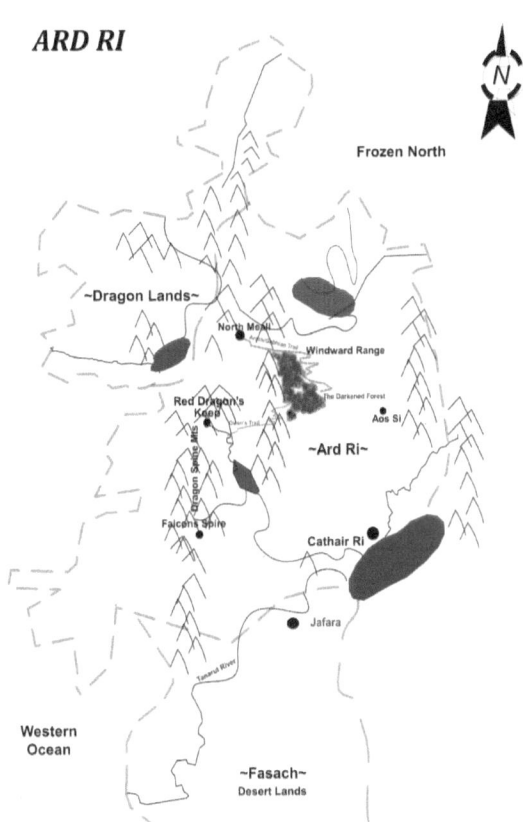

Map of Red Dragon's Keep

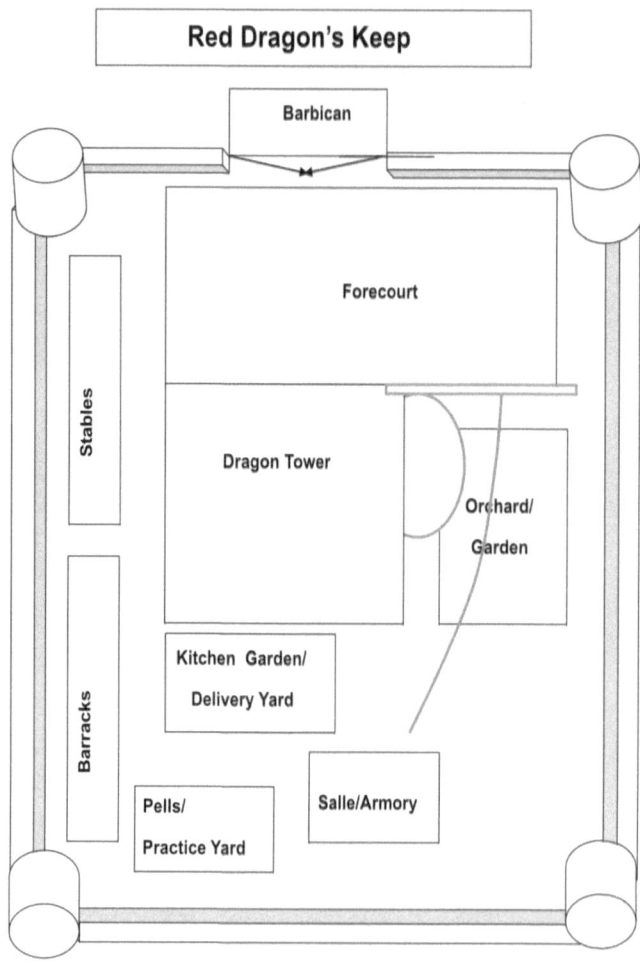

Map of Fasach

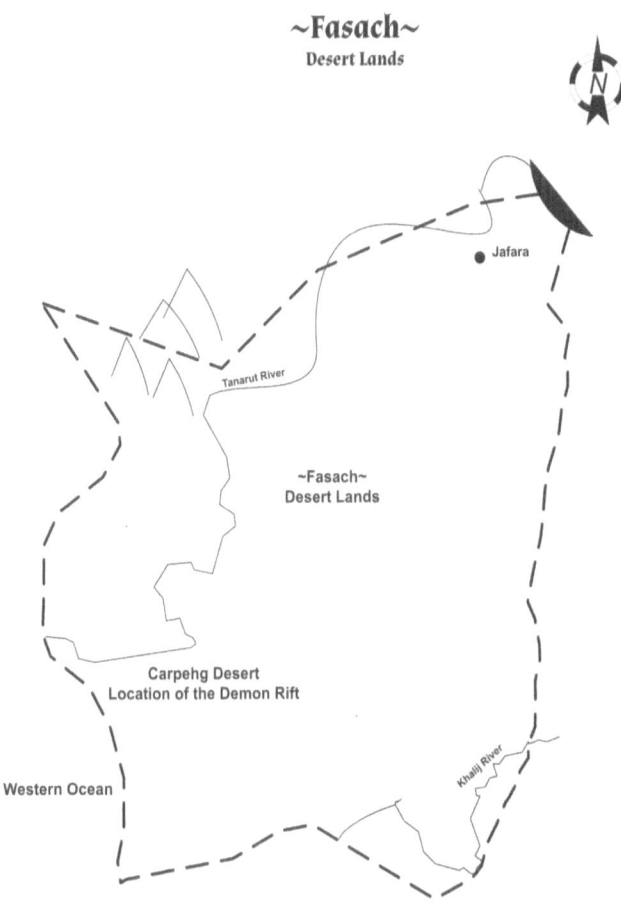

~Fasach~
Desert Lands

Jafara

Tanarut River

~Fasach~
Desert Lands

Carpehg Desert
Location of the Demon Rift

Western Ocean

Khalij River

Map of Aos Si

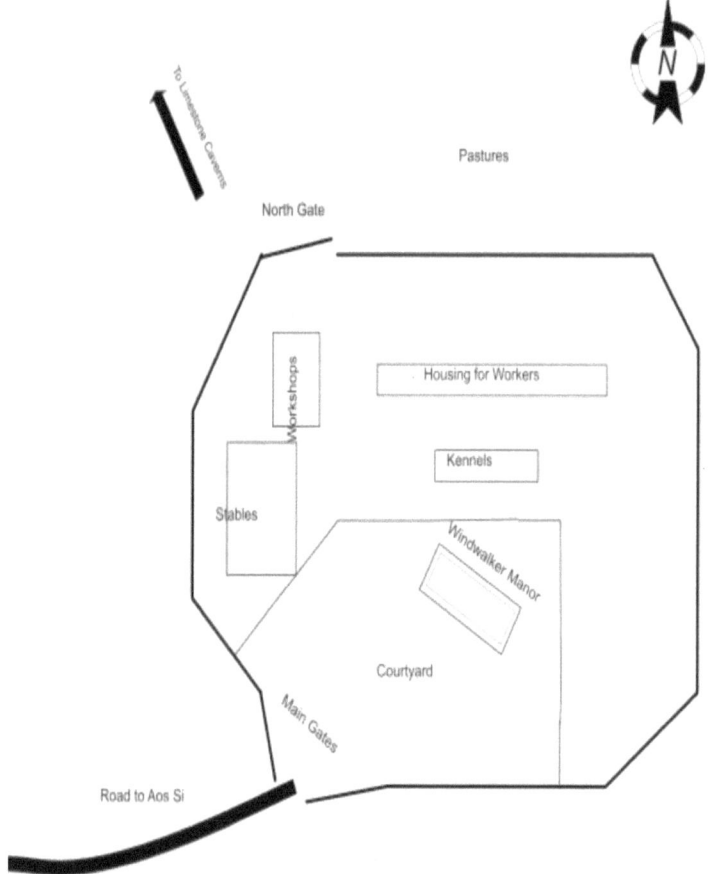

Prologue

Dragons and Demons were myths used to frighten children into obedience. Dragons once flew the skies and fought beside men against Demons in the First Demon War. Men suffered defeat after defeat until Dragons joined the battle and mages created *Claiomh Solas* — the Swords of Light. These Swords, forged by magic and tempered with Dragon fire, partnered with their chosen humans in the last desperate days of the war.

The first mage council designed the *Cumhacht ar Draigoini* Talisman — *the* Power of Dragons — to control the magical beings, binding the fearsome creatures to obedience and to death if need be. Knowing that absolute power corrupts absolutely, the council broke the Talisman into five pieces, hiding them throughout the lands of Ard Ri. For the sake of safety, guardians moved the amulets many times and, as ages passed, their locations were forgotten.

At the end of the last Demon war, the Dragon King gave every Dragon a choice: retire to Dragon lands or stay with humans, losing all knowledge of their heritage and ability to take Dragon form. Aeden, the Dragon King's daughter, chose to stay with her humans, the

Arachs of Red Dragon's Keep. Blocked from her memories, she became the Keep's weapons master and confidant of the Duke.

The King of Ard Ri ordered Lord Tom and Lady Jenni Arach, Duke and Duchess of Red Dragon's Keep as well as Lord Jeremy and Lady Anne Gobhlan of Falcon's Spire to the capital of Ard Ri to advise him on the coming Demon War. On the way, they were ambushed and kidnapped.

Thomas, first-born son and heir to Red Dragon's Keep, chose a Sword of Light when Lady Aeden judged him trained enough to merit a sword of his own. At its choosing, the sword had flashed with runes along the blade. HellReaver awoke when he and Thomas faced a Demon for the first time.

Demons attacked towns and villages, driving survivors to the Keep. As the Demons drew closer, Thomas prepared the Keep as best he could for the coming battle. Sabotage and treason slowed the preparations. Portals allowing Demons entry into the Keep were discovered and destroyed.

The Demons reached Red Dragon's Keep and attacked. Demons used portals to enter the Keep, trying to overwhelm the defenders. The heirs and their cousins fought back in desperate battles to secure the halls of the Dragon Tower.

Aeden shrieked in agony as she lay dying under the Demons clawing and shredding her body. Her agony broke her father's spell and she reclaimed her birthright, transforming into the Red Dragon.

Myths vanished as the first Dragon in a millennium awakened and broke the wardings. Spells binding magic in Red Dragon's Keep shattered. The defenders won the battle.

Thomas found the first amulet, hidden in plain sight. The hunt for the remaining four became desperate.

Chapter 1

Second Son

Owen Arach, second son of Lord Tom Arach, leaned the maul against the stump serving as a splitting block. The heavy wedge used to split logs rested on the ground where it had fallen. He bent and grabbed the split pieces, chucking them into the pile with the others he had already done.

His dark brown hair dripped with sweat and clung to his face. He wiped his face with the tail of his shirt.

I need some water, he thought. Pulling off his leather gloves and tossing them onto the pile of wood, he walked toward the shade of the evergreen trees.

Owen looked around the clearing where the team had set up to cut wood for Red Dragon's Keep. A jumble of rocks and boulders lay scattered across the meadow. The wagon they had brought to carry the wood back to the Keep sat next to two large flat-topped boulders. The men were using them to hold supplies, their own gear, and the wagon harnesses.

His dark blue eyes squinted in the bright afternoon sunlight. Waterskins he helped fill at the Keep hung from a branch in the shade. Owen walked over to the tree, grabbed a skin and poured water into his mouth. He recorked the skin and hung it back on the branch.

Late fall weather chilled the air. Standing in the shade, his sturdy body cooled down quickly. He was still shorter than his brother, but catching up fast. He lifted his grey wool coat from the boulder and shrugged into it. The clean scent of pine filled the clearing.

Owen walked over to a leafless giant of a tree and squatting down, leaned back against its rough bark. He needed a break.

In a quarter of a candlemark, a team of four soldiers dragged the trunk of a tree into the clearing. They lifted it onto the pile of logs. Owen's job was to chop them into lengths that would fit in the fireplaces of the Keep and the village.

He pushed himself to his feet and walked back to the splitting stump.

Teams of ten soldiers and a squire travelled into the forest each day to cut down trees, chop them up, and haul the wood back to the Keep.

I'll go, Owen mocked himself. *I can help get wood for the Keep.* He'd wanted to get away from the Dragon Tower for a little while. He was tired of being around so many people all of the time.

He looked across the clearing at the surrounding trees, not really seeing them. He shook his head in frustration.

What am I going to do? The war with the Demons is here and all I am is a foot soldier for my brother. He gritted his teeth and shook his head again. He needed to get back to work, let the rhythm of the maul swings tire his body and numb his mind, stop its endless recycling of the same old thoughts.

Shadows lengthened as the sun moved down toward the west. Shade shrouded the splitting block by late afternoon, bringing a return of the cold that embraced Ard Ri. Winter tightened its chilly grip on the land. Owen wiped the head of the maul clean and wrapped it in its goatskin covering. He placed it on the tailgate of the wagon. The horses that pulled the wagon grazed on long tethers tied to trees on the sun-side of the clearing.

What is your thought, Owen? HeartStriker challenged him. *You are your father's son and heir, should something happen to Thomas.*

HeartStriker leaned against the wheel of the wagon where Owen had placed it, out of his way. Owen looked sourly at the sheathed *draiochta* sword.

He'd felt as if a missing piece of his soul had fallen into place when he'd chosen the Sword. It had awakened in the presence of Demons in the armory building. Now, he was tired of it, too. It was always telling him what to do and how to feel.

His anger flared. *I'll tell you what the problem is, HeartStriker. I can't do anything to help with defending the Keep, or find Mother and Father, or...anything. I'm useless except for work like this.* He flipped his hand at the meadow, the wagon, and the pile of wood he had cut, waiting to be loaded in to the wagon.

Not true, young Owen. You are helping search the archives for information on how to defeat the Ciardha. You fought well against the Demons in the first battle for Red Dragon's Keep. You continue to train for war. These are all useful things, HeartStriker reminded him.

Owen shook his head in irritation and walked to the wood piled at the back of the wagon. The fresh sharply-sweet scent of cut pine rose from the pile. He grabbed the top piece of firewood and tossed it into the wagon bed.

He'd grown much stronger and more agile since the ambush and kidnapping of his father and mother, Duke Lord Tom and Duchess Lady Jenni Arach, on their way to the King's palace at Cathair Ri. He would turn fourteen in a month. He wanted to do something important.

Bend, grab, launch. Bend, grab, launch. The rhythm of his work soothed his angry thoughts.

He liked weapons practice. He always won when the trainers set the squires against each other. The last time that happened, he'd defeated everyone except his brother. He hoped it was because he was improving, not because HeartStriker was helping him. Marta told him he would need to start training with the soldiers to keep learning. Lady Aeden, watching from the sidelines, smiled at him when he checked to see if she was there.

Owen picked up the last hunk of wood and pitched it onto the top of the pile in the wagon. He walked over and picked up HeartStriker. The sword made no comment as he strapped the belt threaded through the scabbard around his waist. He was confused by his feelings and embarrassed he had insulted the Sword of Light.

I'm sorry, HeartStriker. I don't know what's wrong. I just feel bad, and mad, all the time. I don't want to feel like this.

The other members of the firewood party were filtering into the clearing as the shadows thickened in the forest. Everyone carried armloads of dead branches, tossing them onto the wagon. Two of their number led the horses to the tongue of the wagon and started to harness them.

The Demons that had attacked the Duchy had not returned since the first battle for Red Dragon's Keep, but it paid to be careful. They liked to attack at dawn and dusk, rarely at night. No one knew if they would try again. Owen was sure they stayed away because there was a Dragon living in the Keep, a Dragon that killed most of their horde during the last assault.

The snapping and crashing of breaking brush and small trees echoed across the clearing. The soldiers dragging the last tree trunk into the meadow dropped it and started running toward their stacked pikes and spears. A huge boar almost as tall as Owen, its tusks at least a foot long, charged out of the forest, chasing the running men. The harnessed horses went berserk, kicking and shrilling in fear as they spun around the soldiers holding their bridles.

Owen pulled HeartStriker from the scabbard and ran toward the boar. The corporal in charge of the soldiers raced up beside him, armed with a tri-blade spear. He and Owen reached the boar at the same time. The corporal planted a foot and thrust the spear into the side of the boar. Owen dodged to the other side and sliced down across the wild pig's neck. It squealed in mortal agony. Owen sliced again, almost severing the huge neck. The boar plowed forward another five feet before coming to rest near the wagon.

Owen staggered to the wagon and leaned against it with one hand, desperately pulling in air as he fought down the adrenaline and fear surging through his body. He knew how lucky they were no one had been hurt. That thing could have been Demons.

The others in the firewood party were in much the same condition as Owen. He walked around the wagon to the shaken group. "I'm sorry. I should have set a watch. It won't happen again," he told them.

"Not your fault, my lord. We should have done it ourselves," the corporal responded. "Best we get back quickly. At least we have the boar to show for our scare. It will feed a few for a while."

"Agreed," said Owen, wiping the blood from HeartStriker with leaves lying next to one of the boulders. He slid the sword into his scabbard.

The horses finally calmed. Two soldiers backed them into position on either side of the wagon tongue and buckled harnesses to the doubletree. A private climbed up to the seat at the front of the wagon and gathered the reins of the team. The corporal in charge ordered four men to stay with the body of the boar until he could send a butcher to ready it for transport to the Keep.

The private chirped to the horses and slapped the reins on their rumps. They leaned into their harnesses and with a jerk the wagon started moving. Owen jumped up onto the open end of the wagon. The rest of the men fell into formation to the rear and followed it back to the Dragon Tower.

Chapter 2

WindWalkers

The scout kicked the sides of his horse unmercifully. Desperation hammered his heart. He was the only one left of the squad of scouts sent by Lord Thomas Arach, heir to Red Dragon's Keep, to tell the Lord's aunt and uncle of the first Demon battle for the Keep. The other scouts had fallen away one by one, as men, gear, and horses failed. The horse under him faltered, stumbling badly.

"Easy, easy, Slash. You can do this. It's only another mile." He slowed the horse to a walk to give him a breather.

I am so going to be dead when they see poor Slash's condition. I had to get here as quick as I could.

The horse stumbled again. The scout reached forward and ran a hand down the sweating animal's neck. "Just a little farther, son. Just a little more."

He urged the horse back into a run as they neared the home his mount had left four years before. Slash went to Red Dragon's Keep as a rising two-year-old and had been there ever since.

After crossing mile on mile of WindWalker holdings, rider and horse could see the gates of Aos Si standing at the end of the road. The sun beat down on them as well as the fields of alfalfa and timothy stubble stretching away on either side of the road. Sparse snow covered the fields but the road was dry.

The scout slowed the running horse to a canter. The last few yards he reined Slash back to a trot as they passed through the open gates normally barring the compound. Guards posted there recognized his scout's tunic and badge and watched as he approached, letting him enter unchallenged.

The manor house on the other side of the huge courtyard rose in two stories of grey and white limestone blocks roofed with black slate tiles. A railed porch stretched across the entire front of the structure. Windows with glass panes seemed to stare down into the courtyard. Pine and leafless deciduous trees towered at each end of the building.

Outraged shouts followed the scout as he pulled the exhausted animal to a halt in front of the manor. Stablemen and women, servants and freeholders ran up and surrounded the exhausted horse and its rider. The scout vaulted from the saddle and took the stairs two at a time to pound on the carved dragonwood doors.

"Lady Debra! Lord Scott! Red Dragon's Keep has been attacked by Demons!" He dropped his hands to his knees and crouched panting as he waited.

Shouts erupted from those assembled in reaction to the news. The door wrenched open, revealing Lady Debra holding a napkin. She and her husband had been eating mid-meal. Blond hair bound into a tail by a long piece of rawhide fell to the middle of her back.

"What?" she barked. She glared with piercing blue eyes at the crowd surrounding the sweat-covered mount, blowing like a bellows. Her eyes narrowed as she focused on the scout. "What have you done to that poor horse?" she snarled as she wiped her mouth, stepping out of the door and onto the covered porch. The scout took two steps back. The lady barely came to his shoulder but she was frightening none-the-less.

Lord Scott strode up behind her. He wore rough twill trousers whose ends were stuffed into scuffed boots and a linen shirt covered by an old brown tunic. Well-worn gloves drooped from the left side of his belt where he'd tucked them. The top of Debra's head came to just under his chin.

"Wait," he said. "Come in. Let's hear this after you've had some water." He placed a hand on Debra's shoulder. She stepped back as the scout moved through the door. Lord Scott took the filthy cloak covering the exhausted man and dropped it on the floor. Debra looked back at the crowd and gestured at Slash. "Walk him. Small sips of water, no more. Get that gear off of him." Stablemen hurried to help the exhausted horse.

Debra turned and followed Scott and the scout to the greeting room, down the hall and to the left across from the dining room.

"Get some water and mead with sweetening!" Scott shouted toward the kitchen. "Deb, sit him down quick. He's going to fall."

Lady Debra grabbed the scout's arms as he swayed. He stumbled across the carpet, reeling and almost falling as she pushed him down on the seat of a wingback chair in front of the fieldstone fireplace. Covered with mud, dust and blood, he was close to collapse as the urgency of his mission left his system. She knelt next to him at the side of the chair. Embroidered grasses, vines, and flowers that grew on the Windward Range embellished her skirt, divided so she could ride astride. She had not removed the short black jacket she wore over her linen shirt, waiting for a call at any moment for a WindRunner foaling at the stable.

Quinn, the Range foreman, strode into the room from the back of the stronghold, swearing loudly.

"Who just rode in? Whoever it was, he almost killed that horse!"

Lord Scott held up his hand. "We're just going to find out." He turned to the scout.

"What's your name?"

"Idris, my lord. I'm sorry about Slash. He carried me from Red Dragon's Keep in two days instead of four. I had to reach you as quick as possible."

A maid hurried into the room carrying two tankards and thumped them onto the table next to Lady Debra. She turned and scuttled back to the kitchen.

"Here, drink this." Debra turned to the table, grabbed the tankard filled with water and handed it to Idris. He took it in shaking hands and gulped down two huge swallows. She put her hand on the tankard to keep him from gulping more. "Small sips, just like Slash. We don't want you to founder too." A small smile that did not reach her eyes twitched at the corners of her mouth.

Idris lowered the tankard. "My lord and lady, I've terrible news. Demons attacked Red Dragon's Keep. Lord Thomas ordered six of us scouts to ride to you as they started the attack. I don't know what has happened since." His voice cracked with shock and anxiety, his eyes huge.

Taking a deep breath, Idris marshalled his thoughts as he concentrated on the tankard in his hands.

"The Demons have been raiding closer and closer to the Keep," Idris continued. "Lord Thomas led a sortie to test the Demons a fortnight ago. He learned a lot about killing them."

He fell silent as the enormity of his report settled into the room and about the listeners. He began to shake.

Scott leaned heavily on the back of Debra's chair. Quinn stood rooted in shock.

Scott reached out and took the tankard of water from Idris's hands. He handed him the other tankard.

"Drink this. You need the sweet." The scent of mead filled the air as the scout took a swallow of the fermented honey and water. He stopped shaking almost immediately. He sipped some more.

Deb and Scott glanced at each other. Vague rumors of trouble passed on by the *oirfideach fáin*, the traveling bards who stopped at Aos Si, circulated throughout the home that had sheltered the WindWalker family for generations. The Aos Si fortified limestone manor was the last stop on the bard's way to Talamh or Cathair Ri. The *oirfideach* sang songs and told tales of Demon hordes attacking outlying holds and Steadings, slaughtering everyone within. Here was confirmation.

Deb stood and walked to the chair across from the scout. She gestured for him to continue as she sat.

"Lord Thomas brought back bodies of creatures no one has ever seen before. There is even one that has wings!" Idris shook his head, his face grim. "We lost twenty-two men and the captain of the castle defense. It was only through Lady Aeden's magic they won. Oh, I forgot: and Lord Thomas's Sword of Light."

He looked up to wide eyes and mouths open in wonder. He smiled crookedly.

"I can hardly believe what I'm telling you myself."

"What do you mean 'Lady Aeden's magic'? And what is a Sword of Light?" Debra demanded, incredulity lacing her questions. "Who is Lady Aeden?"

Idris shook his head. "Lady Aeden has been at the Keep for as long as I can remember. She helped Lord Tom with defenses for the Keep and scouted out problems in the duchy. She set magical traps for the ambush against the Demons using magelight. When the Demons triggered the traps, magelight actually killed some of the beasts outright. The light blinded many more so we had an easier time taking them out. I've heard she can read minds and see things we can't. Not sure about that last."

"What about this 'Sword of Light'?" questioned Lady Debra. "I remember stories about Swords of Light from the ancient Wars."

Idris shuddered. "Lady Aeden had Lord Thomas choose a sword from the armory when she decided he had enough training. There was a Demon, a 'Seleigh Soren', imprisoned in the undercroft wellroom. Lord Thomas's sword woke up and helped him kill the Demon. Lady Aeden has one, too.

I heard tell the Swords can talk to people! Masters Owen, Cameron, Evan and Mistress Breanna chose their own Swords of Light stored in the armory. So did the daughter of Faolan Haloran. He's the master sergeant who served with Lord Tom in the last Fasach war decades ago," he told his listeners. "He brought his Steading's people to the Keep when the Demons started attacking outlying towns and villages. Refugees are arriving every day."

"Where is Sir Mathin? Wasn't he in charge of Keep defenses?" Scott asked quietly. "Where are Lord Tom and Lady Jenni?"

Idris dropped his eyes and sat mute, his empty tankard dangling from his fingers. He knew of the connection among the three sisters, Anne, Debra, and Jenni. Strange things seemed to happen around them. Some mistrusted their heritage and the powers they all might have.

Debra reached out and grasped his upper arm. "Tell me," she ordered with a shake to his arm.

Idris hesitated. He spoke in a small voice, almost mumbling in dread. "Lady, your sisters, Lady Jenni and Lady Anne, and Lord Tom and Lord Jeremy were ambushed and kidnapped somewhere between the convergence of the Caladen and Banuisk rivers and Cathair Ri. They answered the order from the palace to consult with the King. Sir Mathin took half the castle guard and rode out to search for them. We'd heard nothing from anyone before we left."

Lady Debra gasped in shock and started to rise from her chair. Scott put a hand on her shoulder, pressing her firmly back into her seat. She looked up at him with a scowl. She pulled her attention back to Idris.

"Steaders and holders are fleeing to the Keep for protection. Magic portals opening paths for Demons were found everywhere in the Keep. Lady Aeden helped find the portals. The head cook tried to kill all of the Arachs and was in league with the Demons. Lord Thomas held a trial and had her hanged."

Lady Debra's fingers pressed against her lips. Tears began to leak from her eyes. She closed them and sat frozen. Scott knelt at the side of her chair and rested his hand on her arm.

"Six of us were sent to you. I'm the only one left." Idris set the empty tankard with careful precision on the table. "Three of the horses collapsed and two of the scouts were shot down as we rode through the Darkened Forest. I don't know who shot at us."

A maid quietly entered the room. "My lady, Jemis says it's time. The foal is on its way."

Rising slowly from her chair, Lady Debra took several slow, deep breaths, visibly calming herself. Idris watched her as she mastered her panic and pain. Those emotions would create havoc within the foal and its mother. Scott rose with her.

A cool gust of wind stirred the window coverings. Though it was late fall, a rare warmer day had prompted the housekeeper to throw open all of the windows to freshen the air in the manor. Lady Debra shook her head and turned to look out the window. Her lips pressed together in a thin line, she turned back to the scout.

"Scott, could you please settle Idris in the hunters hall? We'll talk more after the foaling." Scott nodded in agreement.

"Send for me when you're done," he said with quiet urgency. He reached out and pulled her to him, kissing her on her forehead.

She gave a tremulous smile and raised a hand to his cheek. "I will," she said and turned toward Quinn. "Walk with me," she requested as she took his arm.

Idris watched as they walked out of the room.

Chapter 3

Dragon in the Garden

In the purpling twilight Thomas Arach, Duke Tom Arach's oldest son, stood at the top of the stairs rising from the forecourt to the great doors of the Dragon Tower. He watched as a wagon piled high with firewood rumbled through the gates and into the courtyard. It continued around the west side of the Tower to the receiving area behind the fortress. As it started along the passage between the stables and Tower, his younger brother Owen jumped from the back of the wagon and walked toward him.

Blood splattered Owen's tunic and trousers on his sword-hand side from shoulder to mid-thigh. Thomas's arms, folded across his chest, dropped to his sides as his eyes widened in alarm. He hurried down the stairs and across the forecourt toward his brother. "What happened to you? Are you all right?" He grabbed Owen by the shoulders, stopping him in his tracks.

Owen irritably pushed Thomas away. "I'm fine. A wild boar didn't like our trespassing in his territory. One of the butchers from the village is on his way to get it ready to bring home," he told his brother belligerently.

"Owen, what's wrong? You've been nasty ever since the Keep battle. What's going on?" Thomas asked him quietly.

"Nothing," Owen muttered and stomped past Thomas, taking the stairs two at a time and entering the Tower.

Thomas shook his head in frustration and followed Owen through the doors.

Owen was nowhere to be seen. Thomas bet himself his brother had run through the great hall to escape talking to him. He shook his head again as he made his way to the high table.

His cousins, Cameron and Evan, were already in their chairs, waiting for the Arachs to come to the table. His sister Breanna came hurrying down the stairs on the left side of the hall. She threw a puzzled look at Thomas and hooked a thumb over her shoulder at the stairs. "What's wrong with Owen?" she asked.

Thomas shrugged his shoulders. "I have no idea." He stepped up the two stairs to the dais where the high table stood in front of the huge fireplace heating the room. He automatically looked at the mural painted on the wall above the fireplace opening, searching for the piece of the *Cumhacht ar Draigoini*, the talisman that controlled Dragons. Shrouded in a powerful shielding spell, hidden who knew how long ago within the mural, the amulet deceived by appearing to be a part of the rays of sun falling on some ancient King battling a Demon.

He turned away from the mural and studied the other occupants of the room. The residents who called the Dragon Tower home sat at tables in rows on the floor of the great hall, chatting to each other and eating last-meal. Thomas trusted none of them. He glanced at the four soldiers standing at parade rest on either end of the dais, also watching the residents with alert diligence. He had accepted their assignment as his bodyguards, but he still did not like it.

A hush fell over the room as Lady Aeden entered the great hall through the arch from the kitchen corridor on the west side of the room. Tall and slender, she looked slowly at the occupants of the room, smiled slightly and nodded at everyone. Quiet murmuring started up as she made her way to the high table. She mounted the dais steps and walked to the chair next to Thomas.

"There are those here who are disturbed by my presence," she told him quietly. He smiled and looked at her as if welcoming her to the table. "Can you sense them?"

"The three blacksmiths at the back of the room, two of the jewelers in the blue robes and the group of men-at-arms on the left front by the arch," he told her. "Have you seen Marta?"

She turned to face the room and took her seat next to him. She marked the people whom Thomas had identified. She smiled at the skullies who brought pitchers to the table and poured water into the diner's goblets. "I haven't seen her since weapons practice this morning. Where's Owen?" she asked.

"He got back late with the firewood crew. A wild boar attacked them and he ended up covered with blood. I think he's up taking a bath," Thomas answered her. "Did you see anything while you were 'scouting'?"

Aeden looked at him with a wry twist to her lips and a raised left eyebrow. "No, Thomas, I didn't see anything while I was flying," she murmured quietly to him alone. "I wish I had. Captain Mathin has been missing for a long time and I can't find any trace of him."

Thomas grunted.

Gregory, the seneschal for Red Dragon's Keep, strode up the steps to the high table. "Lord Thomas, I'd like to talk to you after last-meal. Something's come up that you need to know about."

Thomas waved at a chair sitting at the table. "Have you eaten yet, Gregory?"

"No I haven't, my lord. Thank you." He took a seat at the table across from Lady Aeden, nodding to her. "Lady Aeden."

She acknowledged his greeting with a small nod and a smile. "Don't look now, but we have some who wish I wasn't here."

Gregory's back stiffened. He deliberately relaxed. "I'm not surprised. Have you made note of who they are?" he asked her. She nodded. "Good. We'll put a watch on them."

Thomas shifted uneasily in his chair. A frown lowered his eyebrows under dark blond hair that had grown too long. He brushed it impatiently off his forehead.

Skullies arrived, placing bread bowls of chicken stew at each place and platters of roasted tubers and winter squash on the table. Thomas picked up his wooden spoon and started to eat. Hunger burned in his stomach after a full day of weapons practice and reading old records, looking for answers to the mystery of the Dragon Talisman.

"How are Breanna, Cameron, and Evan doing at unarmed combat?" he asked Aeden, just loud enough for her to hear.

"Well enough," she answered. "All of them learned a great deal during the battle. They know what it is to kill Demons."

Thomas shook his head with regret. "I wish they'd been spared that lesson. Just as well, I guess," he said with a sigh. "It's going to be a long war."

The low rise and fall of conversation by those eating last-meal in the great hall masked the conversation at the high table. He spooned a bite of stew into his mouth. "Any ideas about why the Demons haven't attacked again?"

Gregory grinned and nodded toward Aeden. "You're sitting next to her."

Finished with his meal, Thomas checked to see if Aeden and Gregory were done. "Gregory, you mentioned we needed to talk. Let's do it now if you're ready," Thomas said. "Lady Aeden, could you also come with us? I've got some questions I need answered."

"Of course, my lord," Gregory responded. Lady Aeden nodded in agreement.

"I'll see the rest of you in the morning," he told his siblings and cousins.

Following Aeden and Gregory from the great hall, Thomas looked furtively at the others who remained. Several of the men-at-arms were staring steadily at Aeden as she and Gregory left the room. He frowned.

HellReaver, can you keep watch on those men? They feel off, Thomas asked the Sword.

Of course, the Sword responded. *Lady Aeden frightens them. They are afraid she will see into their hearts or read their minds. Fear holds them prisoner, but they plan nothing right now,* HellReaver told him.

I didn't think to ask you about Owen, Thomas said. *I don't understand what is going on with him. Why is he so ... prickly?*

There was silence as Thomas walked toward Gregory's office. *I'm not sure,* HellReaver responded. *He is very confused and angry about something. He is very good at keeping it hidden. He needs a task.*

Thomas's eyes widened in surprise and then narrowed in thought as he walked. "Hmm."

He turned into the door to Gregory's office and stopped abruptly. Gregory and Aeden stood at the window looking out on the Lady Tower garden, staring at what sat at its heart.

A huge black Dragon, twice as large as Lady Aeden in her Dragon form, sat precisely in the middle of the garden. Tail curled neatly around its feet, enormous head dipped to bring shining black eyes level with the window, it stared calmly into the room.

"Oh ... my ... Gods," Thomas whispered in shock.

Aeden strode forward and unlatched the window, pushing it open into the frosty evening twilight. She gave a slight bow to the massive figure.

Straightening, she shook her head in bemusement. "My lord, what brings you to Red Dragon's Keep?"

With a toss of its head, a whirlwind obscured the glittering black eyes and glistening black scales, scarcely stirring the branches of the fruit trees growing in the garden. When the whirlwind died into stillness, a man stood in the Dragon's place. He was clothed in supple black leather, black knee-high riding boots, and a midnight cape seemingly sprinkled with starlight and trimmed with the white fur of mountain dire cats.

I sensed the wards breaking when the Claiomh Solas' woke. I have come to test the binding.

Thomas and Gregory jerked in surprise at the thunderous voice in their minds. Thomas's hand drifted to HellReaver's hilt and grasped it firmly. He started to pull the Sword of Light from its scabbard.

Thomas, you stand before the Arach Ri, the Dragon King. He it was who set the warding to keep your family safe. There is no danger here. HellReaver spoke quietly in his mind. *Be calm and listen.*

The man in the garden shifted to face Thomas. His black eyes, set above a large prominent nose on a long saturnine face, gleamed as he caught Thomas's eyes with his. Thomas felt as if his mind was under attack. Without thought, he slammed his shields into place. He took a step back, away from such power.

A slow smile stretched thin lips on the creature's face. *Well done, Thomas Arach. You are worthy of HellReaver.*

Anger flared at the intrusion into his mind as Thomas glared at this fabulous being out of legend, a Dragon in human form created by the first mages. Thomas turned his head toward Lady Aeden, his eyes still captured by the Dragon.

"Lady, I assume this is your father," he said with rigid politeness. "Would you be so kind as to introduce us? Although, perhaps we don't need introductions, after he's been rummaging in my mind!"

The Dragon King broke eye contact with Thomas, threw his head back and gave a shout of laughter.

"An admirable bearer of the Arach name, daughter. You have taught him well!"

Lady Aeden stepped back from the window toward Thomas, almost in front of him, as if to place herself between Thomas and the Arach Ri. Gregory stepped back to stand beside his shoulder in support. Aeden half turned toward Thomas.

"Lord Thomas Arach, heir to Red Dragon's Keep, may I introduce Lord Neulach, *Dorcha Dubh, Demon Marfoir, Arach Ri*," her voice took on a wry timbre, "My father."

Thomas gave a shallow nod. "Welcome to Red Dragon's Keep," he mocked. Aeden and Gregory inhaled sharply.

Thomas lowered his brows and narrowed his eyes at both of them. "I'll hardly be civil after being treated with such insult."

Neulach narrowed his own eyes. The awkward silence stretched. Finally he rumbled, "I beg your pardon.

Searching your mind without permission was a breach of etiquette. Let us be in good standing."

Aeden's eyes widened. She shook her head and looked at Thomas, a warning in her eyes.

Thomas nodded his head, his manner stiff. He took a deep breath and finally relaxed. "I accept your apology. There is a door to the right of this window. Aeden, will you show him in?"

"Of course, Lord Thomas." Aeden left the room. She returned in a few moments followed by Neulach. As he swept into the room, Thomas fought the urge to back away. Suddenly, the room felt much smaller. Neulach's power pressed against his body and mind, urging him to flee. Gregory turned away and walked to his desk.

"Welcome to Red Dragon's Keep." This time, Thomas's greeting was sincere.

"Thank you for your hospitality," Neulach responded. "I've come to talk with you about Demons."

Gregory riffled through a stack of papers sitting on the corner of the desk, clearly looking for something. At the black Dragon's words, he whipped around, eyes wide. "My lord, do you know where they come from? Why they are attacking? We've searched the records and can't find the answers." He closed his eyes and shook his head. "I'm sorry, my lord," he said quietly. "We've been looking for a long time. Any help would be much appreciated."

Neulach strode to a chair in front of the fireplace across from Gregory's desk. He unfastened the broach at the neck of his glistening black cape and swirled it off his shoulders onto the back of the chair. Thomas walked to the second chair and sat down as the Dragon King took his own seat. Aeden moved to the bookcase on the left side of the fireplace and leaned against it, crossing her arms over her chest.

"Would you like some mead or water, my lord?" Gregory asked.

"A mug of mead would quench my thirst," Neulach answered.

Aeden pushed herself away from the bookcase and walked to the table on the other side of the fireplace. She poured mead into a mug from the pitcher sitting there. She looked at Gregory and Thomas. Both shook their heads in refusal. She took the few steps to Neulach's chair and handed the mug to her father. She returned to the bookcase and leaned against it.

The Dragon King took a sip and nodded in appreciation. "This is very good. It's been a long time since I have had mead."

"My lord — "Thomas started to speak.

Neulach interrupted. "The Demons are coming from south Fasach. There is a tear in reality there that opens from time to time, releasing them from their world into ours. They are searching for a way to keep the Rift open, for more worlds to conquer to feed their hordes. The only thing saving this world is Dragon magic."

Silence echoed in the room.

"How did they find our world? Who controls the Rift and the Demon passage?" Thomas finally asked, a quaver in his voice. *This is worse than I thought. How can we battle a different world? How many are there?*

One step at a time, HellReaver responded, *just as you are doing now. One step at a time.*

Neulach hesitated, a deep frown drawing his brows together. He looked toward the window, avoiding the other's eyes. "In ages past, a Dragon betrayed this world. He has worn many disguises, seeking to take power and rule the lands with the Demon Overlord by his side."

Sharply indrawn breath from the two humans greeted his words.

"Who is the Dragon?" Aeden asked, her voice as hard as the blade of her sword.

"I don't know," the King of the Dragons admitted. "Many of us did not survive the last Demon War. "We think one we assumed dead turned to the dark and hid himself among humans. We have hunted him for long ages and found traces of his magic."

What can kill a Dragon? The irrelevant thought caught at Thomas's mind. He was shaken to his core. "I thought Dragons were indestructible. I guess that doesn't make sense, since the Dragon Talisman can kill them."

Neulach's head swiveled toward Thomas. The thick black brows over his eyes rose almost to his hairline. "You've found the Talisman?" the King questioned.

"No, we haven't," Gregory told him. "We found mention of it in the oldest records of the Keep. Lord Thomas found a piece of it, an amulet, hidden in the mural above the great hall fireplace. We've left it there for safekeeping."

Neulach took a slow sip from his mug. "I remember the *Cumhacht ar Draigoini* and its making. The first mages feared the Dragons and sought a means to control them. The threat of its use was a bitter draught to swallow. Its call cannot be ignored. Nor its danger to Dragons by those who would see us dead. I'd like to look at this amulet when there is time."

He finished the rest of his mead.

"Lord Neulach, I am remiss in offering you hospitality. Have you eaten this evening?" Thomas asked.

"It's kind of you to ask, Lord Thomas. I've already dined," the Dragon responded. He and Aeden shared a look. Dragons needed to hunt and sheep were good eating.

"You'll stay for the night," Thomas invited.

"I will. Thank you. I have much to discuss with Lady Aeden."

Thomas stood, as did the Dragon King.

"Gregory, you and I are done here. Lady, perhaps you can show your father the amulet." He gave a short bow to Neulach and Aeden. "We'll see you in the morning."

"Good night," chorused Aeden and Neulach.

Neulach turned toward Aeden. "It is good to see you again, daughter."

Aeden smiled. "Come. Join me in my quarters. You like the dark red wines, as I recall. We can stop at the mural on the way."

Chapter 4

Mission Assigned

Thomas stormed into the library and slammed his fists onto the table. Owen sat reading one of the Keep's records at the other end. His head jerked up in surprise. He lowered it in shame.

The morning sun shining through the windows made the room warm and cheerful in the deepest days of winter. Thomas's rage seemed to raise the temperature in the room even more.

"What were you thinking? Why didn't you set a guard? That boar could have been Demons!" Thomas shouted at his brother.

Owen fidgeted in his chair. He refused to look at Thomas. "I know," he mumbled. "Look," he spoke through gritted teeth as his own anger started to rise.

He raised his head and glared at Thomas. "I apologized and took the blame. The corporal in charge said he should have set the guard."

Thomas sighed as the rage drained from his body. He shook his head in frustrated resignation.

"I don't know what's going on with you, but it's got to stop. You're going to get somebody killed and we can't afford to lose anyone.

Gregory told me this morning about what happened to you on the firewood assignment. I talked it over with him and I've decided I want you to take twenty soldiers and ride to Aos Si."

Owen's eyes snapped to Thomas's face and remained riveted on him. "We have to get Aunt Debra and Uncle Scott to send us more of their wardogs and warhorses. You can look for Mother and Father and Captain Mathin at the same time."

"Are you sure? You really think I can do this?" he asked, the pitch of his voice rising. "After what you just learned?"

"Yes," said Thomas. "Someone has got to go looking and I can't. I think it is best if you have a task away from the Tower. You should probably leave tomorrow or the next day. I've spoken with Sergeant Haloran and he's putting together a column to ride with you to the Windward Range."

Owen slowly stood up. A wide grin stretched across his face. "I can do this. I know I can. I can really help you. Thanks, Thomas."

"Let's get you started packing," Thomas said. "I don't think you should take a wagon, although the trip is going to take at least five days. Maybe some pack horses."

He stood in thought, arms crossed, lips pursed, looking out the Library window. With a curt nod of his head, he made his decision. "Yes, that's a good plan. Let's get to it."

Owen and Thomas walked out of the Library, discussing Owen's trip.

Chapter 5

WindRunner

Last-meal was finished. Family and guests sat at the head table, quietly discussing ideas for Owen's departure in the morning.

Shouts of alarm echoed from the forecourt into the great hall. Thomas and Aeden rose from their chairs. Gregory twisted around to face the end of the great hall.

The doors slammed open and hit the walls on either side with a resounding crack, rebounding half way closed. A huge animal, black as night, shouldered the heavy wood out of its way.

Owen descended the stairs from the family corridor, returning with a book he wanted to share with Cameron. He stumbled to a halt as he stared at the creature in the doorway. Men drew swords and grabbing for any weapon they could lay their hands on.

"Hold!" The command froze everyone in place. Aeden stood by her chair, looking at the creature.

She took three steps toward it and bowed deeply. "*Gaothsiuloir* – WindRunner – you honor us. How may we help you?" She waved her hand, releasing her spell of immobility. Those assembled in the hall slowly lowered weapons and sat.

The WindRunner resembled a warhorse, but twice again its size. He gazed imperiously over the assembly. A toss of his head sent an impossibly long forelock and mane floating about his head and neck. The WindRunner fastened his glistening black eyes on Owen.

Owen sucked in a breath. The book he was carrying slipped from his fingers and thudded on the stairs.

I have come for you. The WindRunner's voice echoed in the minds of everyone.

Murmurs rippled around the great hall. The WindRunner paced into the room and up the aisle between tables and benches. Owen turned as if to run back up the stairs but hesitated.

What if it follows me up? He stood rooted on the fourth stair from the bottom.

Owen felt he was shrinking as the giant creature approached. He began to tremble with a combination of fear and anticipation. His throat turned dry and his breathing increased, making him light-headed.

I choose you. Gather your things and come with me.

Owen darted his eyes toward the high table. Everyone there sat or stood in absolute silence, eyes wide and some mouths hanging open.

"Lady Aeden, would you please introduce us, since you seem to know ... him?" Thomas asked. He looked wary, thoughtful and concerned, his lips compressed into a thin line.

"Of course, Lord Thomas." She turned to face him." This is a WindRunner from the great plains of the Windward Range."

My name is Navar. I have come for the second son.

Lady Aeden gave a shallow bow to the WindRunner. "As you say, Navar." She kept her eyes on the living legend. "WindRunners choose a rider only in the most dire need. Master Owen has been chosen by Navar for the Windward Range."

"Well then, it's a good thing Owen is already going to Aos Si," Thomas said with iron self-control. "Welcome WindRunner. Would you rest here for one day while Owen prepares?"

The creature from myth swung his head toward the high table and regarded Thomas. Silence stretched.

He finally spoke to the minds of everyone in the hall. *I will wait.*

"What can we do to make your stay more pleasant?" Aeden asked.

I need a warm room and water. The WindRunner looked at the others gathered at the high table.

Greetings, Arach Ri. It has been long since we last spoke.

Neulach gave a small nod of his head. "Greetings, Navar. Need calls us once again."

So it does. Darkness and slaughter march across the land. It is well you have come from your citadels in the wilderness. The waking of the Swords of Light has roused more danger than anyone realizes. He lashed his tail in agitation. *I greet all of you Claiomh Solas. Well met.*

The Swords of Light, never far from their chosen, murmured greetings, causing a shudder to pass through those still lingering in the great hall. Most had slipped away as the highborn spoke.

"What if I don't want to go with him?" Owen spoke loudly into the quiet.

Silence greeted his words.

HeartStriker rebuked him. *Do you want the Dark to swallow your home and this land? You are needed where fate takes you. Be silent and learn.*

Owen clamped his mouth shut and flared his nostrils, crossing his arms over his chest in a display of mulish stubbornness. He looked at his brother, who gave a tiny shake of his head. Thomas's eyes looked up the stairway and then back at Owen.

Owen took the hint. He bowed to the high table and to Navar. "I need to finish packing. Good night." He turned and marched back up the stairs.

"I'm not sure of the protocol, Navar. Do you want a room here in the Dragon Tower or would you prefer a place in the stable?" Thomas asked the WindRunner.

An open box stall will suffice, Navar responded.

"Lady Aeden, would you show Navar to the stables please?" Thomas asked. "He is our honored guest and will have whatever he needs."

"Of course, my lord. If you'd come with me, Navar?" Aeden ushered the WindRunner from the hall.

"Lord Thomas, I shall seek my bed as well," Neulach said. "Thank you for your hospitality. I look forward to seeing you in the morning." He pushed his chair back from the table and left for Aeden's rooms behind the salle.

"I'm off to bed too," Thomas said. He climbed the stairs to the family hall.

Thomas went to Owen's room and knocked on the door.

"Come in," Owen said.

"What was that about?" Thomas asked his brother as he entered the room. "You were willing to go this morning. What changed?"

A grimace twisted Owen's face. "Why should I go with him? Do we even know if this thing is good? What if it just wants to get me away and kill me?" With each question, Owen's voice rose higher and higher. Fury reddened his face.

Thomas reached out to put a hand on Owen's shoulder. Owen flinched and ducked away from him. Thomas clenched his hand into a fist. He was sorely tempted to punch his brother. Slowly he lowered his arm to his side.

"Look," he said. "Fighting won't solve anything. You're mad because you're — concerned — about the future. We all are. We just have to do the best we can and hope everything turns out. I *need* you to get to Aos Si and get more horses and wardogs. I *need* you to look for Father and Mother. Remember the legends? Remember what we read in the records? WindRunners are valuable allies and fighting partners. Don't anger this one."

Owen hung his head. He looked up at his brother with fear in his eyes. "I'm afraid," he whispered.

Thomas took two steps forward and dragged him into a hug. He held tight. "So am I," he muttered back.

Chapter 6

North Meall Escape

Jenni Arach, wife of Lord Tom Arach, Duke of Red Dragon's Keep, moved her fingers back and forth, back and forth. She used a tiny saw, a very thin flexible piece of diamond-dust coated wire with small rings at each end, she had concealed in the hem of her tunic. She scraped the wire against the manacle encircling her right wrist. *Thank the Three Gods Da taught us to be prepared for anything!* She'd already freed her left wrist.

The guards who shoved her into this cell in the dungeons of wherever she was had not searched her or chained her wrists behind her, or chained her to the rings bolted to the walls above her. She'd made sure to set the thought that she was harmless firmly in their minds. The quiet grinding rasp of the saw whispered lower and lower as it bit into the iron. With a final snap, the manacle parted. She stood and set the edge of the opening onto the ring anchored in the wall, slowly allowing her full weight to hang from it to stretch the weak metal. The gap of the cut widened as she watched. She brought her fingers together, making her palm as narrow as possible and carefully pulled her hand through the cuff. She was free.

Jenni shook her aching wrists. The skin was chafed and rubbed raw in several places. She massaged them with careful pressure, trying to relieve the pain from wearing manacles for so long.

The sword-cut on her left thigh burned. The wound had not stopped leaking fluids since she'd taken the cut during her last battle with the kidnappers.

She breathed slowly and deeply, mastering the fury that was her constant companion. Fury that had consumed her ever since she, her husband, sister, and brother-in-law were ambushed on their way to Cathair Ri.

Her cell was filthy. She was filthy. Her clothes were stiff with grime and dried blood. Dirty straw covered the floor of the cell and a bucket for slops sat in the far corner. She walked over to the door of the cell.

Looping the saw around the bolt of the lock, she began to pull on one end followed by the other. She worked for perhaps a quarter of a candlemark. Her efforts were rewarded when the bolt dropped away into two pieces. The door tried to open into her cell. She rested her hands and forehead against the wood and waited. No sounds echoed through the dungeon.

She'd started her work on the manacles when night fell. The starlight through the tiny opening at the top of the wall of her cell told her it was nearing the third candlemark of the morning. It was the time when the night watch was least alert.

Slowly she allowed the weight of the door to swing it inward. Tiny shrieks of ungreased hinges tried to betray her. Had she allowed the door to open more quickly, the hinges would have screeched unbearably. She inched her eye past the frame to check the corridor for guards as soon as the door opened wide enough.

Light flickered from burning torches set in metal brackets mounted along the wall. She saw no guards.

Jenni took the time to tie her brown hair, dirty from her long captivity, into a tail down her back with a strip of cloth torn from the hem of her shirt. She slipped out of her cell and limped to the door at the end of the hall barring the way. The door was unlocked. She pushed the door open with slow deliberation to muffle the shriek of hinges.

A guard was fast asleep at a table set sideways next to the door. Breathing through her mouth to quiet her passage, she inched past the table. She picked up the knife resting by the guard's hand. With a quick thrust, she slipped the knife between his ribs, making sure he would never wake again.

Jenni grabbed the ring of keys dangling from a hook on the wall next to the table and re-entered the corridor. Limping with the pain from her injured thigh, she moved past her cell and beyond it to the next door. She inserted a key that looked like it might fit into the lock and turned. The lock snapped open. She pushed the door into the cell and saw her sister Anne, manacles in pieces on the floor, sleeping on a pile of straw closest to the door.

Jenni squatted down and gently shook Anne's shoulder. She woke up fast, ready to fight whoever had awakened her. "Easy," Jenni cautioned. "It's me. Why are you still in here?"

Anne glared. "I was afraid the guards would hear if I tried to saw the door open. I closed my eyes for just a second and fell asleep."

"It's all right, Anne. Let's get Tom and Jeremy out."

Anne rubbed the sleep from her deep brown eyes. "How long have you been free?" she whispered. Dried blood coated her wrists. Her long brown hair was tangled, dirty, and held bits and pieces of straw. She pushed to her feet.

"About a candlemark, I think," Jenni responded. She limped back out into the hall, making her way to the two doors beyond Anne's cell. She inserted the key and opened the locks. Jeremy sat chained to the wall in the cell next to Anne's, his clothing in shreds. His dark blond hair fell past his shoulders in twisted clumps. His blue eyes squinted as she pushed the door open. No one was in the cell beyond.

Jenni began to panic. *Where is he? If they have done anything to him ...* Her teeth clenched, lips drawn back, baring them in rage.

She stumbled across the hall and opened the door. The cell was empty. She continued opening doors until she came to the last one next to the door at the end of the hall. Lord Tom Arach hung from chains bolted to the wall, his face pressed against it. He was shirtless. The black and red Dragon tattoo riding his right arm, curling up and over his shoulder, echoed the color of the bruises, lash-marks, and dried blood covering his back. With a voiceless wail of dread, Jenni rushed into the cell and over to him, dropping the keys on her way.

"Tom! Tom! Are you all right?"

Slowly he turned his head and looked at her with glazed blue eyes as she laid her hand on the side of his face. "Water," he rasped on a dry throat.

Forgetting the pain burning in her leg, Jenni dashed out of the cell and through the door into the guardroom. She grabbed the bucket sitting next to the table and hurried back to her husband. She cupped her hands and raised them to his mouth, dribbling water onto his tongue. She repeated the motion until he turned his head away, water dripping from his mustache and goatee. Dried blood matted his red-gold hair.

Jenni stepped back and looked at his manacles, finally remembering the keys she'd dropped on the floor. Grabbing up the ring, she sorted through them and found a smaller one that might fit the manacles. She moved to his left arm, fitted the key into the lock and turned it. The lock snapped open. She pulled the manacle apart, releasing his hand and arm. She caught his hand and lowered it to his side. Unlocking the right manacle, Jenni took his weight as he started to slump to the ground.

"Out into the corridor," she ordered. "Come on, Tom. You can do this." She pulled his right arm over her shoulders and helped him hobble into the corridor. She let him slide down to rest against the wall. As his back touched it, he jerked forward with a grunt of pain.

Jenni hurried to Jeremy's cell. "The key to the manacles is on here," she told Anne as she tossed her the keyring. "I've got water down at the end of the hall. Let me know if you need help." She hurried back to Tom's cell and grabbed the bucket of water. She brought it out and squatted next to him. Dipping her hands in the water, she poured a palm-full into his mouth.

"Thanks, Jenni. What time is it? When will the guards change?" Tom mumbled. He was starting to think again.

"We've got maybe a candlemark. I've been free about that long. Can you walk?" she asked him urgently.

"I don't know. Can you help me up?" She stood up and reached down for his hand. They grasped forearms and she heaved him to his feet. He leaned back against the wall, his head hanging, hands on knees, struggling to stand. He slowly straightened and grabbed her in a desperate hug. "Are you all right?"

Jenni nodded. "What happened to you? When did they beat you? I didn't hear anything!" She was almost in tears.

"They took me up to the guard room," Tom told her. "Tilden and his son were there and ordered the beating. They tried to force me to tell them what the King ordered. I almost told them when they threatened the rest of you."

Noise down the hall jerked Jenni's head to the left. She saw Anne support Jeremy out of his cell. He was in better shape than Tom. He could at least walk. Anne helped him hobble to the water bucket. He leaned up against the wall and Anne lifted the bucket to his mouth. He took several deep swallows and pushed the bucket away.

Jenni pointed to the end of the hall. "We've got to get out of here. The guardroom is through that door. Beyond the room are stairs going up. Can you make it?" Jenni asked, looking at the two men.

"Let's go," Jeremy said.

"Yes," Tom responded.

Jenni pulled the door open. The dead guard's head lay on the table, a pool of blood on the floor beneath him. Anne grabbed his sword and the knife as she passed the table. The men gave Jenni a long look. She looked back with narrowed eyes and thin lips.

The four former captives made their way to the top of the stairs. Jenni cautiously pushed the door open and peered into the dim light of a hallway. No one was about.

"Let's get to the end of the hall and see if we can figure out where our equipment is," Jeremy suggested.

They turned left and followed the corridor to its end. No doors opened into the hallway. The corridor ended at another guardroom in front of a room filled with weapons. They had found the armory.

Tom was moving more easily as they entered the guardroom. "Where is everyone?" he asked. "This room should have at least one guard." He eased the door on the other side of the room open and stopped abruptly as heavy snoring echoed from the barracks across the hallway.

"Um," Anne said. "I kind of made everyone extra tired. They're probably all asleep."

Both men looked at her with interest. "I didn't know you could do that," Jeremy remarked.

"I've never needed to use it before," she said quietly.

"Come on. Let's see if our stuff is in there," Jenni's impatience was clear.

Their swords and knives lay in a haphazard pile on top of a table in the center of the room.

"I need a shirt and so does Jeremy. Could someone check in the trunks along the wall?" Tom asked.

Anne went to the chests sitting under pegs holding swords and shields. She rifled through two of them before she found shirts that would fit the men. In the last chest, she found a small bag of silver coins.

Tom gingerly shrugged into the shirt Anne handed to him, trying not to let it touch his lacerated skin. He walked around the table instead of leaning across it to pick up his sword, not wanting to rip open the scabs on his back.

The men strapped on their scabbards. Sliding swords home, they grabbed up their knives and returned them to leg and arm sheaths, strapping those on as well.

"We need to find the stables," Anne said as she slid her sword into its scabbard and flipped its retaining strap into place. Jenni checked to make sure her sword would slide easily from its scabbard.

"By rights, this passage should lead to them," Tom rasped on a dry throat and waved toward the end of the hall

They left the armory, back through the room where cloaks and boots sat waiting for the change of guard. Each of them grabbed a cloak, hood and boots and pulled them on. Tom took four extra cloaks. Footsteps slow and quiet, they moved to the end of the hallway. Pushing the door open into a courtyard, they found the path to the stables and took it. Light snow filtered down from a leaden sky.

As they entered the stables, Tom's warhorse snorted in greeting. A stableman sat fast asleep, leaning against the wall. As they entered, he stirred and shifted position. He fell quiet again.

Anne slowly took down a shielded flickering lantern from a post by the door and made her way to the tack room. Jenni followed close behind.

They gathered saddles and bridles and returned as Tom and Jeremy backed the horses and a packhorse from their stalls. They swung saddles on the horses and loaded the panniers on the packhorse as quickly as they could. Anne went to each stall and untied every horse. She set a compulsion to run from danger deep in their minds. She returned to the others and the four led their horses from the stables, leaving the doors open wide.

"Wait," Jenni hissed. "We need food. Anne, let's go to the kitchen. I think it's right over there."

Leaving the men holding the restive horses, she and Anne hurried across the courtyard and entered the kitchen through a half opened door. The cook and skullies that worked in the kitchen slumped over the center table and along the hall between the kitchen and dining room.

The women stepped carefully over and around them and entered the storerooms. Anne pulled down a small cauldron, frying pan, plates, and utensils, stowing them in a sack she found next to the door. Jenni grabbed flour and salt, dried meat and vegetables and shoved them haphazardly onto a large square of canvas she had grabbed from the stables.

Only a tenth of a candlemark passed before they pushed back through the door with bundles of food and supplies they had difficulty carrying. They hurried across the courtyard to the men and handed out bundles. "Load them on the packhorse. This should last us for at least five days."

As soon as the supplies were loaded, they led the horses toward the main gate. Tom looked at the walls and snorted. "It's not even a castle, just a fortified manor," he said.

Jeremy unbarred the gate and pushed it open with a squeal of neglected hinges. They hurried their horses through as he pushed the gate all the way open, propped the crossbar against it, jamming the opposite end into the ground. It would hold for a while.

They mounted their horses and kicked them into a canter away from their captivity and into the pearl light of the rising sun. As they rode, Anne triggered the compulsion in the horses' minds and listened as the thunder of pounding hooves obliterated their trail.

§ § §

They dared not follow the road that headed south and east from the manor. Someone would surely see them.

"We need to head cross-country," Jenni said as the group trotted along the game trail they had taken into the forest away from the road. Slow and steady movement for two candlemarks had seen them far from the manor.

"I think we're near the eastern edge of North Meall," she said. "Tom, do you recognize those peaks to the northwest?"

Jenni knew he had hunted and scouted all along the Dragon's Spine as a boy and young man. The group slowed to a halt as they came to a clearing in the forest. Tom reined his horse around to look toward the mountains. He glanced at the sky where the sun rose almost to mid-day. He turned his horse in a slow circle and surveyed the terrain.

"That's Sliav Brón, the Mountain of Mourning," he told her. "You're right. We're too far north if we're making for the Windward Range. Southeast will see us to the Plains River and from there it's a two or three day ride to Aos Si. I think there are a couple of villages where we can stop and buy more supplies."

"Tom, you're not looking too good," Jeremy said. "I think it might be time to scout around for a place to lie up. We all need rest."

Anne looked uneasily back down the path they had taken. "I think we need to keep going for at least another candlemark, two if we can. Something follows."

All of them turned to look back down the path. Jeremy reached over and put a hand on her arm, concern roughening his voice. "Do you know what it is?"

Anne shook her head in frustration. "No. I don't think it's human, though. We need to keep moving. Tom, is this the Darkened Forest?"

A shudder visibly ran through all of them. Tom answered, hesitation clear in his voice. "I think it might be. Probably the northern edge. We need to be quiet and careful. We don't want to wake whatever sleeps here. We should get out of it and keep to the grasslands as much as possible."

Jenni reined her horse to the southeast and urged it into a walk toward another game trail leading out of the clearing. "We need to get going." The others followed her lead.

Chapter 7

Owen's Quest

Navar waited impatiently, pacing back and forth in front of the doors of the Dragon Tower. The rising sun slowly lit the forecourt, highlighting the red Dragon laid in stone up the Tower's east wall. He had been away from the Windward Range too long.

This one comes unwillingly. I do not understand. Every rider I have ever called felt honored by the choosing. He tossed his head and laid his ears flat. He stamped his hoof on the stone of the court.

Angry. I am angry! He paused in his pacing, astonished. His ears flicked forward. *It has been too long since I have answered the call to choose.*

From within the hall, HeartStriker spoke to the WindRunner. *Slowly, Navar. Go slowly with him. He is very young.*

Young or not, he should be honored and show his gratitude for the choosing. Have these humans lost all knowledge of us? Navar snapped.

They have, the Sword of Light responded. *We are but legends and myths to them and not thought of often. I am not certain even yet they believe. We must train them and help them remember the truth about us.*

The WindRunner shook his head. *This will be difficult. I am not patient.* He paused and dropped his nose to the ground, searching for stray bits of hay or grain. *Well. A lesson to re-learn.*

The troop of soldiers and pack animals chosen to accompany Navar and Owen on their journey stood quietly near the gates to the forecourt, as far from Navar as possible. The horses shifted uneasily, their riders quieting them with voice and touch.

Everyone waited.

$$ § § § $$

Owen stood at the doorway of his room, looking at all the things he had collected. Rocks, an empty wasp nest, wooden toys, a bunch of knives. His saddlebags slumped at his feet. Doubt tightened his throat. He struggled to breathe around it. *I don't want to go.* Tears threatened to fall and he blinked them back.

HeartStriker spoke to him in the quiet. *All is well, Owen. I would say 'be careful what you wish for', but I think you already know that.*

The gentle mocking of the Sword's voice slid through Owen's mind. The tightness in his throat eased. *I've never been away from home. I don't know if I can do this.*

He wiped the water from his eyes with his sleeve. Reaching down, he hefted the saddlebags onto his shoulder and pulled the door to his room closed. The thump of his riding boots on the stone of the corridor echoed the beat of his heart as he made his way to the stairwell and down to the great hall.

All of his siblings and cousins had gathered behind of the main table to see him off. Lady Aeden and guests of the family stood in front of the table holding mugs of cider. Owen stopped at the bottom stair and just watched them. Another lump closed his throat.

HeartStriker, I might never see them again!

Truth, Owen. But that must not keep us from going forward. None of us are assured of tomorrow. Live each day in itself.

With that thought rolling over in his mind, Owen stepped off the stair and made his way to the table. Thomas turned from talking with Marta and faced him. His movement alerted the others and they looked at him as well. Lady Aeden nodded to him, her face unsmiling.

Breanna ran to him and hugged him tight. He patted her on the shoulder. "It's all right, Breanna." He swallowed the distress in his throat and blinked away the tears that threatened. "I need to do this."

She released him, her lips pressed into a thin line, holding back her own worry. They joined the others, his arm still across her shoulders. Owen picked up a mug and drank it down. "Will we have first-meal as we ride?" he asked his brother as he set the mug back on the table.

"That's the plan," Thomas answered, looking at his own mug as he turned it around and around in his hands. "Navar wants to start as soon as possible." He set the mug on the table next to Owen's and looked at him. "Owen, listen to HeartStriker and Navar. I ..."

"I will. I know they know more than I do. I'll send a scout to report to you when we get to Aos Si," Owen interrupted. He was numb. His life was moving forward as if he had no choice. He started walking toward the forecourt.

"Wait, Owen." Thomas said. Owen stopped and looked back toward his brother.

"I've asked Lady Aeden to scout ahead of your column, at least as far as the Darkened Forest. I'd really like to send her with you, but I need her here. Reports have come in of Demons gathering to the west. I'm not sure the scouts I sent to Aos Si before the Demon battle made it. She'll look for signs of their passage. I've got a bad feeling about this."

"Thanks, Thomas. I'll be fine," Owen said. The family followed him down the aisle between the tables and benches. He reached the doors, pulling open the one on his right. Cold air flowed into the room.

Owen stepped onto the landing at the top of the stairs going down to the forecourt. Lady Aeden followed him as the rest crowded out of the door.

The huge black WindRunner reared and pivoted to face the doors. His eyes locked on Owen as his front hooves found the flagstone of the forecourt. Owen wanted to step back and away as the WindRunner's thoughts pressed on his mind. He shook his head sharply, as if shaking water from his hair, and raised the mind shields Aeden had taught him.

With steps of infinite slowness, the WindRunner moved closer and closer. The pressure of mind against mind increased. A startled cry erupted from Owen as Navar's thoughts began to cascade through a tiny crack in Owen's shield. He reeled back against Thomas. His shields fell. So did Owen, to his knees. His hands reached up and grabbed his temples as if to keep his head from exploding.

A completely new world roared into his mind. He smelled the cold air and the sweet scent of hay and grain in the stables. The scent of men and warm horses distracted him. He caught the Dragon musk clinging to Lady Aeden and Lord Neulach, making him instantly wary. Sounds normally muted rang loudly in his ears. Shouts of dismay echoed around the forecourt.

HeartStriker hastily raised a barrier between Owen and Navar. Owen knelt there, trying to make sense of what had just happened. Slowly he raised his head. The glittering black depths of the WindRunner's stare captured his eyes.

You sense so little. I'm sorry I let you feel so much all at once. It has been a very long time since I have partnered with a human. We must join our minds and learn together. Navar sounded apologetic.

Owen glared at the black creature. He tried hard to bring his anger under control. "It's all right, Navar," Owen spoke aloud through teeth clenched tight. His breath was a harsh panting. "We'll learn from each other."

His mind ached fiercely. As he slowly rose to his feet, HeartStriker took the pain from him. Owen sighed in relief.

Navar raised his head and looked at everyone on the stairway. *We should leave now. Bring another saddle and headstall. As we travel, I will teach you what you need to know to ride a WindRunner. For now, your warhorse will do.*

He sent a picture of what he needed to Owen. Owen called the stableman to his side and relayed Navar's request.

Lady Aeden walked down the stairs. "I'll leave now to scout ahead." She strode to the right side of the forecourt, raised her arms and called her magic.

The air began to swirl around her, growing into a roaring, tearing whirlwind. As it lifted away, the Red Dragon sat in Aeden's place, gold edging each scale and the ridges of her spine, wings folded to her back. Blue eyes glimmered. Deepest black oblong pupils regarded each person. For a breathless moment, all was still.

Aeden opened her wings as she raised her head to the sky and trumpeted a challenge. The horses went mad. Shrilling in fear, they spun around their riders, pulling and rearing, trying to escape from the danger.

The Dragon slammed down her wings, rising into the air. An inhale of breath sounded from those gathered on the stairs as their eyes followed her flight. With another stroke of her wings, she gained the top of the wall and leapt to the roof of the Dragon Tower. Owen gave a nervous laugh, running his fingers through his hair. Neulach watched with a wry twist of his lips and a sparkle in his eyes. The soldiers slowly brought their panicked horses under control.

Lord Neulach turned to Thomas and Owen. "You must leave now, Owen. She can be very impatient."

Thomas pulled Owen into a tight hug. He released him with a small push. "Go on," he said. "You'll be fine."

Owen bounded down the stairs with a lighter heart and jogged to the soldier holding his charger. The dark grey horse snorted as he approached. "Taya, stop it. She won't eat you," he said with a grin as he swung into the saddle. "At least not yet."

The soldier released the reins and mounted his own horse. Owen rode back to the stairs across the forecourt. "Lady Aeden will bring news when she returns, and I'll send word when I reach Aos Si. I'll miss all of you," he said.

"Be safe, Owen," Breanna shouted from the top of the stairs.

He reined his charger back toward the column of twenty soldiers and five heavily laden packhorses. "Let's go, sergeant," he ordered, taking his place at the front of the column.

The tall gates in the center of the wall around the Dragon Tower opened with slow deliberation. The column started forward and rode out of the forecourt. They made their way along the road approaching the heavier gates in the wall surrounding Red Dragon's Keep.

Owen glanced at the tall crenellated battlements and noted the soldiers patrolling along the top. A desperate battle with a horde of Demons happened right here in this space not three months ago. The Keep and village had lost a quarter of its residents during that battle. He shook his head with remembered pain. Thank goodness for Lady Aeden and the Dragon she was.

The shadow of a huge flying creature undulated across the ground. Everyone out in the open looked up at the sky. Owen and his soldiers watched as the Red Dragon flew on whispering wings toward the east. Horses danced uneasily. Riders calmed them.

The column passed through the gates. Owen looked back once before he faced forward — glad to be on his way, but terrified he would fail. Panic clutched at his lungs and heart. He felt light-headed. Taking a deep breath, he let numbness blanket his feelings. If he didn't think about leaving and concentrated instead on what was right in front of him, it didn't hurt so much.

§ § §

The cavalcade alternated between walk, trot and canter for five candlemarks, stopping every candlemark to stretch their legs and rest the horses. Owen had never ridden for such an extended time and soon found it difficult to find a comfortable position on the saddle.

He finally reached the point where the pain was impossible to ignore.

HeartStriker, can you help? he asked his Sword. *I really hurt.*

Yes. Do not wait so long to ask next time, the sword responded. Owen sighed as the pain receded on a wave of magic.

Thank you, he said, his mental voice filled with chagrin.

The column turned away from the Caladen River they were following onto a branch of the road headed down the mountain, northeast toward the foothills and the Darkened Forest waiting beyond. The road became a rough wagon track, a ridge of grass and weeds between two narrow strips of dirt. Not many people traveled this way.

Owen dropped back from the front of the line to take a place in the middle of the column. Navar paced beside him, as quiet and dark as a shadow. At times, he seemed to disappear from sight. HeartStriker kept his own counsel.

The soldiers rode through small dense stands of conifers giving way to patches of deciduous trees lifting their skeletal branches toward the sky. Once across the broad valley separating the heights of the Dragon Spine Mountains from the foothills, the column continued to move through the foothills, riding beside the frozen streams and creeks the trail followed.

By early evening, they had almost reached the Darkened Forest.

"My lord, I think it might be time to stop for the night." The soldier riding next to him interrupted Owen's thoughts. "The men and horses need a break. The Red Dragon landed not far from here. The scout reports there is a likely-looking clearing on the left side of the trail."

Owen came back to the present from his thoughts and looked to his right and left. The trees along this section of the track bordered close. A skift of snow that should have been several inches deep lay along the sides of the wagon ruts, extending into the forest in patches and piles. A shiver of unease coursed up his spine. Something threatened.

He noticed all the soldiers riding in front of him had their hands on the pommels of their swords. It wasn't just him. The others felt the touch of danger as well. Shade across the track deepened the gloom he felt he had been riding through forever. Cold clung to the land.

"Very well, corporal. Thanks. Please pass the order."

As the column reached the opening, the soldiers reined their horses into the meadow and dismounted. Navar ghosted into the clearing, circling the tree line, obviously looking for danger.

A tumble of boulders sat slightly off-center of the meadow. Two of the men began to gather deadwood and kindling from the edges of the forest. Two more began to lead groups of horses to drink from the creek bordering the clearing.

Lady Aeden stepped into the glade from the trees on the north. Navar halted abruptly, his ears rigidly forward. He swung his head back and forth, eyeing the forest. He turned back to her. *I did not hear or sense you coming.*

Lady Aeden gave Navar a small smile and shallow bow. She watched Owen as he dismounted from his warhorse.

"Owen, there are things we need to speak of. The Darkened Forest begins close to this clearing. You need to know what dangers truly lie in wait there, not just rumors and legends."

"Could you tell us while we eat?" Owen asked, nervously coiling and uncoiling the reins he held. "I think everyone should hear this."

Well done, Owen, HeartStriker told him. *Perhaps she will share what she knows of the dark magic dwelling here. It has been a very long time since I have been near the Darkened Forest. I can already feel its heaviness.*

The short hairs on the back of Owen's neck stiffened as a frisson of fear coursed up his spine. *That explains the threat I've been feeling. I suppose we had better find out now so we can get ready.*

He led Taya to the picket line strung between two trees and tied the halter rope to the line. He unsaddled and unbridled the weary horse. He pulled a clump of tall dried grass from the ground, twisted it into a tight knot and began to brush the sweat marks from the horse's coat.

Soldiers cut the dried grass, tossing it into a large pile at the end of the line, ready to feed each horse. Owen gathered a large bundle in his arms, dumping it on the ground in front of Taya. The horse dropped his head and started to eat. Owen glanced around, looking for Navar. He saw the WindRunner grazing on the opposite side of the clearing.

The smell of cooking meat drifted from the fire at the center of the camp. Owen walked through the grass, each step crunching and crackling as he approached the men clustered around the heat. Small two-man tents were set up just far enough back from the fire to leave a narrow path around the fire-pit in the faint hope the heat would help keep the men warm as they slept.

The sergeant in charge met Owen as he walked. "Lord Owen, could we discuss the plan for getting through the Darkened Forest? Lady Aeden will only be scouting this far and I'm not sure what to expect."

"Of course, Sergeant. She's joining us for last-meal and plans to tell us what she knows about the forest."

"That's a relief," the sergeant commented. "Not looking forward to goin' ahead without her."

"What's your name, sergeant?"

"Declan Jory, my lord," he answered. He looked steadily at Owen with brown eyes and a slight frown. His dark brown skin put Owen in mind of the bark of an old maple tree. Crows-feet radiated from the corners of his eyes and deep lines ran from his nose to his mouth.

"How long have you served?" Owen asked.

"Ten years, my lord. Eleven in a few months."

"Thank you for your service," Owen responded.

Jory gave a crooked half smile and bowed slightly, right fist to his heart in salute. "You're welcome, my lord. I'd best be off to check the men." Owen watched as the man walked away to the right.

He reached those gathered around the fire talking quietly to each other. The men gave Lady Aeden a wide berth as she sat on a boulder next to the fire, staring into the flames. Owen glanced toward the edge of the clearing. Navar grazed near the trees, ears swiveling to catch each man's voice. He raised his head and stared steadily at Aeden.

Dragon. What do you know of the Darkened Forest? Navar demanded. His voice thundered in everyone's mind.

Aeden's head slowly swiveled toward him. Her eyes locked with his. The temperature noticeably cooled. The hair all over Owen's body stood on end. He looked at the two fabled beings, eyes wide. He felt the anger rising in Aeden. The men squatting around the fire stood up in alarm. They faced the growing confrontation. One look had them moving quickly around the fire, stopping behind Owen.

"Think they'll fight?" whispered one of the soldiers.

"Who knows," Jory whispered back.

Owen stepped toward Aeden. He gave a small bow, turned to Navar and bowed again. "Lady, Navar." He rested his hand on HeartStriker's pommel.

Draw me, the sword ordered.

With unconscious grace, Owen slid the Sword of Light from its scabbard. The blade burst into white flame, filling the clearing with scintillating waves of brilliance.

Lady Aeden cried out in surprise and threw her arm up over her eyes. Navar shied away from the Sword. The soldiers behind Owen threw up their arms as well and backed away.

Navar! Thee shall stop now this ire. We are allies all, here. Enough. HeartStriker's words echoed in every mind. The sound of chiming bells and a low rumble as of far off thunder followed his demand. The light from the blade dimmed.

Thee? Owen questioned HeartStriker as he held the Sword of Light between the two magical beings. *What was that about?* He distinctly heard his sword give a disgruntled snort.

Lady Aeden was the first to turn back toward Owen and HeartStriker. She shook her head, her lips pressed into a thin line. "I'm sorry HeartStriker. You speak the truth."

She turned with studied calm to face Navar. "WindWalker ... Navar ... we are allies. I do not know what your problem is, but you need to let it go. Danger threatens from every side, regardless of your opinion. Shall we talk?"

Navar stood without movement. No wind rustled a branch or stirred a leaf. In the deafening quiet, the snap of a breaking twig echoed like the crack of a whip.

Everyone in the clearing jerked toward the sound. More cracking and crackling sounded as whatever moved there pushed through the bushes at the edge of the meadow.

Aeden raised her arms, ready to call the whirlwind. Navar's muscles bunched, set to charge. HeartStriker flared blue-white. Swords hissed as soldiers pulled them from scabbards.

A tall figure dressed in brown and green stepped into the firelight, followed closely by the dark grey-black form of a dire wolf.

"No need, Dragon, *Gaothsiuloir, Claiomh Solas*."

A voice filled with irresistible calm and peace spoke to each of them, yet filled the clearing. The stranger glided closer to the fire. The wavering light revealed emerald eyes, a thick fall of light greenish-brown hair and dark skin. He leaned on a tall quarterstaff. The pommel of a long sword strapped on his back rose over his right shoulder. A longbow and quiver rose over the left.

As soon as he spoke, Aeden and Navar relaxed, as if they knew him. HeartStriker abruptly went dark. *Elf*, he told Owen.

The dire wolf came forward, sitting at the stranger's left side. The top of the wolf's head came to the elf's shoulder. Yellow eyes regarded each of those around the fire. His tongue lolled out of his mouth as he began to pant, intelligence gleaming in his eyes.

Schooled by his mother to be polite to guests, Owen stepped forward and bowed to the two creatures. He spoke to the elf but kept his eyes on the wolf. "My name is Owen Arach, second son of Duke Tom Arach. You're welcome to join us."

"Somehow I doubt that, young Owen." A slow smile spread itself across the elf's face. "We know who you are. I am Saleth, scout for the *Tua Dé*." He nodded at the wolf. "This is Samhanach." "The Foraois *Coimeadai* know of your coming. I am to guide you to the Glen."

I have been to the Glen, Navar commented. *It is well to have a guide.*

The hawthorns confuse the unwary and can set them wandering for days, Aeden's OathKeeper added.

"Join us, please," Owen urged. "Lady Aeden is just about to tell us of the Darkened Forest and its inhabitants while we eat last-meal. Would you share what you know?"

Saleth walked to the fire. One of the soldiers stepped up to the cook pot and dished up the stew bubbling within. Everyone moved forward as if unfrozen, filling their own plates. Saleth sat on the ground, Samhanach sprawling next to him. Aeden, Owen and the rest of the soldiers slowly filled in around them, leaving a wide space on either side of the scout and his wolf.

Aeden looked at Saleth across the fire. "Please, Lord Saleth, tell us of your home. It has been many years since I have been to the Darkened Forest."

This is interesting, HeartStriker said to Owen.

Owen frowned. *I'm concerned we didn't know they were there. Why didn't you know they were there?* he asked the Sword.

Saleth glanced to his left and right, watching the soldiers eat. His eyes lingered on Owen and HeartStriker, as if he could hear the conversation between the two. Owen's lips thinned as he frowned at Saleth.

He masks himself and his companion. HeartStriker sounded surprised.

"I'd like to know why it's called the Darkened Forest," Owen asked in a curt voice as his eyes narrowed. The scout and dire wolf did not seem quite right. Suspicion tightened his body and his thoughts.

Saleth leaned forward with a nod to that suspicion. His face carefully blank, he rested his elbows on his knees. As he did, his hair shifted and his pointed ears peeked through. Owen jerked in surprise. Aeden's hand touched his arm. "Steady," she murmured.

This is a creature of great power, she whispered in his mind. *Beware.*

"It is called the Darkened Forest because the Dark Fey are imprisoned here. Mage, Dragon, and elves drove them from Ard An Ri and confined them within the Darkened Forest's borders. We are the guardians of the Forest, keeping the *Unseleigh Sidhe* from breaking the boundaries. We stop their worst depredations on unsuspecting travelers who insist on making their way through the woods, thinking it a faster way to their goal."

At some unseen disturbance, Saleth's head snapped up, as did Samhanach's. Both raised noses and inhaled, as if scenting danger. Saleth rose to his feet. Samhanach stretched and stood up, taking his place at Saleth's shoulder. "There are dangers here no one knows of. I will return in the morning to guide you to the Glen." He and his wolf seemed to fade into the forest.

The clearing was quiet. Navar shook himself and snorted. *Did he just enchant us?*

I believe he did. HeartStriker gave a mental shudder. *I'd forgotten elves can do that.*

"Lady Aeden, should we go with them?" asked Owen in a small voice, his brows furrowed with worry.

"I would remind all here there is a Dragon on this excursion," she replied, chuckling softly. "We do not fear elves. This is unexpected. I think I will remain with you through the Darkened Forest. The *Unseleigh Sidhe* from another world are prisoned here. They have powers that can overwhelm those with no mental protections and then rip them apart with tooth and claw. There are flyers that drop from the trees to smother and kill their victims. We will learn about the other beasts living here together."

"I'll take the first watch with the sergeant," Owen volunteered. "I don't think I'll sleep for a while."

"Fine," Aeden responded. "I'll see everyone in the morning." She walked away into the trees.

Red Dragon's Keep

Neulach stood looking out of the window at the training grounds from Aeden's rooms behind to the salle. He regarded the Tower that, unknown to its inhabitants, bore the image of his daughter on its eastern face. The tower glowed rose-red in the rising sun. He looked at Aeden as she came through the door.

"You look tired, daughter. Are you, or is this just a seeming to mimic humans?" he asked.

"It is a seeming. I've imitated them for so long, I don't remember a time I did not," she responded, straightening her spine and letting the expression flow from her face.

Neulach walked to the table in the center of the room, lifted a pewter cup to his mouth and took a long swallow of wine. Pulling a stool out from under the table, he took a seat.

"Lord Owen and his men have reached the Darkened Forest?"

"They have. A Forest Lord and his dire wolf met us at its border." She stared steadily at him. "I'd forgotten they can shield themselves from our sight."

Neulach's eyes widened. "This elf enchanted *you?*"

"He did. I have come tonight to talk with you about the Darkened Forest. I intend to return to the expedition in the morning. There is a feeling of twisted power in the forest that intrigues me. The magic energy is very wrong there." She moved to the table and poured herself a cup of wine. She took a small sip and lowered the cup while she stared with absent concentration at the weapons hanging on the wall.

Neulach rubbed his chin, gazing steadily at her, while he thought about Aeden's news.

"Interesting. Would that I could go with you, but secrets beckon here. There is hidden power in the Keep that must be found. It tastes of Dragon magic. I would search for it. Think you this will cause problems with the humans?"

Aeden sat on the stool across the table from her father. She did not respond for some time as she sorted through the ramifications of Neulach lurking about the Tower and the Keep.

"I think it would make them uneasy. Perhaps requesting a human guide would make it easier. Breanna or Cameron would do well.

The heirs must continue with their mage training that I have begun. The Haloran girl has continued their weapons training while I've been gone. Could you take on the mage training? It would be a useful facade for your search. Would that interfere with your hunt?"

Neulach canted his head to the side as he considered the idea. "It is a good thought. Training will sharpen their skills. The younglings might not realize they have information about the source of power here. Suspicions will be turned aside as I talk to them."

Aeden shook her head. "Remember. The children are not as— young— as you might think. These 'younglings' have fought and killed Demons. Swords of Light chose each one of them. You will be talking to the Swords as well. And ... they are wary of magic and magical creatures."

"Point taken," Neulach responded. "We have much to do. Shall we go find Lord Thomas and Master Sergeant Haloran to lay this plan before them?"

Aeden smiled.

He rose from his stool and held out his arm. His daughter laid her hand on his wrist as he escorted her from the room.

$$\$\,\$\,\$$$

"Forward, march!" barked Faolan Haloran. The Master Sergeant of troops in Duke Arach's army stood with his arms crossed over his chest. Shaking his head, he watched the ragged lines as the young men and women, and some not so young, marched by. The ranks of recruits, four across and eight rows deep, started forward.

"Other foot, private!" he shouted at a soldier half way down the line. The young woman hesitated. She looked at the feet of the person next to her and picked up the pace on the correct foot.

"Staff Sergeant, this is not acceptable." He turned to the young man, his eldest son, and looked him straight in the eyes. "I want you to take eight recruits at a time and teach them to create an interval in the formation before they ever start marching. They need to learn to watch the shoulder of the soldier on their immediate right. Teach them how to 'dress right'."

"Yes, fa — sir," replied Jaiman Haloran. "Sorry sir. I thought they knew how to do this."

"I'm not surprised they don't. There has been little need for them to learn. It was more important to teach them how to handle weapons. Well, get to it." He waved his hand at the troops and watched as Jaiman called a halt and had the newest recruits gather in a half circle in front of him.

Faolan turned and made his way from the practice field toward the back of the Dragon Tower and up the path to the kitchen. He thought wistfully of the walk to his own kitchen, lost to Demon attack before he ordered the retreat of all his holders to Red Dragon's Keep.

"Father, wait!" Faolan looked back at the salle and armory at the back corner of the Tower grounds and waited as his daughter, Marta, tall and slender, hurried across the salle quadrangle. The black braid falling down her back bounced as she trotted toward him. HellScream, her Sword of Light, rode her hip. "Lady Aeden sent me to ask if you would come to the armory and meet her father, Lord Neulach," Marta gasped out as she reached him. "Lord Thomas is already there."

Faolan went completely still. "When did the King of Dragons come to Red Dragon's Keep? Why would he want to meet me?" he asked quietly.

"I don't know. The Lady just asked me to get you after my training session, so here I am." A frown lowered Marta's brows as she pursed her lips. "Are you all right?"

Faolan's shoulders relaxed. "Yes. Would you go and ask your mother to meet me in the great hall for last-meal? I told her we'd eat in town, but I don't think I'll have time."

"Sure, Da. I'll do it now. I need to see her anyway." Marta turned and jogged toward the tower. Faolan watched her go, a small smile twitching the corners of his mouth. His daughter was growing up. He shook his head and started toward the salle. His long legs made short work of the distance to the large stone building she had come from.

He pulled open the heavy doors of the salle and stepped in. His footsteps echoed from the bricks paving the floor as he walked toward the training area. At his approach, three figures standing at the other end of the room turned to face him.

Lady Aeden stood next to Thomas. Her red hair cascaded down her back like a burning waterfall. The man standing on her other side, dressed entirely in clothing of deepest black, radiated an aura of such power that Faolan could feel it across the room. As he reached them, Faolan bowed deeply. He nodded to each. "How may I be of service?"

Aeden spoke first. "Master Sergeant Haloran, I would like to introduce my father, Lord Neulach. He has brought us critical information about the Demons."

Neulach tilted his head and looked at Faolan with glittering black eyes. "I have heard your name, Haloran. You were instrumental in saving the King's life, along with the elder Lord Tom Arach in the last Fasach skirmish. Am I correct?"

"Yes, my lord. I helped Lord Arach when the nomads tried to kill the King of Ard Ri. For that service, I was given my own Steading," he said, bitterness lacing his words. "The Demons have taken all of it, including my father."

Lord Neulach shook his head. "Much more will be taken if a way is not found to mend the tear in reality in Fasach and seal the Demons back into their own world."

Haloran's eyes opened wide in surprise. "A tear in reality? What do you mean? Is that where they are coming from? Do you know how to close it?"

"The only thing preserving this world from drowning in Demons is the Dragon magic we have woven over the opening into the Demon world. The spells of the renegade Dragon or Dragons whom we have hunted for a very long time weaken that weaving. I ask humans and Dragons to join forces once again— to hunt the renegades and seal the Rifts in this world. Will you join us?

Neulach fell silent and watched him with an intensity Haloran could feel pressing on his mind. He thought of all of the loss he and his — and the world — had endured because of this invasion by the Dark. Anger and resolve stiffened his spine as he looked back steadily at Neulach, Aeden, and the son of his oldest friend.

Thoughts of the danger he faced flashed through Haloran's mind. Dismissing them, he nodded, as if to equals. "I will."

Neulach held out his hand. Haloran stepped forward and rested his hand on top of it. Thomas placed his hand on theirs. Aeden laid her hand on top of them all.

Power surged among the four. Aeden's voice reverberated against the walls.

"The covenant is sealed. The strength is ours."

Power moved in and among them through the union of their hands. Determination forged a bond, linking each with the other. The whole became greater than the parts.

No human could hold such power for long. Their hands fell away from each other.

Haloran stiffened with dread, shaken to his core. He knew with certainty beyond his understanding that the power they raised would call them again and again to sacrifice and pain. He buried that understanding deep within his heart.

"I would search for the hint of Dragon magic I feel within your Keep, Lord Thomas. Might I train your sister and cousins to fight the Demons with magic? And perhaps ask one of them to guide me through the Tower?" the Arach Dubh asked the heir to Red Dragon's Keep.

Thomas gave a short bow to Neulach. "Of course, sir. When would you like to start?"

Chapter 9

The Glen

Owen stretched in the warmth of his blankets. He felt like he had tossed and turned all night after his turn on watch. No sound or movement disturbed the camp or the clearing. He rolled over and bumped into another warm body. He jolted fully awake.

Navar's back faced Owen. Owen threw his blankets aside in a panic. Grabbing HeartStriker in its scabbard, he scrambled to his feet in alarm.

What are you doing? he demanded.

Navar stretched out his front legs and lunged up onto his hooves. He shook himself and turned to face Owen. *I thought to share warmth. Were you cold last night?*

Owen paused, his outrage subsiding. *No.* Another, longer pause. *Thank you.*

At their abrupt movements, the others in the clearing began to stir.

Owen leaned his Sword against the boulder next to him. He pulled on his boots and rolled up the blankets he'd used as a bed. The nip of cold in the air had him pulling on his coat for warmth as he carried the blankets to the pile of equipment near the fire.

Now would be a good time to learn how to ride a WindRunner, HeartStriker suggested. *Owen, the tack we brought for Navar is next to the supplies.*

Navar looked at Owen and the Sword of Light. *Perhaps this is a good time.*

Navar walked to the pile of gear next to the horse-line. Owen followed, dragging his feet. *Are you sure this is a good idea?* he asked HeartStriker.

Better now than later. There is much we do not know about the Darkened Forest. Trying to master riding a WindRunner and fighting at the same time could prove perilous. Time is short.

Owen rolled his eyes. He looked around the clearing searching for Lady Aeden. He frowned. *Where is she?*

She has taken to the sky to look for danger, HeartStriker answered.

Navar nosed the saddle he wanted Owen to use. *Put this on my back,* he ordered.

Owen lifted the saddle by the pommel and carried it over to Navar's left side. He struggled to swing it above the WindRunner's tall back, finally settling it carefully over his spine. He reached under Navar and grabbed the girth, threaded the straps through the billets and buckled it into place. He tightened the straps and checked that he had correctly positioned the breast band and crupper.

"What about the headstall?" he asked.

Not today. Today is for balance. Remove the stirrups. Get on.

Owen complied, unbuckling the stirrup straps, unthreading them from the saddle and buckling the two together. He placed them next to the bucket that held grooming brushes and combs.

He looked around the clearing, searching for a reason not to get on the back of the giant creature standing next to him. Reluctantly he faced the WindRunner.

How?

The same way you would get on a pony. Navar's sarcasm was clear.

Angered, Owen grabbed the front of the saddle with his left hand, stepped back with his right foot and pushed off with his left. Using his momentum, he swung his right leg up and over the cantle of the saddle and hooked his heel on the other side. He pulled himself on to the WindRunner's back.

Navar snorted. *Not bad. We'll practice that.*

$$\S \S \S$$

For the next hour, Owen and Navar worked on Owen's balance in the saddle.

Lean into the turn as we move, Navar demanded. He increased his speed from trot to canter and shouldered into a small circle. He changed leads abruptly and circled in the opposite direction. Owen unbalanced to the side and fell off. Navar stopped, spun and walked back to him.

This is the sixth time you have fallen off. What is wrong?

Owen didn't move, lying on his back on the ground, staring at the sky. *I don't know. It isn't the same as riding Taya. I give the signal to turn, he turns, and I don't fall off. I do not know what is going on.*

There is the answer, Navar responded. *You give the signal so you are prepared. You must start feeling the movement before it happens.* He stood still in thought. *Remove the saddle. We will practice without it.*

Owen swiveled his eyes to look at Navar. He pushed himself up onto his elbows with a groan. He rolled to his feet and unbuckled the girth, pulled the saddle from the WindRunner's back and dropped it to the ground.

A wry smile crossed his face. *How do I get on?* he asked.

Navar stretch out his left foreleg and bent his right knee to the ground. *Get on.*

Owen's eyes bugged out. *Why didn't you do that before?* he demanded.

You needed to learn how to get on a tall WindRunner, was Navar's dry response.

§ § §

By the time they finished, Owen's middle felt as if the WindRunner had kicked him in the stomach. His knees could no longer lift him clear of Navar's bare back at a trot. He had fallen off so many times he had lost count.

Navar walked sedately over to the picket line from the edge of the clearing where they'd been working.

Owen swung his leg over the WindRunner's withers and slid to the ground along Navar's side with a groan of pain. He almost fell as his feet met the ground and his legs started to buckle.

Navar, did you forget there is a full day of riding to the Glen? HeartStriker chided the WindRunner. The Sword sent a surge of healing through Owen, removing the pain. Owen's legs still ached.

There is much to learn, Navar responded, frost in his voice. *His life will depend on what he masters here.*

Owen picked up a brush and began to run it over the satin coat, removing the sweat stains that had formed under the saddle, and under his backside. Finished, he hobbled to the fire for breakfast, grumbling curses.

One of the men stirred a pot of porridge. Another soldier fried bacon in a pan. Owen was not even close to hungry. He felt a little sick. Grabbing up a waterskin, he poured a stream of water into his dry mouth. He swished the water around and spat it out.

He straightened his back, stretching muscles threatening to cramp. Taking another swig of water, he winced as he limped to one of the large rocks set back from the fire and gingerly sat down. He noticed Aeden sitting on one of the boulders to his left.

"That was hard," he grumbled to her. *Did she see me fall off?* he wondered.

I did, she responded to the thought. *But you got back up and got back on. That's how you learn. You have better balance now than you did when you started this morning,* Aeden told him. *You need to shield your thoughts at all times. You reveal too much when you don't.*

"You should eat, Owen," she said aloud. "It's a long ride to the Glen. I'll be with you for most of the rest of the journey. Thomas approves."

Owen swung his head toward her. "How do you know?" he demanded.

"I have wings, Owen. I returned to the Keep last night and sought counsel of my father and Thomas, as well as Haloran. They approve. Should I be needed, my father will call. Twisted power threatens in the Darkened Forest. I must find out what has changed it."

Owen stared at her. He was too tired to respond.

§ § §

By mid-morning, the troops were ready to leave. The only thing they lacked was their guide. Owen paced back and forth between the fire-pit and the horse-line.

Lady Aeden watched him from the top of a boulder. Navar watched him from across the meadow. The soldiers watched him as they stood near the horses.

Owen stopped next to the fire-pit as Aeden hopped down from her seat and walked toward him. He crossed his arms in stubborn anger.

"Why are we waiting? The elf is not coming back. This was just a trick to keep us here. I'll bet there's an army coming this way," he snarled.

"Because it is better to be invited, than to try to sneak in," she said, glancing at the soldiers by the horses. "As if we could sneak anywhere with this number of men." She shook her head. "There are dangers here not even I know about. The Forest Lords were set as sentinels to confine the *Unseleigh Sidhe* to the Darkened Forest and keep others out."

"So this forest is a prison? How is that possible?"

"As I said yesterday, the Forest Lords are very powerful. Tread lightly," Aeden murmured as she faced the trees.

Saleth stepped into the clearing from the east. Sunlight slanted across the meadow into the watchers eyes, obscuring the elf's shape and cloaking everything in shadow beyond the meadow's edge. A darker shadow shaped itself into his dire wolf, Samhanach. "Come. The way is open, but not for long. Lead your horses."

He stood waiting as men took up reins and led their horses into a ragged line. Aeden moved toward the elf and waited for Owen to walk his warhorse up next to her. She took a place at his left shoulder. Navar ghosted up on his right. His warhorse tossed its head in agitation at Navar's presence.

Saleth looked steadily at Owen, waiting for some comment. Owen looked steadily back. Saleth glanced at Aeden and Navar, spun away and strode into the forest on a path that had not been there until he stepped forward.

Owen choked on a cough. "Was that there all along?" he whispered to Aeden.

"I think it was," she murmured back. "He is even more powerful than I thought."

Owen, Aeden and Navar stepped forward onto the path. It seemed to widen to accommodate all three of them. Owen looked back at Sergeant Jory and ordered,

"Two abreast. Be ready. Pass the word." The command whispered back along the line of men.

Darkness pressed toward the trail. No birds called, no wind stirred the branches of trees or undergrowth. A faint rustling and snapping of twigs and dried brush betrayed the creatures shadowing the column.

Two candlemarks passed, maybe three. A mournful hooting echoed through the trees. Owen began to walk faster as his spine prickled with uneasiness. Navar's ears moved constantly, his head held high. Soldiers gripped their swords tighter. Horses jigged nervously, alerted by sound, scent, and the nervousness of the men leading them.

Snarls swept around them from both sides of the trail.

Saleth hurried back to the column from his position as scout. "Quickly. We are almost there. The *Unseleigh* have gathered. My power to hold the path is waning."

As if to prove his point, Owen watched as a monster from one of his nightmares paced beside the column. Its neck stuck out from a humped back sloping down to muscular hind legs. Massive canines protruded from a wrinkled muzzle. Orange eyes gleamed and glittered as the beast tried to capture his gaze.

"Do not look in their eyes," exclaimed Aeden, loud enough to be heard at the end of the line of soldiers. "Many of the Fey trap the unwary with their gaze."

Owen locked his eyes on the monster's feet. Five-inch claws dug into the ground with each step.

He shuddered, feeling sick. HeartStriker sent a jolt of power through his body.

Shield your mind, the Sword warned.

Shaken, Owen sent his *ki* deep into the earth. Power welled up through his body. He used it to raise his mental shields. As soon as he did, the pain he hadn't been aware of began to recede. His hand tightened around HeartStriker's pommel. "Lady Aeden, can you shield the men?" he asked.

"Yes," she answered. Men and horses visibly relaxed as their fear and pain subsided.

The trees began to thin. Owen, Aeden, and Navar sprinted after Saleth out of the forest and into a golden sunlit expanse of rolling hills, the spires of an ethereal castle rising in the far distance. The sun was still rising in the east.

Samhanach bounded out of the trees, following the last of the men. Shrieks and horrendous growls followed the column as they rushed into the Glen. A flood of misshapen beasts raced after them. Everyone whirled to face the forest and drew their swords. HeartStriker and OathKeeper blazed with light. Samhanach leapt aside and slashed down with his teeth as a large boar with enormous tusks and glittering red eyes charged toward Saleth. His teeth found their mark and the boar squealed in pain and outrage. The wolf landed, spun on his hind legs and lunged for the boar's throat. He slashed through arteries and windpipe. Blood fountained as the light died in the monster's eyes.

Saleth sprinted past the column back toward the forest and Samhanach. He nocked an arrow as he ran and raised his bow. A flying horror, mostly grey teeth, tail, and wings, sprang from the tree nearest the men with a snarling hiss. Saleth loosed his arrow. A flash of brilliant blue light arced from his bow.

The arrow, gilded in brilliance, took the flyer in its mouth. The creature exploded into a grey spray of powder. The men scrambled away with cries of fear.

Saleth nocked another arrow, prepared to let it fly if any more Fey tried to enter the Glen. Samhanach crouched at his feet, prepared to leap and kill. The flood of monsters stopped and milled at the edge of the forest. A coughing roar from the depths of the trees had them turning and slinking back into the shadows.

"Mount up," ordered Aeden. Everyone threw themselves onto their horses, ready to flee. Coughing, growls and grunting boomed from the forest and slowly faded away as the unseen horde moved back among the trees.

Saleth released the tension on his bowstring and looked at Samhanach. "Thank you, my friend. That was close." The dire wolf slanted a glance at him and seemed to grin.

Returning the arrow to the quiver on his back, Saleth swung the bow over his shoulder. He held out his hand and his staff appeared.

The men shifted uneasily in their saddles. "That's a pretty trick," whispered Sergeant Jory. "Wish we had the doing of it."

Saleth looked at the sergeant.

"Meaning no disrespect, sir," Jory added.

"It is perhaps a candlemark and a half to the Citadel. We should go," Saleth told the group.

"I'll leave you here," Aeden responded. "We are close to whatever has disturbed the Forest and given its prisoners more power. I want to find out what it is."

Saleth gave a slight bow to Aeden. He and Samhanach started down the track toward the distant castle. The patrol from Red Dragon's Keep followed.

Aeden waited until they were but specks in the distance. Raising her arms, she called the whirlwind. The Red Dragon spread her wings and flew over the towering trees, back the way they had come.

Chapter 10

Danger Close

Lord Tom's horse stumbled over nothing. Tom jerked awake, his mind befuddled. He scanned the landscape, looking for danger. Reassured, he drew in a deep breath and flung his arms out to either side, rolled his head from shoulder to shoulder and straightened his spine. He gave a huge yawn, pulling air deep into his lungs and pushed the air out with a grunt. Snow fell gently, a dusting covering the ground. Not much yet, but he knew more was on the way. He shivered in the cold and pulled his cloak tighter around his body. They'd been running from North Meall for three days straight, heading for the home of his wife's family.

His movement and yawn roused the others. Snorts and yawns echoed his. He bent his head from side to side, adjusting his neck. Pops and cracks followed his movement. He pulled his horse to a stop.

"We need a rest, and so do the horses."

Anne, Jeremy and Jenni stopped their own horses. They stood at the bottom of a shallow swale leading to the east, trying to stay out of sight of anyone following. Tom looked at the trees towering on their right about half a mile away. The Darkened Forest. He shook his head. *Best not enter there.*

He dismounted and led his horse up the side of the swale, closer to the trees. As he topped the rise, he saw a circle of nine standing stones. A jumble of boulders blocked the space between each stone, except for the two facing directly east, where the opening became an entrance to the circle. Inside, the ground was clear of snow. Green grass grew within as if it were spring. He led his horse through the opening, giving a sharp two-toned whistle as he did. The tension he had been carrying so long dropped away.

He lifted the rope he carried across his body over his head and knelt, twisting it into a set of hobbles around the horse's fetlocks. He stood and looped the excess rope over the saddle horn. He slipped the bridle off the horse's head, hanging the headstall on top of the rope. The horse dropped its head, eagerly lipping the grass.

At the sound of his whistle, his companions followed him over the crest of the swale and into the circle of stone. Jeremy slid from his horse with a groan, straightened his legs and leaned against its side for a few moments. He reached out and lifted Anne from her horse. She swayed with exhaustion as her feet touched the ground and she almost crumpled where she stood. He swung her up in his arms and carried her to the standing stones that ringed the clearing, setting her carefully on one of the flat boulders between them.

Tom walked to Jenni, still sitting on her horse. He put his hand on her leg, reaching up with the other to help her down.

"I don't think I can get off," she told him. "The wound on my leg is infected."

Tom held out both arms. "I'll catch you," he said.

Jenni leaned over and fell from the saddle into his arms with a cry of pain. He stumbled forward into the side of the horse as his whipped back sent daggers of agony to his brain. His breath left him in an explosive gasp.

"Jeremy," he choked out. "Help!"

Jeremy rushed to his side and slid his arm around Jenni's waist, pulling her arm over his shoulders. Tom used the horse for support, panting in short shallow breaths, trying to control the throbbing in his back. As it subsided, he straightened.

"Thanks," he told his brother-in-law. Jeremy nodded at him.

He took Jenni's other side and together they helped her to the boulder where Anne sat. Tom lowered her to sit next to her sister.

He looked around the circle at the standing stones and back to Jenni. "Let me see your leg," he said. She began to roll up her left pant leg, revealing dried blood and damp fluids sluggishly flowing down her leg from the wound. As she rolled higher, the slash she had received from one of the kidnappers appeared. It sliced diagonally down her thigh from hip to knee. Tom sucked in his breath.

Her leg was swollen, the lips of the wound bright red all the way along it. Yellow and green pus filled the cut and trickled from its lower end. The purple lines of blood poisoning hadn't appeared yet.

"That needs cauterizing," Jeremy said with grim certainty.

"Start a fire, Jeremy. We need to clean it first," Anne told him. "Let's lay her on the ground." Tom spread a blanket by the rock where Jenni sat and helped her to sit down on it. He supported her back as she lay down.

Anne stood and, too tired to hurry, made her way to her horse. She pulled the saddlebags from behind the cantle while Jeremy left the circle to search for anything burnable. She grabbed waterskins from all of the saddles and walked back to the boulder. "We need to do this while there's still light," she insisted.

"I've got some mold salve in my saddlebags," Jenni told her through gritted teeth. Her breathing was shallow, her face pale with pain.

"Why didn't you say something," Tom demanded. "We should have done this yesterday."

"We can't stop. We've got to get to Aos Si as soon as we can," she slurred her words.

"You won't get to Aos Si at all if you keep on like this," was his curt reply. He strode to her horse and pulled the saddlebags off. He stomped back, anger in every step, and dropped the bags next to his wife.

Jeremy returned to the circle with an armful of deadfall and tinder. He scraped the grass away from the ground a few feet from his companions and built a fire pyramid. As soon as he'd finished, he looked at Anne. A tiny flame appeared in the tinder as she used her mind to call fire. He fed it with larger and larger branches until the fire burned brightly. Already, coals were forming.

Jenni pulled her knife from its sheath and handed it to him. He took it and laid the blade on the coals to heat. Tom joined him.

Anne turned to her sister and grasped her shoulder. "What did Da always tell us? Take care of yourself first else you can't take care of others." She gave a gentle shake. She knelt down next to the injured leg and began rummaging through the saddlebags. "Where's the salve?"

"On the right side under my tunic," Jenni responded. "Do you feel the magic in the circle?" she asked with quiet intensity.

With a cautious glance at the men, Anne nodded. "Yes. I'm beginning to feel a little better. I think I can use it."

"Good. Clean out first, cauterize, then the salve. Save the magic as a last resort. Can you banish the pain?"

Anne nodded. She went back to the packhorse, pulled the small pot from its pack, and grabbed one of the extra cloaks they had taken. She placed the pot on the fire and poured water from two of the skins into it. She tore the cloak into strips. She used the last strip to remove the pot of boiling water from the fire and took it to Jenni's side.

Anne dampened a strip in the water and began to wipe the pus from the wound. Jenni clenched her teeth and her fists, nostrils flaring with pain she refused to acknowledge.

Tom picked up the knife from the fire. The blade held a dull red glow. Anne put her hand on Jenni's shoulder and the other on her leg above the cut.

"I'm sorry," Tom said.

Anne sent tendrils of magic into Jenni's mind, blocking the pain messages her body was sending. She sent pulses of magic through her hand on Jenni's leg, further disrupting the throbbing spreading from the wound.

Tom laid the blade on the right side of the cut. The stench of burning flesh filled the circle. Jenni inhaled sharply as her leg spasmed. Tears rolled down her cheeks. She made no sound. Tom rolled the knife to the opposite side, burning the infection from the wound.

He lifted the knife away from her leg and handed it to Jeremy. Jeremy set it next to the fire.

Tom sat down next to Jenni and gathered her into his arms, her head on his chest, rocking her slowly. "It will be all right. I promise." Tears leaked from her eyes and dampened his shirt.

Anne sent the magic she had used into the earth of the circle, allowing Jenni's pain to dissipate into the ground. She gently spread the salve on the wound from the tiny jar she'd found in Jenni's saddlebag. Folding one of the strips into a large pad, she placed it on the wound and bound it to Jenni's thigh with the remaining strips of fabric.

"Done." She dropped her hands to her knees. "We need to rest here tonight," she said, a bit of hesitancy in her voice. She looked at Tom. He gave a slight nod. "Jeremy, could you dump the water and refill it with fresh? We'll have soup tonight, not just dry rations."

§ § §

The next morning Tom woke as the sun cleared the horizon and sent light streaming through the opening into the circle. He stretched in the cloaks he'd spread on the grass next to the fire for his and Jenni's bed. He listened to the horses grazing across the circle. He stretched again, relishing the strength he felt. He sat up with an abrupt jerk, astonished. "It doesn't hurt," he whispered. He twisted slowly side to side. "I can't believe this."

Jenni slept on, oblivious to his elation. Anne's eyes opened and she looked around the circle guarded by stones, then at him. She rolled out from under the cloak she'd shared with Jeremy, who was already up and busy at the fire preparing first-meal. She smiled. "I feel good."

"My back doesn't hurt. Why don't I hurt? Is there magic here?" he asked.

Anne hesitated before giving him the affirmative. "Yes," she said. "I can feel it like a pool of light and happiness. Men and women worship the Three Gods here. Over time, the power of that worship has filled and protected this ring we've used as shelter," she said.

She faced the entrance and raised her arms.

"Lord of Light, Lady of Night,
Thank you for this day so bright.
Bless the Earth within my sight,
Bless us here with all your might.
Keep us safe, guard our way,
This we ask and always pray."

Subtle energy rolled its way around the circle.

Anne smiled.

Tom shook his head.

He knelt next to Jenni and shook her shoulder with a gentle hand. She blinked blearily up at him and smiled. She sat up and stretched her arms over her head. The chafe wounds from the irons she had worn were gone. Tom's eyes widened.

"Let's see your leg," he said, his voice filled with sudden urgency.

Jenni pushed the blanket down and rolled her pant leg up. The cut was still red along its edges, but looked much better than the day before.

"I wish we could stay for another day. Maybe that would be healed by then," he said as he pointed at the wound. "Unfortunately, we need to leave this morning." His head came up as the smell of baking flatbread and eggs filled the air. "We'll eat before we leave."

He held his hand down to Jenni. She grasped it and he pulled her to her feet. They took the few steps to the fire and sat down for first-meal.

§ § §

Tom kicked dirt over the fire and watched as the flames died. Urgency tightened his stomach. He raised his head and looked at the Darkened Forest looming south of the circle. Nothing moved within the shadowed depths under the trees.

The others sat on their horses, waiting for him. He took one last look around the circle. *Thank you for your blessing and your healing. By the Three Gods, thank you.*

The circle enfolded him in a sense of peace.

He swung into his saddle with new ease and urged his horse through the standing stone gateway. The companions signaled their horses into a trot, heading east.

Chapter 11

Traders Road

Travelers filled the caravanserai to overflowing. Maaike paid for the space her wagons would need. She left the office and went in search of her caravan master. "Make sure the horses and mules are groomed and fed. The horses need a measure of grain. Check the wagons for wear and see after replacement parts. I'll be back as soon as I am able."

"I will," he responded in his dour way.

A guard from the gates leaned against the side of one of the wagons, arms crossed, watching the hustle and bustle of her people. Maaike started toward him and he pushed himself away from the wagon. She gestured with an imperious sweep of her arm. "Lead on," she ordered.

Together, the two made their way through the town. The signs of spring arriving lined the road, with tulips and daffodils nodding their blooms to the sun. Greening grass softened the winter-dried verge. Maaike's stomach contracted painfully when she caught the scent of roasting lamb as they passed one of the inns along the main road. It had been a full day since she had last eaten. Worry during the journey about her mission had killed any appetite she might have. Merchants displayed goods and every kind of food imaginable on almost every street corner. The hubbub of too many people in too small a space threatened to overwhelm her senses.

She felt plucking fingers at her belt. A snap of her wrist against the offending hand drove the pickpocket away. She whirled with a snarl, but no one was there. The guard turned as she did and watched in amusement. "We try to keep the petty theft down, but they *will* try at every opportunity. Sorry," he commiserated with her.

They made their way up the main road to the gates of the Dragon Tower. Maaike stumbled to a stop. A dark whirlwind seemed to engulf the figure of a woman standing with her arms raised to the sky. As the churning darkness lifted away, a red Dragon almost two stories tall stretched out its front legs and lashed its tail like a cat. With a mighty yawn showing gleaming white teeth, the Dragon shook itself and stretched its hind legs, shaking each in turn.

Maaike clutched at her chest. She could not breathe. She groped for the guard with her other hand, grabbing his arm for balance.

The Dragon spread its huge wings and thunder rumbled on the downstroke. The wind those wings created pushed against Maaike and the guard, molding her clothes to her body. Dust filled the air as the Dragon rose into the morning sky. It rapidly gained altitude and glided out of view over the wall. Maaike felt the blood draining from her head and she came close to fainting. The guard grabbed her around the waist and held her as she struggled to draw in air.

"First time seeing our Dragon?" he asked with a chuckle. "It does this to most people. There. Feel better?"

"I had no idea. Tales are told along the Traders Road, but ..." her voice was faint with shock. Her mind struggled to find words.

"Well, thank the Gods for her. We'd have lost the first Demon battle without her fire and magic. We almost did lose," he admitted, loosening his hold. She stepped away from him as she regained her balance.

"Thank you." She gave him a short bow. She hated showing weakness in front of anyone, but the truth of the Dragon had shocked her and filled her with dread.

They continued on to the gates of the wall surrounding the Dragon Tower. "We're here to see Lord Thomas", her guard told the men on duty at the gates. He led her through them, across the forecourt and through the double doors into the Tower.

The guard stopped a skully carrying an armful of rushes for the floor and told him to find the seneschal.

"Quick now. We've news from the Traders Road."

"Yes sir." The skully scuttled away, dropping his burden next to the stairs rising on the left side of the room.

Maaike watched as he disappeared through the arches on the right side of the room. The guard fidgeted.

The sound of booted footsteps echoed through the arches. A tall, grey-haired, ramrod straight man swung into view. He walked across the room to Maaike and her guard.

"You came along the Traders Road?" he asked.

"I did, sir," she answered.

"Welcome. I am Gregory Anur, seneschal for Red Dragon's Keep. Please, join me in my office," the seneschal invited. He looked at the guard. "Locate Lord Thomas and have him join us," he ordered. "I think he's in the training yard."

The seneschal took Maaike's arm and guided her through the arches, turned left and walked with her down the hall.

The guard followed Maaike and Gregory through the arches. He turned right and walked down the passage, letting himself out through the door at its end.

Gregory pushed the door to his office open and motioned to Maaike to enter.

Long and narrow bookshelves filled to overflowing lined the walls. A cabinet sat between two of the shelves on the right. A narrow table sat in the center of the room. Tall windows at the end let in abundant light. In front of the windows, a desk stretched across the room, its front facing the door. Two chairs sat there. Gregory poured water into goblets sitting on the cabinet and handed one to her as he made his way around the desk. "Sit, please," he invited. She chose the chair on the left.

Very clever, Maaike thought. *The light blinds those on this side of the desk, shadowing his face and making his expression difficult to see.*

"Would you like a glass of wine or mead, perhaps food?" Gregory asked her.

"Thank you for the offer. I'm fine," she responded, sipping from her goblet.

The door into the room opened and Gregory rose to his feet. Maaike twisted in her chair and stood up in turn. A young man walked through the door, pulling off well-used gloves, tucking them into his belt.

"Lord Thomas, a trader has arrived by the Trader's Road from Fasach. I thought you should know immediately." He looked at Maaike. "Trader, this is Lord Thomas Arach, heir to Red Dragon's Keep. You are?"

Maaike bowed to Thomas. "I am Maaike Soth Lahri," she said, lifting her head with pride. "I am the daughter of Centak Soth Lahri, the greatest trader that ever lived."

Amused by her self-importance, Lord Thomas strode across the carpet toward her. He held out his hand and grasped the hand she extended. "Welcome, Maaike. What news do you bring?

He sat in the chair next to hers. The others followed his lead.

She took a sip from her goblet, thinking of responses that would keep her safe. Should she tell the truth about the Demon attacks or make them seem inconsequential? Which would benefit her the most? She decided the truth would make its way from her caravan to the Keep, so lying served no purpose.

"Appalling news, my lord. We lost half our wagons and a third of our handlers. The spells I purchased in Jafara were useless. Small packs of Demons attacked almost every night from the time we left the last oasis south of the border with Ard Ri until four days past Falcon's Spire."

Gregory gave her a long look. "I'm sorry for your loss." He paused. "You purchased spells? I was not aware one could do that."

"Of course you can purchase spells," Maaike responded with indignation. He sounded as if he thought she was making it up. "Everyone knows you must purchase them or you are vulnerable to attack. Mages have been selling them forever."

A deep frown lowered Thomas's eyebrows and tugged down the corners of his mouth. "How do you buy spells?" he asked, his voice filled with suspicion.

"My lord, they are sold at the Mages Enclave in Jafara, each one crafted for the individual. I purchased protection from Demons. Ha." She took another sip of water. "Usually the spells do the job, but considering what happened on this trip, perhaps well-armed guards would have provided better protection."

A half smile lifted a corner of Gregory's mouth. He snorted softly. "I'm sure you're right."

"Demons are on the move," Maaike continued. "The spells I bought did little to stop them."

Thomas glanced at Gregory.

"Do the mages live at the enclave? How many are there? Have there been other failures? How many? What happens when the spell fails? How do you carry them

with you? Are they set into an object or are they verbal?"
His questions bombarded Maaike.

She looked at her interrogators in feigned confusion, inner glee quickening her breathing. She fought the smile threatening to cross her face. These were questions she wanted to encourage. She preferred to answer them to avert more troubling questions, questions the Sheikh of Fasach did not want asked nor answered. His Minister of Spies had made that more than clear.

"My lord, do you not have a Mages Enclave in Ard Ri? I'm sure I've heard of it," she asked, innocence evident in every word.

Thomas's eyes narrowed. He looked at Gregory, his left eyebrow rising.

"There is a Mages Enclave at the capital," Gregory responded. As far as I know, they do not sell spells or charms. The King supports mages, much as he does artists and musicians."

"Ah, I see," Maaike said, her tone condescending. "The mages in Fasach lock their spells in objects, things like rods or jewels or disks, things that can be easily carried by a person. For larger groups, a large spellstone is used."

The spread of disinformation was explicit in the sheikh's orders, under pain of death.

Maaike had no wish to die.

The trader has a very tight shield over her mind. I do not think she knows it is there. Perhaps seeing this object will reveal some of its secrets, HellReaver spoke to Thomas.

"Trader Lahri, would you be willing to show us this 'spellstone' you carry?" Thomas asked Maaike.

Maaike bowed her head in acquiescence. "Of course, my lord."

$ $ $

Maaike walked with the two men, followed by two guards, toward the caravanserai.

"Have you been to Red Dragon's Keep before, Trader Maaike?" Gregory asked.

"Yes, I have. My father brought me many times as I was growing up. It's the first time I've seen a Dragon, though."

"A Dragon is a new thing for all of us." Gregory chuckled and Thomas laughed aloud.

Maaike's mind churned with questions she wanted to ask. "How long has the Dragon—?

"Demons attacked us three months ago," Gregory interrupted her, his voice somber.

"Lady Aeden transformed into her true form as they were killing her. Had she not, we would all be dead and the Keep overrun." His grim words silenced Maaike more effectively than a shout. She glanced at both men, a frown marring her forehead.

She led them to the far side of the caravanserai where her wagons stood in ordered rows. The scents of foreign spices and roasting lamb filled the air. The painted sides of her own wagon stood out gaily from the drab utility of the others. For the first time, she noticed how *much* it stuck out. *Perhaps I should hide its uniqueness,* she thought.

She removed the key from her belt and unlocked the door. Pausing on the steps, she turned to the men. "It is a very small space. We may not all fit," she apologized.

Thomas grasped HellReaver's hilt as he looked at Gregory. Gregory noted the gesture and glanced into his eyes. "I'll go, Gregory," Thomas said.

Gregory gave a curt nod and stepped back. Maaike unlocked the door and walked into her home. Thomas followed her up the stairs and through the door.

§ § §

He stopped, his mouth dropping open in astonishment.

The interior of the wagon looked at least twice as large on the inside as it did on the outside. On the wall opposite the door, cabinets hung over a counter laid on top of more cabinets. To Thomas's right, a wooden plank folded down from the wall, forming a table under which sat four stools. Thick brocade curtains hung on either side of windows fitted with glass panes. A fabric roof curved over his head. Dried herbs, hams and other sundries hung from the curved wooden ribs holding the roof fabric taut.

A platform holding a mattress covered with thick blankets and pillows lay on top of more cabinets stretched across the width of the wagon at its far end. More cabinets over the bed provided even more storage. Painted symbols and pictures covered every surface.

"This is amazing." Thomas shook his head, eyes wide in wonder. He stepped farther into the wagon.

HellReaver sent a stab of magic to his hand resting on the pommel. *An amulet lies here!* the Sword exclaimed. Thomas covered his jerk of surprise with a stumble.

"Welcome to my home, my lord." Maaike gave a shallow curtsey. "Here. This is the chest holding the spellstone."

She opened one of the cabinet doors under her bed and removed a mahogany box from the shelf where it rested. She placed it carefully on the counter and opened the lid. Lifting out the silk-wrapped object from within, she placed it on the counter next to the box.

"It's obviously lost its power. Demons wouldn't have attacked had it worked," disappointment coloring her words. She flipped open the silk fabric covering the object.

Thomas gave a quiet sigh. With difficulty, he kept his face smooth.

Yes! hissed HellReaver.

A triangular amulet, studded with golden tiger-eye jewels, rested on the silk. Thomas pulled the silk back over the object.

"Too bad it didn't work. It is a beautiful thing, though. Would you be willing to part with it?" he asked, struggling to be casual. "I'd be willing to pay."

Maaike cocked her head in speculation. A slow smile widened her mouth. "No need to pay, my lord. Anything for the Lord of Red Dragon's Keep." She lifted the silk covered bundle, replaced it in its box and handed the box to Thomas.

"Do you have charms or spells on any of the other wagons?" asked Thomas.

"There's a round spellstone carved with runes in another wagon. The mages recommended I position it halfway along the caravan. Demons did not attack that wagon. Maybe I should have bought one of those for each wagon, but the mage assured me these were enough."

Thomas shook his head in commiseration. "Do you know if other caravans have had this kind of bad luck?"

"I haven't heard of any. Ah well. What is done is done.

§ § §

Her mission to deliver what she thought was a spellstone to the Dragon Tower complete she needed to fade into the background as quickly as possible. "If you would excuse me, my lord? I must be about my tasks." She wanted to get her booth set up and start gathering information.

"Of course, Trader Lahri. Good luck," Thomas responded as he stepped down from the vardo.

§ § §

Thomas felt her watching as he, Gregory, and the guards walked back toward the Dragon Tower.

"Not a word," murmured Thomas to Gregory.

In silence, the four men made their way through the interior gate, across the forecourt of Dragon Tower, and into the great hall.

"To your office," Thomas ordered.

The guards that followed Thomas everywhere took up their positions on either side of the door into Gregory's office. Thomas hurried to the table in the middle of the room and carefully placed the box on the table.

"It's got to be the Fasach Amulet!" he exclaimed.

Wait. Do not uncover it here. The silk has dampened its power. Had the Demons sensed it they would have surely destroyed the entire caravan to possess it, HellReaver spoke to both men.

"Perhaps I can help." A deep voice, smooth as velvet, spoke from the doorway.

Thomas and Gregory looked to the speaker. Neulach stood in the opening.

"Please, my lord. We have the second amulet," Thomas told him. Excitement laced his words.

"I felt its power a short time ago, as did any magical being within the Keep and perhaps beyond," Neulach's dry observation made Thomas blush.

"I didn't know it was the amulet, and Trader Lahri uncovered it while we were in her wagon," he answered. "I re-covered it as quickly as I could."

Neulach nodded. "Not your fault then, Lord Thomas."

Thomas shook his head. "Trader Lahri said she bought it from the Mage Enclave in Fasach. How could a mage not feel its power? Why would they send it north with her, out of Fasach, especially if that's where the Demons are entering our world?"

"A good question. There may be more to the amulet than we can see right now. I would like to inspect it more closely as time allows."

"Of course," Thomas agreed.

A guard knocked on the doorframe. "Lord Thomas, a messenger from the King has arrived. He says it's urgent."

"Gregory, hide this in the corridor behind the mural. I'll be back as soon as I see the messenger. We need a plan," he told the seneschal and Neulach as he hurried from the room.

Chapter 12

Sir Mathin's Trail

The Forest Lord Citadel was farther away than Owen thought. They had been riding for at least two and a half candlemarks through fields of waving grass. Owen finally realized what had been bothering him since they entered the Glen. Here it was mid-summer. Everywhere else, it was the end of winter, possibly the beginning of spring. He shook his head in wonder. He knew powerful magic ruled here from that alone.

He urged his warhorse into a trot and quickly into a canter, catching up with Saleth and his wolf at the head of the column. "We need to take a break. The men and horses should rest before we reach the Citadel." *I'd like to make a good impression*, he thought.

Saleth grinned at him, the corners of his eyes crinkling in amusement. "As you wish. There's a stream to the right up ahead at that line of trees." He and Samhanach slowed from the lope they had maintained the entire time, leading the column toward the Citadel. Owen reined his horse to the right and looked back along the column, searching for the black and white horse Sergeant Jory rode. He motioned the sergeant forward.

The sergeant moved out of the column, booted his horse into a trot and quickly closing the distance to Owen. "We'll take a break and let everyone eat and drink."

"Yes sir," Sergeant Jory responded. He moved his horse away from Owen and bellowed down the line, "Fall out at the stream ahead."

The trees gave welcome shade to the soldiers and horses. Men stepped out of their saddles and led the horses to the stream to drink. When they were finished, they moved them out into the fields filled with spring grass. Bridles removed, the animals dropped their heads and began to graze.

The men stretched to loosen tired backs and legs. They pulled jerky and dried fruit from their saddlebags. The men talked quietly among themselves. Owen dropped the reins he held, using them to ground-tie his horse, listening with half an ear as he straightened his clothing and beat the dust of travel from his trousers.

Using the horses' shadows for shade out in the meadow, the men squatted near each other. "What do you think the elves will do when we arrive?" Owen overheard one of the men ask his companion.

"Don't know," the corporal responded. "I don't trust 'em, though. They can mess with us any way they want. I don't like 'em."

"Hope Lord Owen knows what he's doin' with them," the other responded.

I hope so, too, thought Owen as he chewing on a piece of jerky.

He walked to the stream and filled his waterskin with cool water. Standing, he wrapped the binding around the neck of the dripping skin, absently looking along the line of trees that followed the stream. His eyes paused at movement on the other side.

Flashes of color and sparkle dazzled his eyes. Frowning, he looked back at Saleth. The elf was watching him steadily. Owen looked back toward the other side of the trees. He stepped across the stream, using the stones placed to create a path. He couldn't remember if they had been there when he'd filled the waterskin or not.

He shook his head and pinched his wrist. Yes, he was awake.

HeartStriker, is this real?

As real as you are, the sword answered quietly.

Owen reached the other side of the creek. Pushing through the last edge of brush and trees, he stopped in astonishment.

"Ah—" the breath escaped him in absolute wonder.

White horses whose coats shimmered and sparkled in the sunlight filled the grasslands on the other side of the trees.

No, they weren't horses and they weren't white. The sun struck every color from those glittering coats, as if diamonds covered every hair. These beings were more slender than any horse though they stood as tall as his charger. Their eyes were huge. Delicate ears swiveled constantly on a head that looked more goat than horse. Their babies bounced and hopped among the grazers.

The movement of a large body pushing through the brush could not turn him from what he watched. Navar joined him at the edge of the trees. Navar snorted.

At his sound, every head jerked up and around in his direction. The creatures flowed together, babies in the center of the group, wary adults facing what they perceived as a threat.

Fairy mounts, used for the Great Hunt, Navar told him, dismissal in his tone. *They would eat you as quick as look at you.*

No, they would not, responded HeartStriker. *They sense the magic in his blood and in me. Walk forward, Owen.*

Owen obeyed HeartStriker's request. He started walking toward the herd. *What are they?* he asked the Sword of Light.

They are Agni. They have served the elves as long as the elves have lived.

Owen continued walking. His heart picked up speed. The herd moved forward, many heads tossing in agitation. One of the Agni, larger than the others, pushed to the front as the herd began to circle around

Owen. He could feel the magic building, he knew not to what end.

He locked eyes with the leader of the herd. The circling Agni ran faster and faster, raising a cloud of dust around him. With a bugling call, as clear and sweet as a bell, the leader trumpeted. The circling animals stopped as one, turned to the center of the circle and bent a knee, bowing to Owen.

He stood bemused. Keeping his eyes on the leader, he bowed deeply. Recognition passed between them.

Well done, Lord Owen. HeartStriker and Navar spoke as one.

Owen looked back to the tree line. Navar, Saleth, and Samhanach stood watching him.

The shadow of something huge swept over the tableau.

The Agni reacted instantly.

Pushing the babies to the middle, they grouped themselves in a circle, heads raised to confront the danger. Teeth bared, heads tossing, squeals of anger filled the air.

The Red Dragon glided in to land between the Agni and Owen. She moved to Owen, her long neck snaking down to his side to claim him as hers. Waves of magical power rolled from her body.

Owen turned and bowed deeply to her.

The Agni stopped as if frozen in place. Eyes wide, they watched as the Dragon raised her head and roared to power. The whirlwind whipped around her form, raging in a mad swirl of dust and chaff, then dissipated.

Owen stood firm against the wind.

Aeden, OathKeeper in her hands, crouched ready to fight beside him.

"Lady, all is well," he told her, cautiously reaching out to touch her on the shoulder.

Eyes fierce, she looked at the Agni as she straightened with slow deliberation.

The leader narrowed his own eyes, tossed his nose in dismissal and turned his back on both of them. He gave a snorted command and the rest of the herd whirled and galloped away toward the Citadel.

§ § §

In silence, the companions made their way back through the brush and trees and crossed the stream. The soldiers desperately tried to control the rearing, squealing horses. Owen sent calming magic through the gathering with a wave of his hand.

Aeden stopped. As she did, so did the others. She looked at him, eyes wide, left eyebrow raised. He swung around to face them. "What?"

"What did you just do?" she asked, her head cocked to the side. "I've not felt that power in you before." Her hand rested on OathKeeper's pommel. Saleth leaned on his quarterstaff next to Aeden.

"I told them to calm down, to not be afraid—oh." Owen's eyes went wide as well. "Wait. Where did that come from?"

"It is part of your power now," Saleth told him. "There was a change when you bowed to the Agni. Powerful or no, they do not recognize many, especially not humans."

Samhanach walked up behind Owen and thrust his head under Owen's right hand. Owen absently began to scratch behind the wolf's ears. Navar snorted loudly. Owen realized what he was doing and jerked his hand back. The dire wolf pushed against his side until Owen lowered his hand and began to scratch again, eyes wide, mouth hanging open in astonishment.

Aeden compressed her lips, trying not to laugh at his expression. Saleth just shook his head in resignation. "Samhanach chooses whom he wants to bestow his friendship on."

No accounting for some people's tastes, Navar told them nastily. Samhanach wrinkled his lips at the WindRunner, showing teeth. Navar bared his in return.

"Stop it, both of you," Owen demanded. He lifted his hand from Samhanach's neck and deliberately replaced it. "Navar, I can befriend whomever I wish. It doesn't make me any less your companion."

"Magic, fighting over the boy. Who would have thought," Aeden murmured, mostly to herself.

"Sergeant Jory, have the men mount up. We need to get going," ordered Owen.

Chapter 13

Pack Attack

Lord Scott WindWalker shrugged into his wool jacket, quickly fastening the horn buttons made to keep it closed. He pulled on a pair of thin leather gloves followed by a pair of woolen mittens.

Winter had returned with a vengeance to the Windward Range. Five inches of snow covered the ground. Visibility was down to a quarter of a mile in some places as the wind blew the top layer into a ground blizzard. The men had waited as long as they could to go out and hunt for meat for the stronghold. Scott would go with them, regardless of unwanted advice from his wife.

He stalked down the hallway to the door that faced the kennels. The dogs began to bark and howl as soon as he stepped out onto the porch, pulling the door shut behind him. He scowled in irritation, certain Debra would hear the racket and come to investigate.

Moving quickly, he strode down the shoveled walk to the kennel. He slipped through the door facing the manor and closed it firmly against the freezing wind. A gust rattled the door in its frame, as if some ravening beast sought to enter.

He stamped the snow from his boots and pounded his gloves together. Just that short walk had chilled his hands and feet.

The dogs' barking fell to quiet whining and yipping as Scott walked down the center aisle between stalls sized to fit the dogs in them, murmuring to each of the creatures as he passed. He and Debra raised war, hunting, and herding dogs. Each type required different housing, feed, and training. The WindWalker animals were the envy of the kingdom.

He reached the open training area at the end of the aisle.

"Good morning, Jokan. Cold out today. I'm looking forward to the hunt," Scott greeted the youngish man who stood in the center of a milling pack of dogs. "Who have you chosen for the sweep?"

"I'm thinking these fifteen wardogs need a run, and ten of the hunting dogs will do well in the snow, my lord," Jokan responded.

Scott ran an expert glance over the dogs. The wardogs were huge, heavy coated black and sable animals standing thigh-high to a man at their shoulders. Bred to take out horses and men during battle, they could run them down to exhaustion when needed.

The hunting dogs had coats of red, brown, blue roan, and black, some with white patches and spots. Sleek and lithe, meant for running and retrieving, these dogs carried unusually dense coats in the winter that kept them warm in the coldest weather.

"We'll take four of the warhorses as well," Scott told him. "Meet me at the edge of the pastures. Tristan and Brody are at the stable with the horses. They'll come with us as archers."

Jokan nodded in understanding. "Let's go, boys," he said quietly to the dogs.

Scott snugged his hat down over his ears and pulled the scarf tighter around his neck. He stepped out into the cold from the relative warmth of the kennel. For an instant, the cold took his breath away. Hands covering his nose and mouth, he hurried down the shoveled path to the stable. Quinn met him at the double doors.

"Lord Scott, this isn't a good idea." Quinn's voice was deep with disapproval. His bright red wool coat covered him from shoulders to mid-calf. A red cap with earflaps covered his bald head. "There are too many things that can go wrong with a hunt at this time of year. I've told you about travelers heading south seeing strange creatures moving across the range and finding slaughtered game that's been killed by nothing they recognize. I've seen things myself."

"We need the meat. I'm going." Scott spoke with crisp command.

Resigned, Quinn did not argue further. Once the lord used that tone, it was impossible to change his mind.

"Tristan and Brody have the horses at the other end of the stable. They're ready to go. I knew you'd want to go out through the fields."

Shaking his head, Quinn walked beside him. "Lord, for my sake would you at least take another archer? Please?"

Scott stopped and turned to the person whom he trusted more than anyone else he knew, except for his wife. He searched Quinn's face and saw real disquiet there. "What have you heard?"

"Strange sounds out in the fields, especially toward the old quarry. Herds of antelope killed and ripped apart, but not eaten. I've heard in the village that the badlands send the rare human who ventures there fleeing in fear for no reason they can name."

Scott frowned. "Anything from the WindRunners?" he asked.

"No," Quinn almost barked out. "And that's even more suspicious. I can see they are nervous when they come in for feed, but there's nothing I can put my finger on."

Scott shook his head. "We're still low on meat. I need this as much as the dogs and horses do," he told him. "We'll not go far. Half a day out. Back by tonight."

Quinn snorted in resignation. "Aye, my lord. Travel careful."

Scott thumped his range foreman on the shoulder and walked to the end of the stable. Five warhorses stood at the doors, saddled and ready to go, held by the two archers Scott had requested, and Idris.

"My lord, I know you asked for two, but I'd like to help. I've not been out since I arrived. I'm a fair archer when I'm not scouting for the duke," the man from Red Dragon's Keep hurried to tell him.

"Fine. Mount up. Let's go," Scott's words were short with impatience.

The archers led the warhorses out of the stable onto the shoveled entryway paved with stone. The ground shuddered under the ponderous beat of huge hooves as they followed their riders. The wind had died down but the snow continued to fall. The horses snorted and moved restlessly as men stepped up on mounting blocks, put their feet in stirrups and pulled themselves up into saddles.

Each archer carried a bow, arrows, and a sword. Two of them carried pikes. Scott made sure the crossbow he had requested was bound to his saddle.

He tightened his legs, urging his horse to a trot. The others followed, Tristan leading Jokan's horse. They soon reached the pack of dogs sniffing, barking and playing in the snow. Jokan stood watching them. The riders stopped next to him. He sprang up, grabbed the horn of the saddle on the left side of his horse and pulled himself up far enough to find the stirrup. He swung his other leg over the saddle.

"That was impressive," Tristan teased the younger man.

Jokan grinned. He shouted out "Watch Me" to the dogs that immediately stopped what they were doing and turned to look at him. He swung his arm out from his body and silently signaled 'hunt'. The dogs took off to the northwest, away from Aos Si. Riders touched heels to sides, cueing the horses to follow.

Dogs and horses soon settled into a working trot each could sustain for a very long time. Within a candlemark, one of the hunting dogs belled out in its deep tracking voice. Once on the trail, it fell silent. It veered to the right of the pack, leading them toward the quarry.

A relatively deep canyon riddled with caves and tunnels, the quarry was an outcropping of limestone worked by men for as long as anyone could remember. It provided the blocks of stone used to build the fortified manor for Aos Si.

Predator and prey alike made it their home. Plains red bear, prairie wolves and great cats with huge canine teeth prowled its depths. Small hills and valleys surrounded the quarry, offering shelter and grazing for larger game. Herds of antelope and bison pawed through the snow to tear at the frozen grasses.

Stands of deciduous trees and evergreens grew along the edges of the quarry. An ice-free stream flowed at the bottom. Where water was, trees grew. Thickets of alder and yew lined its banks, leafless at this time of year.

The racing dogs startled a herd of antelope from behind one of the rolling hills leading to the canyon. Bunching in a panic, the antelope rushed toward what they thought was the safety of the trees.

Without a sound, the wardogs put on a burst of speed and drew even with the panicked animals. They cut off six of the runners from the herd and leapt forward to hamstring each one. The archers raised bows and shot the struggling creatures behind the front leg, piercing their hearts, putting them out of their pain. Blood stained the snow.

"Good hunt," Scott shouted. The warhorses thundered past the bloody site, slowed and turned back. The group trotted toward the carnage.

The dogs faced the canyon as one. Tails tucked, none of them took a step toward what stood at the top of it. They began to bark, whine, and howl.

The men looked back over their shoulders toward the top of the canyon walls.

Huge black shapes stood in silhouette against the white snow on the ground. The shapes began to move toward the hunt.

The men swung their horses toward those shapes. As they drew closer, the figures resolved into a roiling horde of beasts. Beasts the men could not identify.

"Demons," gasped Idris.

The Demons, black as midnight, flowed like hot tar over the snow. Enormous eyes glowing green in some, red in others, were set at the front of heavy rounded skulls. Powerful jaws on short muzzles hung open as the monsters panted, revealing massive teeth and canines. A short neck rose to a hump at the withers, the back sloping down to powerful hind legs that drove them forward. Huge clawed paws carried them effortlessly over the snow. The stench of rotting, putrid death rolled in a wave before them.

Scott raised his eyes from the charging line to look at the Rift. He watched, frozen in place, as three creatures from nightmares unfurled wings and launched into the sky. He groped at the side of his saddle, releasing the crossbow it carried.

"Go Out," shrieked Jokan. He threw his arms wide. Half the wardogs bolted to his right, the other half to his left. The hunting dogs dropped back to surround the riders. "Hunt, kill," he ordered them. The dogs sprang toward the monsters.

Scott cocked the crossbow and aimed at the creature running easily at the front of the Demons. He pulled the trigger, launching the bolt. With a thwack, the arrow sped away. The bow recoiled back into his shoulder. The iron bolt took the Demon in the chest, dropping it without a sound.

The others loosed arrow after arrow. Most found their mark. Tristan and Brody pulled the pikes from the straps on their saddles. Idris hefted his war axe. Scott cocked the bow and shot another bolt, killing another Demon. Unable to cock and load the bow quick enough, he dropped it in the snow.

The flying Demons rose above the running horde. "Way to me," shouted Jokan, telling the wardogs to attack from the flanks. The wardogs turned as one and charged into the sides of the attacking horde. Bone crunched, blood sprayed, shrieks exploded as the two groups met in a slashing, snarling, clawing, ripping mass.

"Charge!" bellowed Scott, yanking his heavy sword from its scabbard. Tristan and Brody lowered their pikes and kicked the warhorses into motion. Ignoring the smells of death, blood, and dying, the five horses surged forward. The pikes skewered two and three Demons at a time. The horses slammed into the beasts, cleaving heads, breaking bodies and smashing bones with hooves larger than a man's head. Idris swung his axe to deadly effect, chopping off heads, bodies and legs.

The flying Demons dove on the melee. One swooped and grabbed Tristan by the shoulders with clawed hind feet, attempting to pull him from the saddle. Tristan's horse reared and hopped forward on its hind legs, crushing Demons as it went. Tristen thrust his pike up into the flying horror. It slid down along the pike, slashing and biting at his head and chest, cutting his throat.

It pushed off Tristan's body as he fell from his horse, flapping awkwardly away. Blood gushed around the pike. It finally dropped dead to the ground.

Scott kicked his horse toward the flyer diving to attack Jokan. Brody desperately tried to stab the other flyer dropping toward Scott's back. Scott's horse shrieked and reared as Demons attacked its flanks and hind legs. The flyer slammed into Scott, claws ripping at his sides, teeth tearing at his shoulders and back.

Flyer, rider and horse fell over backward, crushing the flyer. Scott's horse struggled to its feet, rearing and pounding down again and again, using its front feet like sledge hammers.

Brody ran his pike through a Demon as it leapt at Scott, killing it. He jumped from his horse, pulling his sword from the saddle scabbard as he fell and stood over Scott, killing Demons right and left as they pushed in to kill the men.

The remaining flyer hovered above those from Aos Si as if studying them. It turned and flew off toward the northeast. Without warning, the three remaining Demons broke off their attack, as if following orders from the flyer. They sped away from the battleground, racing back toward the limestone caverns.

"Leave it," Jokan croaked. The wardogs broke off the attack as the Demons ran. They struggled back to the humans. Every one of them was injured. Not a single hunting dog survived.

"Tristan! Idris! Jokan! Help," shouted Brody. "Lord Scott is down!"

The two remaining men swung their warhorses around and galloped to where Scott lay on the blood-soaked ground, Brody kneeling next to him. He carefully pulled his lord over onto his side. He shrugged out of his coat and rolled it up, carefully lifting Scott's head and pushing it under him.

Scott groaned and opened his eyes. Idris pulled the waterskin off his saddle as he dismounted next to the two men. He crouched down next to them, handing the waterskin to Brody.

"My lord, can you hear me?" he asked.

Scott groaned again. "Yes," he whispered.

"Can you move your legs?"

"Yes."

"How about your arms?"

"Yes."

Idris reached out and parted Scott's hair. Blood seeped from punctures and scratches. He slid the shoulder of the shredded jacket away from Scott's body, revealing deep cuts on his shoulder and sides.

Idris gave a gusty sigh. Gently Brody lifted Scott's head and tilted the waterskin, sending a trickle into his mouth. Scott gulped down the liquid. He struggled to sit up.

"Rest now," Idris told him, pressing gently on his shoulder.

"Jokan, light a fire. We need to close some of these wounds. The dogs and horses need water and food. I'll set up a windbreak. We have to clean the antelope and get them ready for transport. I'll bring Tristan's body here."

Brody gasped and looked out at the carcass-covered field, searching for his friend. The Demon bodies were bubbling and smoking, dissolving as he watched.

Idris reached out and shook Brody's shoulder. "I'm sorry, lad. Stay next to Lord Scott and make sure he stays down, at least for a little while, maybe a half-candlemark." He heaved himself with weary resolve to his feet. "We still have to get home."

$$\S \S \S$$

The sun had long set by the time the weary group of archers, dogs and horses returned to Aos Si. The wind had died completely, but snow continued to fall, blanketing them all in a layer of cold.

Tristan's body lay over the saddle of his warhorse, hands tied to his feet with rope to keep the body from

sliding off. Every horse carried an antelope carcass.
Scott had lost a lot of blood before Idris and Brody
cauterized the worst of the wounds. Scott slumped
forward over the front of his saddle, holding on to the
pommel as tight as he could as his horse stumbled often
from the slashes on its legs. Everyone in the group bore
signs of the battle. Jokan's horse limped badly from
Demon wounds. Six of the wardogs died on the way
back.

A shout went up from the guards standing watch at
the wall between the pastures and the stable as the men,
horses and dogs entered through the gate. Groomsmen
pushed opened the doors to the stable. When they saw
the condition of the group, one split off and ran to the
manor, the others running out into the cold to help the
injured.

Jokan threw his leg over the saddle and slid to the
ground. Brody caught the reins he tossed as the
kennelman knelt to comfort the remaining wardogs. He
trailed fingers over heads and down spines, silently
telling the dogs all was well. He wearily turned and
trudged up the walkway to the kennel building, what
was left of the pack trailing after.

The horses halted at the stable entrance. Quinn
appeared from the depths of the barn, took one look at
them and ran to the doors. Brody stepped down from
his horse, almost falling as he landed. He caught himself
by the stirrup and leaned against the giant horse.

"Use the mounting blocks to help them down," Idris
ordered the grooms. "Watch the bundle behind Tristan.
It's a Demon." Stablemen recoiled from the horse.

"Don't worry. It's dead," he told them. He untied the ropes holding Tristan across the saddle and slid the body into his arms. He laid it gently on the ground, out of the way.

Quinn and two stablemen carefully lifted Scott from his saddle. They supported him into the barn. Quinn threw a horse blanket over a short stack of hay bales and helped Scott lie down. He gently laid more blankets over the injured man.

"Get Lady Debra and the healer now." Quinn sent a groomsman running. "You and you, bring the horses in, untack them and get them brushed. Check their wounds and bind them up. Warm mash and hay. Get the antelope meat to the butcher." The grooms jumped to obey, gathering reins and leading the horses into the warmer stable.

"I told him not to go," a voice filled with anger echoed down the center aisle. "We need him here. I need him here," the voice broke with fear.

Lady Debra, bundled in wool and leather, rushed down the aisle toward Quinn and Scott. The healer trailed after her at a more sedate pace.

Debra slowed as she approached the makeshift bed, taking in the extent of his injuries. Scott reached out for her hand, lifting it to his lips as she came to stand next to him.

"Husband, what were you thinking?" she asked in a much gentler tone as she reached out and rested her hand on his chest. "What caused these injuries?"

"We needed meat," he grimaced as he answered in a very weak voice. "Now we know, Debra. The Demon War is here."

Chapter 14

The Tolling
of the Bell

In a candlemark, the troops arrived at the gates of the Forest Lords Citadel. The column stopped, barred by a lowered portcullis and gleaming silver gates at least three men high, washed to gold by the setting sun. Four Forest Lords stood guard, two to either side of the portcullis. White marble walls held a rose-orange blush as the sun sank lower. Flags flew from the peaks of the towers along and within the walls.

Owen let his head fall back as he marveled at the beauty of the Citadel. *I've always thought Red Dragon's Keep was wonderful, but this, this is gorgeous.* He felt HeartStriker's laugh through their bond.

He'd kept his shields very tight since the Agni in the meadow. He didn't want any hint of power or thought leaking out or getting in.

Navar stood next to him, his head held high, looking expectantly at the gates. Aeden sat on her warhorse on his other side, her crossed arms resting on the horn of her saddle. Saleth stood talking with the guards. The Agni had arrived well before them, obviously telling tales.

With a groan deep in the walls and the clash of links of chain on a windlass, the portcullis slowly began to rise. The gates swung out, revealing the courtyard beyond. As soon as the portcullis rose high enough, Saleth motioned for them to follow him.

Owen took note of the murder holes in the short passage leading from the gate to the courtyard.

The view of the courtyard opened up before them. A layer of crushed white marble chips covered the ground. On the far right, white marble veined with broad blue rivers of stone rose into a tall slender tower. Set into the tower wall, wide high doors sweeping to an elegant peak at their center stood at the top of stairs ascending from the courtyard. Curved walls spread to the left and right, forming an arc around the courtyard.

Broad marble stairs threaded with gold descended from the entrance to an apron of rose marble. Intricately carved wooden brackets held globes of magefire around the walls of the court. Tall Forest Lords lined the perimeter, both men and women, most armed with spears and bows, arrow-filled quivers slung over their shoulders.

Saleth leaned on his staff at the edge of the apron. Samhanach sat at his side, ears swiveled forward and flicked back.

"Dismount," murmured Owen.

Sergeant Jory heard him and gave the signal. As if rehearsed, the men dismounted at the same time. They stepped forward to hold the horses' reins next to the bit. Navar moved to stand on Owen's left side. Aeden joined him on his right.

As she did, the doors of the tower slowly swept open to the left and right.

Within their embrace, a tall, slender figure stood, dressed in a sleeveless light green robe, covered with a forest green tabard picked out with golden thread highlighting unending loops and swirls. Blood red thread bordered its edges, gleaming like the liquid itself. Black sandals studded with jewels protected his feet. White hair swept behind his pointed ears and hung to the middle of his chest.

He held his hands clasped at his waist. Gold and silver rings glittered on every finger and silver filigree circled up his bare muscled arms to his shoulders. The thin band of his crown held every color of powerful beryl gems. They flashed in the light. A slender sword of silver hung from a silver chain fastened around his waist.

He seemed to glide down the stairs to the apron. Guards with bows, arrows and tall, wickedly tri-tipped spears followed him. Each took a place on the stairs, ranging in a wedge behind their ruler.

Saleth stepped forward onto the apron. "My King, I bring to you the Second Son, Owen Arach, as you ordered." He gave a short bow. He straightened and, with a sweep of his arm, motioned to his right. "I also bring honored guests, Lady Aeden, The Red Dragon." He gestured to the left. "Navar, WindRunner of the Great Plains."

A quiet whispering, as of leaves in a breeze, circled the courtyard. The High King's deep amethyst eyes, set at an oblique angle above high, chiseled cheeks, flicked over Owen and settled on Aeden and Navar. Without expression, he nodded his head to them.

His deep voice filled the enclosure. "Welcome, Owen Arach, second son of the Lord of Red Dragon's Keep. Welcome, daughter of the Black King. Welcome, WindRunner. Welcome indeed. Join me." He turned his head a tiny fraction. "See to their men." He turned and ascended the stairway, not once looking back to see if they followed.

Owen and Aeden glanced at each other and at Navar. They handed the reins of their horses to Sergeant Jory. The three stepped forward onto the rose marble apron. HeartStriker began to vibrate, but did not speak. The deep voice of a bell tolled, its sound reverberating across the Citadel, filling Owen with dread. He and his companions halted. Indrawn breath circled the enclosure. Murmurs whispered.

Saleth looked at them with wide eyes. "The Bell of Prophecy has not tolled for a thousand years," he told them in a low voice.

The High King hesitated on the stairs as if he wanted to turn, but continued into the tower.

Saleth nodded at them. "Come. He awaits you."

Alberick, High King of the Forest Lords, swept through the entry to the Citadel. The tolling of the Bell troubled him deeply. Legend held the tolling foretold the breaking of the Darkened Forest. He could not let that happen. He'd felt the quickening of power as these strangers had entered his court.

The Agni told a tale of magic and potency surrounding the second son. Owen. He must remember his name. And he came with a Dragon and a WindRunner.

"Show them to their rooms," he told the seneschal. "I would meet with them at last-meal."

He continued through the entry and down the hall to his chambers. Ceremony demanded he wear these clothes denoting his status and power, but not to last-meal. His chamberlain glided up to him as he entered the room. He raised his arms and the chamberlain removed the tabard, laying it out on the couch at the foot of the bed.

The wall of the room on the right stood open to a forest glade, turning the room into a peaceful retreat. Birds flitted among the branches of the trees. A bowl of fruit sat on the table next to the armoire that held his clothing. He chose an apple still glistening with dew. Biting into its sweetness, he gazed deep into the shadows of the trees, searching for an answer to the tolling Bell of Prophecy. *What great power has come to break this Forest prison?* he wondered. He never doubted the foretelling.

Uncertain and concerned, he shook his head as he flicked the apple core into the air. It disappeared.

"The white tunic and trousers," he told his chamberlain. "And some wine."

§ § §

Owen and his companions stood just inside the great doors opening into the foyer. They stared at the great trees rising around the space, upper branches interwoven to create a cool and serene bower. Beautifully carved tables and chairs sat in openings among the trunks of the trees, creating secluded alcoves. Large silk pillows in jewel tones rested in groups on the floor. Magelight globes hung from silver chains wound through the upper branches of the trees.

The companions had little time to marvel at the beauty of the foyer as a tall elf approached and introduced himself as the Citadel's seneschal.

"Windrunner, how may we serve you?" he asked Navar.

Do you have an ungated room? Navar answered. *I am content with deep straw, water and grain. I will join my companions for this meeting at last-meal.*

"As you wish, WindRunner Navar," the seneschal bowed to him.

"Please. Follow me, honored guests." He bowed to Owen and Aeden.

The three trailed him down a hall opening to the right. Its walls were massive tree trunks, their branches arching and interweaving over the top to form a ceiling. Soft, gently moving lengths of silk fabric in every color of the rainbow lined the corridor, somehow anchored to the trees behind them. Owen reached out in wonder to run his hand along the shimmering lengths.

"It's beautiful," he murmured.

"It is," Aeden agreed.

The seneschal stopped at a doorway on the left created by slender saplings bent at the top into an arch. Fabric draped the entry. He raised his hand and pulled the fabric back, hooking it over a small limb bent to that purpose.

Within, the chamber opened out to the vista of a meadow. Rippling waves of grass rolled to the edge of the forest. Sitting in the middle of the room was a couch covered in soft green satin fabric. A low, ornately carved table stood in front of it. Several large jewel-toned pillows lay on the floor beside the table.

A crystal-clear pool of water, surface moving with ripples caused by a waterfall, beckoned the weary travelers from the other side of the couch. Doorways, again created by saplings, opened into rooms on the left and right. A bed, table, chairs, and an armoire were visible, promising tranquility and peace.

"You may refresh yourselves. The King wishes to meet with you at last-meal, in perhaps two candlemarks."

"Thank you," Aeden and Owen spoke together.

The seneschal withdrew, letting the curtains fall. Owen listened as Navar's hoofbeats faded into the distance.

He looked at Aeden, shaking his head.

"Lady, I have a question," he said as he unhooked HeartStriker's scabbard from his belt. He laid the sword on the table in front of the couch. "Why didn't you, umm, flame the Agni when you flew over the meadow?"

With a crooked smile, Aeden sat on the couch.

"I try not to kill those who are allies of allies. The Agni are one among many of the magical beings set to guard the Darkened Forest. They are as unpredictable as any magical creature. They often lure the unwary traveler into their territory and kill him. Had they attacked you, I most assuredly would have 'flamed them'."

Silence filled the room as Owen thought about what she had said.

"What did you find on your flight over the Forest," he asked quietly.

"I found where Sir Mathin is held. It is close to the edge of the Forest near the Windward Range. There is something there I have never sensed before, perhaps a beast grown to monstrous proportions. We must ask the King," she responded.

§ § §

Owen ran the whetstone along HeartStriker's length one last time.

Sharp enough, he thought.

Yes I am, HeartStriker replied, a smug note in his response.

Owen snorted. He slid the sword into its scabbard. He glanced up from his seat on the couch in the main chamber as Aeden slid through the silk draping the doorway to her room.

She wore a pale green dress that hugged her body, its length brushing the floor. Long sleeves ended at her wrists. A garnet ring surrounded by diamonds graced her left hand. A necklace of water pearls spilled down the front of the dress. Hair banded at the crown of her head cascaded down her back like a fall of fire. OathKeeper hung from a silver chain belted at her waist. Owen's mouth fell open.

He jumped to his feet. "Lady?"

Aeden grinned at him. "Yes, it's me. Thank you."

Owen blushed. He brushed self-consciously at the front of his court clothes. He'd carried a tunic and trousers in deepest brown for just such an occasion as this meeting. The sigil of his house emblazoned the front of the tunic: a red dragon spreading its wings, preparing to fly.

He clipped HeartStriker's scabbard to his leather belt and held out his arm. "Shall we go?" he asked formally.

Lady Aeden placed her hand on his arm. "I believe we shall," she said primly. A smile lit her face.

Owen brushed back the silk at the doorway. The seneschal waited beyond the opening. He led them back to the foyer and down a long hallway that branched from the entry. He left them at the arched doorway of the banquet hall.

Murmuring voices filled the hall as the gathering of elves talked quietly to each other. Tables were set in intimate groups throughout the room. Servants circulated with trays of refreshments. Navar stood next to the high table, waiting for Owen and Aeden. His ears swiveled in constant movement.

Cool eyes watched as Owen and Aeden made their way through the room. Owen stole glances at the elves they passed. Expressionless faces gave nothing away. Owen's back itched. Pressure on his arm from Aeden's fingers kept him from turning around to see who was staring at them with such animosity. He slanted a glance at Aeden whose serenity calmed his nerves. They mounted three stairs to the platform that held the high table. A servant bowed and led them to their chairs.

The High King entered the room as soon as they were in place. He wore a white tunic and trousers under a blue silk over-robe that shimmered with glints of silver and gold as he moved. A silver circlet rested on his white hair drawn back behind his pointed ears. Those gathered in the room fell silent. Owen watched as his companion gave a gracious nod. Owen made a shallow bow from the waist.

Owen locked eyes with the King. His blue eyes stared into the amethyst eyes of the elf. Owen felt a small trickle of pressure against his mind shield. He strengthened it. HeartStriker sent power to the shield. The King's eyebrows rose as he broke the stare and looked at the Sword hanging from Owen's belt. He glanced at Lady Aeden's Sword. He looked away with an odd smile on his face. Owen saw a tiny look of satisfaction cross Aeden's face.

"I see we have neglected to acknowledge beings even older than I. Welcome, Swords of Light."

Sharply indrawn breath from around the room greeted this welcome. Whispers filled the air.

Thank you for your greeting. HeartStriker spoke to every mind in the room. The volume of murmurs intensified.

The King raised his hand. Instant silence.

"WindRunner, what news do you bring of the Great Plains?"

Magic quickens everywhere across the plains. Some dark magic stirs, north of Aos Si. Those who have gone to test it have not returned, Navar responded.

The silence and tension in the hall intensified, if that was possible. Owen felt it as a tightening across his skin. His hand moved reflexively to HeartStriker's pommel at the perceived threat. Aeden glanced at him, giving a minute shake of her head. Owen did not remove his hand.

The King noted Owen's unease. He pulled out his chair and took his seat. His movement broke the tension in the room. Owen and Aeden sat. The King looked at the servants standing at the side of the room holding trays of food. They hurried forward and placed the trays on the table between the diners.

Owen served himself a slice of nicely browned roast chicken swimming in its own juice. The tubers and greens looked delicious, so he dished some up.

"May I serve you, Lady?" he asked Aeden.

"Thank you, no, Owen. I'll serve myself."

Duty done, Owen looked to the King to make sure he had started to eat. His mother would kill him if she ever found out he had been disrespectful to the King of anywhere.

If she's still alive. The thought surfaced, morbid and morose.

Don't think of it now, HeartStriker told him quietly. *Not that your mother isn't important,* the Sword of Light said, *but paying attention now could reveal things leading to answers we need.*

Owen sighed and took a bite of his chicken. *I know, HeartStriker. Things have been moving so fast, I haven't had a chance to think about finding them. Working with Navar has been hard. What can I do?* Even his mind voice sounded plaintive.

Listen. Watch. Perhaps some answers are here, his companion replied.

Owen glanced around the room. Several of the elves were watching the high table and the strangers who had sounded the Bell. When Owen caught their eyes, they averted their gaze or turned to their companions.

Interesting. HeartStriker told him. *They are thinking about the prophecy that foretells the breaking of the Darkened Forest. I have just remembered what the tolling of the Bell means.*

Owen slowly replaced his fork on the plate. *Should we be worried?*

HeartStriker was silent. *I take it we should be,* Owen thought grimly. *Aeden, have you been following this? Do you know of the prophecy?*

I have, she answered, *now that you have mentioned it. The prophecy tells of the breaking of the Darkened Forest by the Gathering of Heroes.*

Owen whipped his head around toward her. *What?* he exclaimed.

I must think on this, Owen. There are many paths stretching from this prophecy and this moment. Peace, for now.

Owen forked a bite of tuber into his mouth.

The King turned to him. "How came you to be in the company of a WindRunner, Lord Owen?" Owen finished chewing as quickly as he could. The amethyst color of the King's eyes glowed, seeming to compel him to speak.

"Sire, Navar appeared at the doors of the great hall at Red Dragon's Keep and told everyone he'd come for the second son." He poured mead from the flagon in front of him into his mug. "I didn't want to go. He insisted." He took a small sip from the mug.

The King looked at Owen, his eyes unblinking. He shifted his gaze to the WindRunner standing at the end of the table.

Owen decided to ask the question that had burned in his mind since his troop had entered the Glen. "Sire, have you heard anything, any rumor or tiniest bit of report about my parents? Lady Aeden ... um," He changed the question about Aeden's discovery he'd been about to ask. "Or the men my brother sent out to look for them? We've had no report since they were taken."

The King's eyes returned to Owen. "I know your parents were kidnapped." His voice held only sympathy. "I would speak of this with you after last-meal. For now, Lady Aeden, your presence here is ... astonishing. Has the Binding been broken?"

Owen watched in dismay as Aeden, whom he'd know all his life, became something else.

Utter silence descended on the room. A single indrawn breath.

Magic danced in the air, strong, pure, yet somehow filled with peril.

A stillness of feature removing every trace of emotion from her face or hint of movement from her body, supplanting the seeming of humanity she had shown to the world for so very long. An ancient alien presence, beyond powerful, looked out of her eyes and answered the Elven High King.

"The Binding is broken. The days of waiting are fulfilled. The Demons come, and with them, the traitors who have waited to doom us all."

The Bell began to toll. It rang seven times, reverberations fading between each ring. The sound trailed into silence.

The King stood abruptly and bowed deeply to the Red Dragon. "Lady, you honor us with your presence." Rustling filled the room as those present rose and bowed to magic incarnate in their midst.

Navar snorted loudly. Aeden slowly turned her head to gaze at the WindRunner. When her eyes met his, he shuddered once, bent one knee, and bowed to her as well.

Owen sat frozen in place, afraid to move.

The moment passed.

Aeden returned to humanity. Magic swirled in the air and was gone.

The King stood and waved his hand at the assembly. "Thank you, my friends, for joining us this night." The others in the room slipped quietly away, murmuring among themselves.

He turned to his guests. "If you would join me in the study?"

Two elven guards armored in silver stood behind the King. Armed with tall sharp spears, they fell into step on either side of their monarch. The five companions followed them from the room. As they entered the hall and turned toward the King's wing, Navar stopped. *I will return to my room. I can follow this meeting as easily from there.*

As you wish, the King responded.

§ § §

Once settled in his comfortable chair, part of a grouping of six arranged in front of the King's desk, Owen pressed his concern.

"Sire, have you heard about my parents?"

"Call me Alberick," the King requested. "We must work together to face that which comes."

"Y ... y ... yes, Sire. I mean Alberick," Owen stuttered.

With a small shake of his head, Alberick sighed heavily. He stood up from the chair to join the others and began to pace. Hands clasped behind his back, a frown marring his forehead, he was the very picture of agitation. He stopped and faced the group.

"The Darkened Forest is more vast than you can imagine. It exists, not just in this world, but also into the world of the Fey. The grove forming most of the Citadel opens into it.

We, the *Seleigh Sidhe*, the Forest Lords, seek to contain the dark and evil always threatening to creep out of our world into yours. We cannot close the Rift that connects us. We have tried, and lost too many in the effort.

I have information that may or may not be true. The Mymarida has taken your men and holds them, undying, in her lair."

Owen jerked forward in his chair, almost standing in his need for more. Aeden reached out and rested a calming hand on his arm. He slowed down enough for his mind to catch up with the surge of adrenaline threatening to overwhelm him.

"S—Alberick, what is a Mymarida and where is its lair? How do we get there? Can you help us find them? Is it in our world or yours? What do we need to do to get the men? How long has the Rift been open? What is a Rift?"

Alberick raised his hand. Owen's tumble of questions trailed into silence.

"I will answer your questions," the High King told him. "We have been planning a scouting mission to discover if the reports are true." He glanced at a servant who waited discretely against the wall. "Perhaps a small drink to settle us?" He spoke to the guard standing at the opening to the room. "Please request the presence of Saleth and Samhanach."

Chapter 15

Neulach's Search

The ball of magelight created by the Dragon in human form floated along the ceiling in front of he and Cameron, perhaps thirty paces away, casting a pale golden light along the walls and floor. Dampness and the musty, salty smell of old stone filled the air.

The hairs on Cameron's arms and neck stood on end. He felt something pressing on him. He shivered, not in fear, but in dread. He knew dark magic waited ahead.

"Do you feel that, Lord Neulach?" he whispering to the tall, dark man who walked with him on his right.

Neulach glanced down at him as they followed the tunnel, a tunnel that should not be there. Cameron had played in the undercroft of the Keep with his cousins many times. He knew all of the corridors and he'd never seen this one. He could tell by the stone floor that it wasn't new. Was it hidden all this time?

"I do, indeed, Cameron," Aeden's father, the Dragon King, responded in his deep voice. "Tell me again of the search for the Demon portals before the Demons attacked the Keep." He asked the question to distract his companion from what lay ahead.

"Well, sir, there are rune portals and disk portals." Cameron shook his head, sending his dark blond hair flying. He frowned with concentration, trying to remember every little detail from the first Demon attack.

"Breanna and I found the first disk. Thomas sent us to search the Keep, looking and, I guess 'feeling' is the best word, for any magic or things out of place. We saw a rat carrying a disk running along the wall of the family corridor. It went into Evan's room and we watched it try to stick the disk to the wall behind his wardrobe."

Make sure you tell him about killing the rat and SunWalker's part in the tale. Cameron's Sword of Light laughed into his thoughts.

I haven't forgotten, Cameron told his sword with grumpy shortness. *We were the ones who figured out how the Demons got into the Keep.*

Neulach canted his head in inquiry, as if he could hear GhostWalker. Cameron looked back in consternation. *He can hear me, Cameron. He is, after all, a Dragon.*

Oh, Cameron responded.

GhostWalker sent a smile through their link.

"Breanna and I killed the rat and SunWalker pried the disk off the wall. Both of our swords created a shield around the disk and we took it to Lady Aeden. Is she really your daughter? Anyway, she made the disk show a picture of the person who made it. Haloran recognized him. It was a man named Mannan. He's a counselor for the King. Then the Demons attacked, Aeden turned into a Dragon, we won the battle, Navar arrived for Owen and we haven't had time since to figure out why Mannan would make portals Demons can come through."

§ § §

Neulach listened closely to the tale Cameron spun for him. The boy was rail thin and growing quickly as he entered his fourteenth year, made evident by the too-short tunic and trousers he wore.

Thomas had agreed with enthusiasm when Neulach asked Cameron to accompany him on his search. More important to Neulach was the power he felt from the youngling, even when they were not close together.

Neulach shook his head. "I'm amazed at all you have done, young Gobhlan." He raised his head and drew in a deep breath, scenting the air. Reaching out, he put his hand on Cameron's shoulder. "Wait. There is something not far ahead."

The two stopped in the middle of the corridor. Cameron stepped away to the left, putting his back to the wall. Neulach looked at him, turned his head and looked down the corridor. He stepped to the other wall, brightening his magelight.

They stood silent, listening. The sound of a heavy body dragging on the stone floor of the passage started and stopped, started and stopped. Cameron looked at Neulach, eyes wide. He shivered.

"I feel its magic," Neulach told him. He cocked his head to the right.

A reflection at the farthest reaches of his magelight alerted both of them. There was a loud exhalation of air, almost a whistle. Two tiny globes of red light flickered into being. White dagger shapes beneath the globes flared in the light.

Without warning, an explosion of sound and motion hurtled down the corridor toward them. Neulach raised his right hand. Fire burst from his palm. The creature blew through the magical blaze. Its black hairless body ignited and flames began to stream behind it.

The white daggers became fangs. The red orbs turned into eyes glaring with hate and malice. Its mouth opened as it approached. Its throat was a portal to a place of ice and cold.

Neulach raised his left hand and added a second stream of fire. He pushed away from the wall with his shoulder and aimed the fire at the Demon's maw, directing the flames down its throat.

§ § §

Cameron trembled as he tried to burrow into the wall behind him. His breath came short and fast. Sweat dripped down his face.

Draw me, GhostWalker demanded.

Cameron gasped. He'd completely forgotten his Sword of Light.

With a shaking hand, he tried to pull the Sword out of the scabbard. It took two tries to finally slide free. He pointed it at the charging Demon, blade wavering wildly.

A roar of incandescent fire burst from the point of the sword, streaking to join Neulach's magic. GhostWalker's fire amplified the flames into an inferno.

The conflagration struck down the throat of the Demon.

Cameron flung his forearm up as if gutting a hanging deer. GhostWalker's flame rose up through the head of the Demon and winked out. The monster collapsed, momentum sliding it at terrible speed toward them. Dust billowed out and around its hurtling body. Neulach took one step back.

The body came to rest one foot away from them. Cameron's exhale of relief sounded very loud in the sudden quiet. He collapsed back against the wall. His arm loosened and the Sword's tip lowered toward the ground.

"What was that?" he hissed.

Neulach stood unmoving.

A step forward brought him to the Demon's muzzle. He knelt and laid his hand on the side of the creature's jaw.

"This is a *romhair tochail* Demon, brought to this world to dig this tunnel and create a Rift for others of its kind to enter. Why here? Why now? Why is Red Dragon's Keep so important? Who wants it to fall?"

Cameron stood silent, more interested in regaining his breath than answering questions. He leaned over and braced himself, a hand on each knee. Sweat dripped from his hair to the floor as he hung his head.

"What do we do now?" he asked.

"Move back," Neulach ordered, waving his hand up the corridor.

Cameron pushed himself up and shuffled away from Neulach, keeping his back to the wall, watching him over his shoulder.

Neulach straightened and stepped away from body. A sweeping movement of his right arm brought fire along the length of the Demon's body. Ethereal flames consumed it as they grew. In a heartbeat, the entire Demon lay masked in flickering light that gave no heat. The last of the beast faded away.

Cameron watched in astonishment.

"We go forward," Neulach told him.

Chapter 16

The King's Messenger

The King's messenger stood at the door of the Duke's office, a room Thomas had avoided since his father's kidnapping. The guard who watched the man came to attention as Thomas approached.

The messenger gave a short bow to Thomas. "My lord, the King requests your presence at Cathair Ri." A smirk twisted his lips and his eyes narrowed. The hair on the back of Thomas's neck lifted and a shudder passed down his spine. He looked at the man for what seemed like ages.

HellReaver, call Neulach. We need his wisdom here. Summon Gregory. Something's wrong.

Thomas pushed open the door to the room where his father spent so much time. A quick stab of sorrow tightened his chest and throat. Walking to his father's desk, he turned. "Where is the King's message?"

The man reached for the pouch at his side. He lifted the front flap and pulled a scroll from inside, extending it toward Thomas. The red wax seal of the King looked like a large drop of blood. "The King's Mage instructed that I personally deliver this into your hands."

Don't touch that! HellReaver and Neulach ordered him with a mental shout.

Thomas pushed his mental shield out toward the messenger, catching the man's hand and the scroll in its field. HellReaver augmented the shield's strength. The messenger's eyes widened as he tried to pull his hand back.

"Let me go," he gasped, twisting and turning his arm.

Neulach strode into the office. His black eyes glittered.

The person who sent this seeks to harm you. His voice whispered in all of their minds.

Thomas's shield recoiled as Neulach's magic wrapped the messenger's chest in a vice of power. The messenger shrieked. Gregory hit the doorway at a run and stopped abruptly.

Thomas drew a shaky breath into lungs that had suddenly emptied. He swayed. Neulach reached out and grasped his left shoulder, giving him much needed support.

"Who sent you?" Neulach asked as he turned his head and locked eyes with the man.

The messenger's gaze fixed on Neulach's eyes. His struggles ceased.

"The King commanded I deliver this. The King's Mage gave me the scroll. She demanded I hand it directly to the Lord of Red Dragon's Keep."

Gregory and Thomas looked at each other, eyebrows rising. Gregory shook his head.

Neulach released the man from his bondage. Without pause or movement, the messenger disappeared.

Thomas gaped. Gregory gasped.

"No trace of his existence remains. Spell and greed bound him. It is simpler this way."

"But ... but ... you can't just ... disappear someone," Gregory protested, his hands waving toward where the messenger had been standing.

"I have, and I will again when the need arises," Neulach said without emotion.

He cocked his head and looked intently at both men. "What would you have done? It is clear the King, King's Mage, and this messenger seek to kill you. Is that not a capital crime? He would have hung. Better to finish quick and quiet."

Neulach was right. Thomas shook his head with regret. "I wish you had asked. I agree with your decision, but I feel like I should have made it."

Setting that feeling aside, he paused in thought. "Why would the King want to kill me? I sent messages to him, telling him what had happened with Father, and again after the First Demon Battle. Why? Why would he do this? Unless ..."

"He's in league with whoever is working with the Demons," Gregory continued the sentence. "We know someone is. Demons would not know to attack Red Dragon's Keep without direction from someone here in Ard Ri."

Thomas sank into his father's chair behind the desk. He rested his elbow on the desk and rubbed his hand over his mouth and chin, thinking hard. "That could mean the King or the King's Mage or both are working against us, against the kingdom."

"Against the world," he whispered with dread.

Silent fear filled the room.

"Neulach, can you call the Dragons?" he asked quietly.

"I cannot. Once each Dragon made the choice to either stay or go, an ancient spell was set in motion. Someone must reunite the five amulets into the *Cumhacht ar Draigoini*, the Power of Dragons Talisman. Only then can that one who holds the Talisman call them. I was able to return because the *Claiomh* spell shrouding the *Claiomh Solas* was broken. It is the task of you and yours to find the amulets."

"Damn." Thomas stared into the distance. "We have two. I'm hoping someone in Fasach is on our side, someone in their Mages Enclave. Owen is on his way to Aos Si. We think one might be there." He stared at Neulach.

"Is one hidden in the Dragon Lands?" he asked the King of the Dragons.

Neulach stood, silent and still, giving no answer.

"I thought so," Thomas murmured. He pushed himself up from his father's chair. He put those thoughts aside as well.

"The messenger never arrived. We did not get an order to go to the capital. I'm going to protect Red Dragon's Keep," he told the man and the Dragon.

"No one will remember him," Neulach assured them.

Chapter 17

The Forest King's Choice

The Forest Lord King took his seat again. "I have no news of your parents, Owen," the King told Owen, his face drawn in lines of sympathy. "I'm sorry."

"To answer your question about the Rift, there are worlds beyond our own," Alberick began. "In some places, the barrier between the worlds is weak and can be further thinned by those with power. Once the Rift opens, it takes a great deal of strength to close it, often more than it took to create it. There are sealed Rifts all across your world leading to other realms.

The Rift in the Darkened Forest opened when the mage council created the *Cumhacht ar Draigoini*. The

Unseleigh Sidhe, to you the Dark Fey, entered your world on the gust front of that breach. Our world sent the Forest Lords to contain them lest they ravage your world past repair. Dark magic from this side of the Rift has kept us from closing it time and again. I wish we knew who wields such power."

Alberick pushed himself up from his chair and walked to the edge of the glade making up the left wall of his study. He clasped his hands behind his back and stared out into the meadow beyond the trees. With a shake of his head and a weary sigh, he turned back to Aeden and Owen.

"Mymaridae are flying beasts that sting their prey, paralyzing them. Many call them fairyflies. It carries the bodies back to its lair and binds them in an egg case for future use. This is the largest of such we have ever seen. There is a smell of Dragon magic to this monster."

Owen's eyes were huge. "Does that mean Sir Mathin and his men are dead?"

The King glanced at Owen and the others. "No," he admitted. "Once the prey is paralyzed, they are alive until the fairyfly lays her eggs in the body or eats it. The body will also die if damaged or left too long in the cocoon."

Owen gagged.

"The Mymarida lair is close to the Rift on this world's side," he told them. "The Rift itself is perhaps six candlemarks from the Citadel."

The servant returned carrying a tray of delicate glasses filled with amber liquid. Each of those in the room took a glass. A throat cleared at the opening to the room and someone sneezed.

The King motioned for the guard to draw back the silk covering the opening. Saleth and Samhanach waited until Alberick gestured for them to enter. Saleth nodded to those in the room. Samhanach's golden eyes flashed from the King to Owen and came to rest on Aeden. He stared steadily at her.

"Welcome, Saleth and Samhanach," the King greeted them. "I have a mission for you."

Aeden took a small sip of the liquid. Owen followed her lead. The wine was very sweet and tasted of plums.

Saleth's face betrayed no emotion. "As you will, Your Majesty. What is the mission?"

"You will accompany the envoy from Red Dragon's Keep to the reported lair of the Mymarida and, if it is true it has captured the humans, help them retrieve the men they search for."

Saleth's lips thinned and his eyes narrowed as he contemplated Alberick. "I appreciate your confidence in my prowess, Sire, but I think more than just we four will be needed to complete this quest."

Five, Navar's voice reminded everyone he was listening.

Six, chimed in OathKeeper.

Seven, added HeartStriker

"Seven," Saleth conceded with a nod.

The Bell tolled seven times, startling those in the room, its deep reverberations seeming to shake their bodies. The ringing faded into silence as those in the room traded glances.

"It appears the Bell of Prophecy agrees," Alberick said with a shake of his head and a raised eyebrow.

"Still, Sire, more of us would have a greater chance of success against the fairyfly," Saleth pressed him.

The King seated himself, resting his arms on the armrests and leaned back in the chair. He nodded his head as he considered Saleth's words. "I agree. You may ask for volunteers among the warriors. Take no more than ten."

Saleth gave a short bow. "As you command, Sire. I'll see to it now." He swept his eyes over Owen and Aeden. "We must leave tomorrow. Can you be ready?"

"Of course," Aeden spoke for the first time since his arrival.

"Very well. In the courtyard in the morning, first candlemark after sunrise." He nodded to those in the room. "Until then." Saleth rested his hand on the dire wolf's head as the two left the room.

Alberick turned to Owen and Aeden. "I suggest you leave your men here. They have no magic and cannot protect themselves from the *Unseleigh Sidhe* or the *Mymarida*. I will make sure they are well taken care of while you are gone."

Owen glanced at Aeden, who gave a tiny nod. "As you think wise, Alberick. We'll leave them here."

§ § §

As the rising sun's light finally filtered into his room the next morning, Owen checked his saddlebags for the third time. Cloak, socks, change of clothing, packets of food sent from the kitchen with a servant. It was all there.

His stomach clenched and rolled as he thought about the coming journey.

He pulled on his brown leather jerkin over the linen shirt he'd been wearing. He wrapped his brown leather belt around his waist, sliding HeartStriker's scabbard to his left side. He hoped he'd be warm enough on the journey. He stuffed his dark brown riding pants into his riding boots as he pulled them on. He'd been up for hours, too nervous to sleep.

Aeden stuck her head into his room. "Are you ready?"

Owen turned to look at her. "I'm not sure. I don't really know what to take."

"May I come in?" she asked.

"Of course," Owen waved her in. "You, especially, need not ask."

"Owen, what do you feel? I can tell more is going on than your concern about our task. What is it?"

Startled, Owen paused in thought, turned to face her and cocked his head in astonishment as he identified the source of his irritation.

"The King is afraid we will succeed," he said. "He's thinking about the end of his world. The tolling of the Bell foretells the ending of his world!" His voice rose. "How can I know this?"

Aeden looked at him, a wry grimace confirming his revelation. "I suspect you are clairvoyant. You pick up on what others are feeling and, sometimes, thinking." She picked an apple from a bowl sitting on the table beside the door. Without warning, she threw it straight at Owen.

With a shout, he threw his arm up, hand facing the apple. It stopped in mid-air.

"And telekinetic, as well."

Owen dropped his hand. The apple fell.

"Think about how you can use these powers to help us find and free Sir Mathin and his men. I'll practice with you while we travel. You must always be wary of entering another's mind. Someone can easily seize control of your body with their power, especially the Fey. When was the last time you practiced your mind shield?"

Owen stared at the apple. "I didn't know I could do that."

Aeden walked over and touched his arm. He shook his head and looked up at her. "What did you ask?" He bent over and picked up the apple. He rubbed it against the front of his jerkin and took a bite.

"Let's go," Aeden said with a sigh of resignation.

Owen picked up HeartStriker and slid the Sword into his scabbard. He lifted the saddlebags and, draping them over his arm, followed Aeden from the room as he took another bite of the apple.

Chapter 18

The FairyFly

Owen rode Navar along the game trail winding its way to the northwest from the Citadel. The WindRunner insisted Owen leave his warhorse behind.

Ten elven warriors sat astride Agni mounts who had agreed to carry them. The Agni kept turning their heads to check on Owen. He frowned.

Navar, HeartStriker, why do they keep looking at me? It's making me nervous.

There is a power in you that draws them. HeartStriker's comment held a puzzled tone.

Perhaps it is the bond between you and I. Navar's smug comment grated on Owen.

Perhaps it is the prophecy. Aeden's sharp response silenced everyone.

Do you really think we seven will break the bonds that have held the Darkened Forest for all this time? Owen asked. *Really, Aeden?*

"Yes," she answered aloud, a growl in her voice.

Owen looked over at her, suddenly wary. He had not heard that tone before.

Aeden raised an eyebrow as she looked back, her lips compressed. "You need to change your attitude and your perception, young man. These *Seleigh Sidhe* have agreed to help you find your men. Mocking their beliefs belittles them and diminishes you in their eyes."

Dragon, if you please, throw a rock at Owen. Let us work on his telekinesis, Navar requested in an attempt to divert Aeden.

Gladly, she responded. For the next several hours, both Aeden and Navar launched branches, rocks, pinecones, and various other objects toward Owen. Most he was able to deflect, but some got through, hitting him unexpectedly, leaving bruises.

He learned to expand his situational awareness all around himself. By the time they were close to the Rift in the Forest, he was able to deflect almost everything they threw at him. The Agni and elves watched with amusement.

As they approached the Mymarida's lair, and the Rift somewhere beyond it, reality seemed to pulse, as if it were breathing. Smells intensified and slowly dwindled to nothing. Light strengthened and dimmed. Vision wavered, sharp and clear one moment, misty and faded the next. Uneasiness tightened chests, dried mouths and caused nervous glances into the forest on either side of the path.

As the sun reached its zenith, it shown straight down on the party, filtered by the trees into moving shadows. Saleth glided by them, Samhanach running close behind. The dire wolf's tongue hung out the side of his mouth, seeming to laugh at Owen as he passed. Owen sent a glower after them. Envy raised its ugly head, reminding him he didn't have much experience and could never hope to move like that.

The Agni slowed from trot to walk. Saleth reached the front of the column as the Agni stopped. He spoke to the leader of the column. He glanced back along the line until his eyes reached Owen and Aeden.

"Come on," Aeden told Owen. She reined her warhorse to the side of the column and kicked it into a canter. Navar followed, cantering after her.

To the consternation of their elven riders, every Agni turned and watched as they passed. "They must be in love with him," one of the elves murmured in a disgruntled tone to the others. A ripple of shudders coursed down the line of Agni, as if trying to dislodge flies. "Sorry," the elf said in contrition.

Aeden and Owen reached the head of the line.

"The fairyfly's lair is half a candlemark down this trail," Saleth reported. "I suggested half the column dismount, spread out. Slip in on a broad front. The rest of the elves and Agni form flanks to the left and right, with Owen, Navar, and Aeden at the center. Samhanach and I will back them up," Saleth told them.

Do not forget the strategic advantage HeartStriker and OathKeeper bring. The fairyfly will not know of their power, Navar reminded them.

Saleth nodded. "Good advice. HeartStriker, OathKeeper, please be ready to back everyone up."

We shall. The Swords of Light's words echoed in everyone's mind.

Elves and Agni faded into the trees. Silence descended.

The remaining elves formed up, two on the left and three on the right. Samhanach and Saleth joined the two on the left.

Owen and Navar started down the trail, Aeden to their right. The rest fanned out and slipped through the trees on either side. Hooves made no sound on the wet fallen leaves littering the ground.

They moved forward. The hair on the back of Owen's neck lifted. A shiver of dread and excitement moved up his spine, raising goosebumps. He hoped with everything he had that Sir Mathin and his men were still alive.

The gloom under the trees began to lift as the trees thinned. Owen extended his awareness out in front of the group. A light pressure on his mind made him throw his shields up in reflex.

"Aeden, did you feel that? It is a very light touch. Almost like the brush of a feather." Fear and chagrin made his voice squeak higher. He should have been on alert long before this.

"I do," she responded. "It's been tracking us since we split up. It may be the Mymarida can sense us.

Although," she murmured, "this feels like Dragon magic." She frowned and shook her head.

The forest was quiet, as if it held its breath. Not a rustle of brush or sound of birds disturbed the silence. A high whining sound began, coming down the path in front of them.

Owen leaned back in his saddle. Navar stopped at the edge of a small clearing opening before them. A huge tree had fallen an age ago and lay rotting across its center. It had pulled down other trees when it fell, opening the forest to new growth.

Aeden swung down from her warhorse and drew OathKeeper. Owen pulled HeartStriker from his scabbard as he slid from Navar's back.

"Do we need the Dragon?" Owen asked in a very quiet voice to Aeden.

Aeden shook her head once. "There are too many trees here. I will change should the need become dire, but my flames will only start a forest fire. Best to handle this with Swords and Magic.

The whine grew louder as whatever it was drew closer. It slowly appeared from the shadows and hovered in the last line of trees on the other side of the clearing.

This was no delicate fairy conjured in the mind. This was a ravening beast set to destroy those that opposed it. It was larger than a man, almost as big as Navar. Its abdomen was bilious yellow-green and grossly swollen, a stinger hanging from the rear. Drops of liquid glistened at its tip. The rest of its body was black. The wings appeared too small to lift it, yet it flew. Ten legs covered with coarse bristles hung below its body, each tipped with a huge claw.

Antennae that looked like feathers projecting from its forehead swept in arcs above huge multifaceted eyes that reflected the light falling through the upper branches of the forest. Black mandibles gaped wide, dripping fluid. Where the drops landed, the ground bubbled and smoked.

Owen reached out with his mind and felt for the Agni and elves on either side of the clearing. They crept toward the beast, almost encircling it.

The whine from the fairyfly increased. Owen wanted to cover his ears. He glanced at Aeden. She nodded. "Don't look in its eyes," she whispered to him.

Navar laid back his ears and prepared to charge. "Go," Owen spoke to everyone. "Go," echoed HeartStriker.

The quiet of the forest exploded into chaos.

Navar screamed with rage and launched into the clearing. Spears with tri-blade heads flew from the trees on either side of the beast. Most bounced harmlessly off its body. Three found their way to the places where its legs joined the thorax.

The whine rose higher, resonating in Owen's chest, almost forcing him to run away. The mandibles spread wide as the creature began to extrude white foam from its mouth. It spat the foam toward him. Owen deflected it with his mind, thrusting it into the branches of the tree standing at his back. The tree began to smoke as the acid in the foam began to burn.

He shouted and ran into the meadow, pointing HeartStriker at the eyes of the fairyfly. Flame ignited along the blade and speared to its target. Magefire bathed the head of the beast. The sound of its whine rose higher as it reared back in pain.

Navar raced past the Mymarida's left side. He whirled and lashed out with his hind legs, a move that could kill man and beast alike in battle. His hooves, larger than a man's head, connected with the abdomen, punching through and into horror's guts. The whine faltered, dropping to silence. A leg lashed out and scored the WindRunner along his side as he raced away. He stumbled and fell, rolled, and staggered upright. Owen grabbed at his side, joined with the WindRunner in his pain. His magefire died. He pushed forward through the pain toward the Mymarida.

Aeden reached her hand out, projecting a rope of magic, wrapping it around the joining of head to thorax. The fairyfly reversed course, flying backward, pulling Aeden with it.

Owen ran to the right and along the monster's side. The beast tried to swing to its left to follow him. Elves ran from the forest, attacking thrashing legs with swords sharpened by magic.

Reaching its rear, Owen raised HeartStriker and brought the Sword of Light down in a two-handed swing, severing the stinger from the Mymarida's body. The severed stinger flew in a short arc, piercing the chest of an elf as he ran past. He died as he fell. The remaining elves hacked at joints and claws, severing them from Mymarida's body. Its wings stopped beating in unison and it wobbled wildly from side to side.

The Agni raced in an ever-tightening circle around the beast, holding it in place with their magic, preventing its retreat back into the Forest.

Saleth and Samhanach sped to the rear of the fairyfly. Saleth thrust his knife into the abdomen above the wound where the stinger had been. The beast heaved and swung rapidly side to side, trying to dislodge him. Saleth pulled himself up onto the creature and ran up the curve of the abdomen toward the thorax. Samhanach lunged at a leg threatening to knock Saleth off. He clamped his jaws on the appendage and held it to the ground.

When Saleth reached the top, he slammed his knife into the abdomen and threw himself off, holding tight to the knife's handle. As he fell, the knife sliced through the shell of the insect, top to bottom. A wave of insect gore followed his path to the ground.

The wings of the Mymarida stopped beating. With a last shudder, it fell to the earth. Aeden's magic rope tightened and tightened, strangling the fairyfly. With a final pop, the head separated from the thorax, bounding across the ground.

All movement stopped. Aeden stood silent and still. Elves leaned on staffs, panting. Owen staggered and sat down hard. Saleth crouched on hands and knees, head hanging, not a hands-breadth from the body of the Mymarida. Samhanach trotted around the back end of the beast and went to join Saleth. The Agni slowed and stopped circling. Navar limped with faltering steps toward Owen. Aeden moved to join him.

The rustling of brush and snapping of litter on the forest floor told of the presence of those who had watched the battle. The Agni swung to face outward. A wall of magic arced out from their bodies. Squalls and squeals erupted and dwindled into the distant trees as the watchers fled.

"We are not done," Aeden said. "We must find the men. Now, before whatever else is out there finds them first." She looked off into the trees. "And us."

Owen pushed himself to his feet and walked over to Saleth. He held his hand down. Saleth reached up and clasped it, letting Owen pull him to his feet.

"That was the craziest move I've ever seen," he said to the elf.

Saleth looked at him; face straight, but a sparkle in his eyes. "Not my best performance," he admitted.

The Agni and elves drifted closer as they talked. Navar stopped by Owen.

"Thank you, WindRunner. We could not have done this without your help." Owen raised his voice. "We could not have done it without all of your help." His eyes swept all those in the clearing. He bowed to them.

A tired chuckle ran around the circle.

"One more thing to do. Get the men this creature captured. Will you help?"

"Yes." Saleth spoke for them all. "Water and some food will do much to fortify us before we leave here."

Owen turned to Navar. He reached out and laid his hand gently on the WindRunner's shoulder. "I know you're hurt. What can I do?" he asked with quiet determination.

Navar stood still, looking Owen in the eyes. The slash along his ribs on his right side cut from hip to the elbow above his right leg. Blood ran in a slow sluggish stream down that leg, over his hoof, and pooled on the ground.

Would you ask HeartStriker to help heal my side?

Owen's eyes widened. This was the first time Navar had asked, not demanded.

Of course. HeartStriker, will you heal him? He kept the conversation between just the three of them.

Lay my blade along his side, the Sword of Light responded.

Magic met magic and healed the WindRunner.

§ § §

Within a candlemark, the band left the clearing, slowly following the trail the fairyfly had created as it flew through the forest. The pace gave the injured more time to heal.

Tree trunks were marked with slashes from claws and acid. Saplings felled by those claws lay across the path. Smoke from acid still rose from the leaves piled at the sides of the trail and along its course.

Owen glanced into the trees on the left. "Stop," he shouted. Navar swung to look into the trees, as did the rest of the party. A monstrous moth's cocoon the size of a man hung from a branch. Navar strode into the trees and up to the object. Owen looked around and saw other cocoons hanging from branches farther into the forest.

Flies crawled across parts of the cocoon. Owen drew HeartStriker and cut the thick piece of webbing holding the cocoon to the branch. The cocoon fell to the ground with a thud and shattered.

Owen swung his right leg over the pommel of Navar's saddle, kicked his left foot from the stirrup and slid down to the ground. He landed with bent knees, HeartStriker extended toward what lay on the ground.

Large pieces of cocoon covered what lay within. A skeletal foot projected from the end of the pieces. Owen walked with cautious steps to the head of the case. He picked up a broken branch and flipped away the piece covering the head. A skull rolled to the side. Owen straightened slowly.

He raised his head and looked at the rest of the hanging cocoons. His shoulders slumped with dejection. "We're too late."

"You don't know who that is," responded Aeden. "The newer captives should be closer to the lair." Owen followed her glance as she looked for Saleth. He saw the elf examining another cocoon perhaps thirty paces away. Saleth turned and started back to them.

"Saleth, would you have your brothers cut down every cocoon they find? If the victims are alive, could you bring them to the fairyfly lair? I cannot feel life through the weaving of the Mymarida."

Saleth turned to the other elves. Raised eyebrows and glittering eyes met his. Everyone felt the rejection of his request.

Every Agni gave a thunderous snort and began to buck, throwing the elves from their backs. Shouts of surprise and consternation filled the forest. The elves rolled to their feet and looked at the Agni in shock.

A wry smile crossed Saleth's face. "Apparently, the Agni disagree with your decision. Perhaps you should rethink it?" Samhanach's yips sounded like laughter. Navar snorted in agreement.

The elves looked at each other. A tall elf, bulkier than the others, stepped forward and bowed to the Agni. "Forgive us," he said to them. "We will help cut down the cocoons and find the missing men."

The shaking heads of the Agni greeted this statement, as if they did not believe what was promised. Every Agni head turned to look at Owen.

Eyes widening, he looked back. "I think you should trust them to keep their word," he stammered to the elven steeds. The lead Agni stamped his front hoof. The demand was clear: do it or you do not ride.

The Agni watched as elves moved away from the trail and deeper into the woods. Magic lowered the cocoons to the ground as elves cut them from the branches. The Agni dropped their heads and began to graze.

Aeden went to help the elves. Owen hung back, guilt gnawing at his mind, not wanting to see what was in the shrouds of web. He leaned against Navar's shoulder for comfort.

Magic shattered the cocoons, revealing the bodies of the creatures held within. Some were human, others not. All were just skeletal remains.

As the group moved closer to the fairyfly lair, the bodies became fresher: fewer skeletons, more flesh remaining on the bones.

The sun had set by the time they finished cutting down the cocoons. All of the creatures, Fey and human, encased within were dead, and most decayed. Saleth drew Owen to the side, watching Aeden and the elves work. "What do you wish done with the bodies," he asked.

Owen flinched. He had not thought that far ahead. "We bury our dead," he finally answered. "What of the elves and Fey? What do you want to do?"

"Magefire," was the prompt response. "Quick and clean."

"Aeden, could you come here?" Owen called to her where she worked with a group of elves.

She looked over at Owen, laid a hand on the shoulder of the elf next to her and came to stand beside him.

"Saleth has asked what should be done with the bodies." He hesitated. "He says the elves burn their dead with magefire. Humans normally bury bodies and mark the graves. What do you think we should do?"

Aeden pondered the question for a few moments.

"We do not know who these are. Perhaps magefire is the kinder thing," she answered.

Owen nodded slowly. "You're right. I think magefire is the answer. We're almost done. We'll gather the remains and burn them all at once."

Aeden looked back through the trees at the ground they had covered and the multitudes of cocoons lying on the ground. "Perhaps a better plan is to send a team of two or four elves and have them use magefire on each where it lies. We should continue as quickly as possible. Saleth, can you keep the Dark Fey at bay?"

"I can," he responded, "but there is power stirring in the Forest. It is not of this place or my world. We must hurry. I feel it growing stronger."

Aeden stilled. Owen knew she searched the surrounding area with her mind and magic.

He threw a small tendril of his own magic chasing after hers. With a gasp, he stepped back in alarm. His magic winked out of existence. "It's Demons," his voice rose, shuddering in panic.

Aeden, her eyes fixed on the trees, laid a hand on his shoulder. "Yes, but they are far away. Coming toward us, I think. We need to finish this and find out why they are here."

Saleth called the elves to him. "You two and you two," he pointed at four of the elves, "burn the remains where they lie and rejoin us as soon as possible."

The rest of the group could see the lair through gaps in the trees, about a hundred lengths away. They started toward it as the four held out their arms and called magefire to consume kin and strangers alike. Flickering flames of blue, red, orange, and white filled the forest with light.

Chapter 19

Sir Mathin's Men

The mouth of the Mymarida lair gaped in front of Owen and Aeden. It had created a cave using the trees as supports for hardened webbing. The stench was overwhelming. The smell of rotting meat and fairyfly feces combined to create an acrid miasma that had Owen and Aeden, and even the elves, coughing and gagging.

Owen yanked the scarf around his neck up and over his nose and breathed very shallowly. Navar threw his head up and backed away. *I'll wait with the Agni*, he said, his mind projecting disgust. He spun away and trotted back toward the elven steeds.

Owen felt a surge of magic from Aeden. The stench eased dramatically as she sent a gust of wind into the lair, flushing the bad air out and sweeping fresh air in. Owen wanted to smack himself for not thinking of doing the same. "Thank you, Aeden. I wish I'd thought to do that," he told her in a small voice. She gave a crooked smile and waved her hand toward the cavern. "After you, my lord."

Each one in the band conjured a ball of white light, illuminating the area. They moved cautiously along the walls into the cavern. Owen guided his magelight to the roof of the lair. At least fifteen cocoons hung there. More lay shattered on the ground along the back wall.

He wanted to hurry over to what lay on the ground, yet his feet would not move. Fear of what he would find held him in place. He gave a snort of disgust at himself and started forward.

The first shell held the remains of one of his father's soldiers. He gasped and reeled away, his hands covering his mouth. "It's them," he choked out in anguish.

He hid his face in his hands. He did not want the others to see his tears. Agony gripped his heart. Pain choked him. The same feelings that devastated him after the battle at the Keep overwhelmed him; so many friends and people he knew gone forever.

Fury exploded in his mind. With a shout of rage, he drew HeartStriker and released that rage against the lair itself. The webbing caught fire. He felt HeartStriker withdraw the magic from their bond.

"No," roared Aeden and Saleth in unison. Magic snapped out and shrouded the flames, smothering them for lack of air. Aeden slammed a shield around Owen, preventing his magic from expanding.

Owen slowly lowered HeartStriker until the sword's tip touched the ground. His face flushed and he panted, eyes darting around the cavern. Fury against the Dark burned in his veins. "I need to kill them," he said in a low deadly voice. "I will kill them wherever I find them."

Rage strengthened his resolve and seemed to burn deep into his heart and mind. He struggled for control over it. HeartStriker helped him create a barrier that removed the immediacy of his feelings, set the rage a step away from him. His struggle to contain it finally succeeded. Aeden released the shield around him.

Saleth and the others watched his struggle for a short time, turning away one by one, resuming the work of lowering the cocoons from the ceiling to the floor. Only Aeden remained at his side. She stood, taut and silent, arms crossed over her chest.

"I thought I taught you and the others control," she said, her voice sharp, each word filled with contempt. "I failed."

Owen looked everywhere but at her. "I'm sorry. I ... don't know what happened," he choked out the words.

"You lost control of yourself and your magic. We who hold this great power cannot, do not have the right, to ever lose our control. You must be as cold with it as the snow in winter. Rage may fuel it but wielding it must be cold. Cold as ice. Do you understand?"

He nodded, eyes focused to the ground. Misery and embarrassment kept him silent.

"Owen, look at me," Aeden demanded.

He raised his eyes to her face. Her face softened with sympathy. He felt it flowing from her in waves. With a cry of despair, he flung himself into her arms, weeping uncontrollably for all he had lost.

Aeden held him tight. She laid her head on his. "It's all right, Owen. It's all right," She murmured to him.

One of the elves gave a shout of surprise. "These two still live," he exclaimed.

Owen stepped away from Aeden, wiped the tears from his face with his hands and dried them on his trousers. He and Aeden walked over to the row of cocoons laid out in the middle of the lair.

He knelt between the two cocoons the elf indicated. He laid two fingers on the neck of the man to the right. There was a very faint flutter of a heartbeat against them. He swiveled to the left and did the same. He felt another very slow heartbeat. He looked up at Aeden, excitement widening his eyes. "Can we bring them back, Lady?" He rose and backed away from the bodies.

Aeden stood in thought for several minutes. "There is an herb that grows in this type of forest. It will speed his heartrate and perhaps awaken him."

"Saleth," she called across the cavern. "Do you know of any crataegus close to us?"

"There should be some near," Saleth told her. He looked at the elf working next to him. "Can you go and look?" he asked.

Without a word, the other walked out of the cave. He returned within a quarter-candlemark, carrying a large handful of the roots and leaves Aeden had requested.

She knelt next to the men. The elves stripped away the cocoons. The bodies looked dead, faces grey, thin from starvation.

She picked up a piece of wood from the floor of the cave and used her magic to form it into the shape of a bowl. She put the plants in the hollow and held her hand out over them. They began to deform as she applied pressure, becoming a paste and finally a liquid. She set the bowl on the ground and picked up a piece of bark curved into the shape of a spoon. She carefully scooped out some of the liquid.

She swung on her knees to the closest man.

"Owen, come hold his lips open. I'm going to dribble this onto his teeth. Hopefully he'll swallow it."

Owen knelt by the soldier. He used his thumbs to push the lips back from the teeth. Aeden knelt and tipped the piece of bark. A very thin stream of liquid ran from the bark to the teeth and back into the corners of the mouth. The man's throat worked as he swallowed.

Aeden continued to pour until all of the liquid was gone. She swiveled back to the bowl and scooped up more liquid.

Owen moved to the next man's body. He knelt and pulled the soldier's lips back. Aeden repeated the slow pour, watching as this one's throat worked as he swallowed.

Aeden leaned back on her heels. "Now we wait. They should gradually regain their minds and bodies within a candlemark, perhaps sooner."

"I'll go and help with the other cocoons," Owen volunteered.

He spent the next candlemark building a small fire near the survivors, then removing webbing from the remainder of the bodies. His heart dropped as he shattered the next to last of them. Sir Mathin's body lay revealed. He was clearly dead.

Owen drew in a deep, shuddering breath. Memories of the man working with his father and training his father's guard sent his thoughts back to Red Dragon's Keep. Mathin had taught Owen how to whittle when he was ten, using a soft piece of firewood.

Of all the men Mathin had taken to search for his father and mother, only two remained. Owen felt completely numb.

He looked over at Aeden. She was helping one of the men to sit up. The other was still down.

He thought about going over. He did not want to know what had happened just yet. He walked out of the lair to find Navar.

Chapter 20

Running Battle

Anne Gobhlan shifted wearily in her saddle. Her legs and seat ached with a bone-deep hurt. The pain never stopped, no matter how she tried to ease it.

The Arachs and Gobhlans rode steadily east, away from North Meall. Except for the stop to attend to Jenni's wound at the standing stones, they had kept riding: eating in the saddle, choking down the hard journey bread and jerky they had taken. The horses were suffering as much as their rider's.

They lit no fires when darkness forced them to stop and sleep. Shallow streams that infrequently flowed through the prairie gave an excuse to pause, fill waterskins, and stretch tired muscles. The snow was intermittent, sometimes drifting down gently, at other times weighing down horse and rider with a thick heavy fall.

Time and again Anne sent her magic questing for the faint touch of that which trailed them. It was always there, driving them closer and closer to the looming Forest.

The Darkened Forest bordered their route to the south. Anne watched it uneasily as she kept her horse moving. Pressure on the shields she had spent decades building around her mind signaled danger in the shadows. She squeezed her legs against the sides of the horse, urging it up next to Jenni.

"Can you sense anything?" she asked her sister.

Jenni sat slumped in her saddle. She looked at Anne, eyes dull, furrows of pain bracketing her mouth. Alarmed, Anne reached out and laid the back of her hand against Jenni's forehead. Her heart began to race as she realized just how sick her sister was.

"Jeremy, Tom," she shouted. "We need to stop."

She reached down, grabbed the reins of Jenni's horse next to the bit, and pulled both of the horses to a stop. She vaulted from the saddle and stood next to Jenni. "Come on. Let me help you down. We'll stop here for a break."

Jeremy and Tom dismounted next to Anne. Tom hurried to Jenni's side. He lifted her from her horse. She slid into his arms, completely limp. Jeremy took charge of the animals.

Tom fell to his knees, holding Jenni across his lap. Anguished eyes met Anne's.

Jeremy tethered the horses, nose to tail, creating a small windbreak for Jenni and Tom. Anne calmed the animals' minds with swift precision, keeping them steady.

Jeremy dragged the sack of dried dung he had collected from the packhorse. He quickly cleared out a circle through the dead grass for a fire. He shook three pats out of the bag into its center. Anne sent a tendril of power from her mind to the pile. It burst into flames. Jeremy sat back on his heels and shook his head with an astonished grunt.

"Jeremy, please stand by the horses," she ordered with brisk authority. "I'm going to try to heal Jenni. When I withdraw my mind from theirs, they might spook." Jeremy walked over to stand by the animals.

Anne sat down across from Tom, Jenni between them. Releasing her hold on the horses' minds, she placed her right hand on Jenni's forehead, left hand on her sister's stomach. The horses shifted uneasily. Anne closed her eyes and calmed her thoughts. Slowly she matched her breathing and heartbeat to Jenni's. She let her awareness open and felt the pain coursing through her sister's body.

She flinched, struggling to quiet her own body and thoughts. Moments passed. She created a place of peace in her mind, letting it fill her. She raised her right hand from Jenni's stomach until she could just feel the muddied aura outlining the body. She pushed the pain, fever, and fear down the legs and away from the wound on her sister's thigh. At the bottom of Jenni's feet, Anne flicking her fingers, as if throwing the disruption of health into the earth. She repeated the cleansing.

As she worked, she chanted:

> Lord of Light, Lady of Night,
> Bless this work I do by right.
> Clean the wound,
> Remove the pain,
> Drain the infection,
> Fever restrain.
> Close the cut,
> Make whole the leg,
> Cease the torment of her I beg.
> As I will it, three by three,
> As I will it, so shall it be."

Gradually she sensed the fever cooling. She sent her awareness deep into the wound, helping the rejoining cells knit together. As they did, pain became tolerable, then faded away. Anne gently let her awareness of her sister's body flow away. Jenni opened her eyes. They were clear.

Jeremy watched as his wife used her magic to save another.

Tom's eyes went wide with astonishment.

Pale skin bloomed with the pink of good health. Jenni looked up at Tom. "I didn't think I would see you again," she whispered. She reached up and laid her hand gently on his cheek.

Anne leaned back with a weary sigh. She rested her hands on her knees and straightened, stretching her back, lifting her chin to the sky. She lowered her head and looked at Jenni. "We need to check your wound and we both need to eat as soon as possible," she said to all of them.

She looked over at Jeremy. He looked back, eyes wide with wonder and astonishment. "It's something my mother taught me when I was very young," she said with an apologetic shrug of her shoulders. She pushed herself to her feet with a groan. She felt dizzy and slightly sick. "Give me some jerky, quick." He pulled a piece from the bag looped over his shoulder and handed it to her. She ate it with ravenous intensity.

Tom helped Jenni sit up. "This is the first time I've felt like I'm all here since the kidnapping," she told him. "Anne's right. I really do need something to eat."

"You sit here. I'll help put a meal together," he told her as he scrambled to his feet. Remembering, he turned back. "Let's look at your leg."

Jenni rolled up the leg of her trouser. A long line of healed scar tissue came into view. She pushed on it with hesitant fingers, gently at first and, when no pain met that probe, pushed more firmly. "It doesn't hurt at all," she exclaimed.

"I've never seen anything like this," Tom admitted. "Our wise-woman can heal with herbs, charms, and oils, but not with spells, and never this quickly." As soon as Jenni lowered her trouser leg, he reached down and grabbed her hand, pulling her to her feet.

Hand in hand, they walked to the bundles Jeremy had pulled from the packhorse while Anne worked. They rummaged through the bundles, looking for supplies for a proper meal. Jeremy held the pot he'd retrieved as Anne scooped snow into it.

Tom walked over to Anne and pulled her into a tight hug. "Thank you," he whispered.

Jeremy set the pot next to the fire to heat, shoving it partially into the flames. The only thing to do now was wait.

§ § §

Jeremy swallowed the last of the jerky soup, relishing its warmth.

"We need to find shelter for tonight," he said. The others looked up from their own cups, more concerned with eating than thinking ahead.

"You're right. We have to get out of this weather," Tom agreed.

"Do we dare enter the Darkened Forest? Maybe just inside the tree line?" Anne asked. "We can put up a shelter to get out of the snow using the blankets and some branches for a lean-to."

Tom and Jenni looked doubtful, frowns ridging both of their foreheads. "We don't know what kinds of beasts are in there," Tom said. "If they're anything like what's been chasing us, I don't think we should." He looked toward the trees looming to the south and made his decision. "But, we'd better go now, before dark, if we're going to do it."

The men loaded the packhorse as Jenni and Anne tightened girths and slid bridles over the heads of their horses. They all mounted and turned toward the trees. A half candlemark later, Jeremy pulled his horse to a stop.

He watched Anne's face, looking for any warning of danger.

"What?" she asked irritably. "What are you looking at?"

"Can you tell if there are any dangers close by in there?" he nodded his head toward the edge of the forest.

Anne scowled. Her face cleared and she gave a wicked grin. "Of course. There's a giant spider half way up the trees, waiting for us to enter."

Jeremy's eyes widened in shock. Realizing she was poking fun at him, he narrowed his eyes and pressed his lips together in irritation. Anne laughed aloud. Her delight drew a reluctant smile from him. "Ask Jenni. She's better at clairvoyance than I am."

"Jenni?" he turned to his sister-in-law. "Anything?"

Tom, sitting on his horse on the other side of Jenni, leaned forward and rolled his eyes at Jeremy.

"I can't sense anything close by, although there is a strange presence coming from the northwest. It's pretty far away and I can't tell what it is. I think we're safe for now," Jenni told him with a forthrightness he now distrusted after Anne's teasing.

"Well, let's get in there then." He drew his sword, prompting the others to do so as well. He squeezed his knees into the horse's sides, urging it forward into a slow walk.

They rode into the Darkened Forest. The trees were bigger around than five men could stretch. They towered into the sky. As the four passed beneath the first trees, the wind died and the snowfall ceased.

"I think this is far enough," Tom said when they were past the first border of trees. They stopped as one.

"I want to be able to get out of here fast if we need to," Jenni said. She swung her leg over the horse and stepped to the ground. "Let's set up here and get some rest."

$ $ $

Anne woke from a restless sleep, plagued by dreams filled with dread but nothing she could clearly remember. She had stood the middle watch, somewhere around midnight. Jenni had replaced her, sitting down in front of the lean-to they had cobbled together under which the others slept. Jeremy sat in front of it now, watching as the sun rose to a clear morning.

Nothing had stirred in the depths of the forest behind them. The horses stood hipshot, tied to a picket line strung between two of the trees adjacent to the lean-to.

Anne crawled out of the shelter. She sat next to her husband and watched the sky brighten from very pale yellow to pink and orange until the disk of the sun pushed above the horizon. Snow-covered hills and valleys refracted the sunlight into brilliant points of color.

"I wish we were home," she whispered to him. He put his arm over her shoulders and pulled her close. He kissed her hair. "Me, too," he told her.

Sunlight filtered through the edge of the forest, shining onto Tom and Jenni's faces. They woke at its touch and joined the others.

Jenni stiffened. "We need to leave. Now," she told them with quiet urgency. "There's a pack of beasts running through the Forest toward us. I don't know what they are, but they have been commanded to hunt and kill us."

They all jumped to their feet. The men loaded the packhorse while the women saddled and bridled the horses. They mounted and rode out of the trees. Jenni's head snapped up and turned toward the northwest.

"Those creatures I told you about last night are almost here. We need to run," she told them abruptly. "I don't know why I didn't feel them before, but I suspect the influence of the Forest. Go. Go!" she urged.

The four kicked their horses into a trot and quickly into a canter. Tom rode behind them as tail guard. He looked back over his shoulder just as a black dot crested the hillock defining the border between forest and prairie, perhaps three miles behind.

Two more dots joined the first. They raced down the side of the hill and arrowed straight toward the fleeing group. A horde of misshapen beasts poured from the edge of the Forest, chasing the cantering horses.

"They've seen us," Tom shouted and urged his horse into a gallop. The others did the same, the packhorse catching their panic, galloping next to Jenni's horse instead of trailing behind. They raced across the dazzling hills and swales. Snow flew in chunks and clods behind them. At least fifteen *Unseleigh Sidhe* pressed toward them, gaining ground with every leap.

Everyone pulled swords from scabbards, ready to slash anything that came close.

"We need to make a stand up ahead," Tom shouted, "By that copse of trees."

Jenni raised her sword in acknowledgement and reined her horse toward the trees standing on a small rise. The others followed. As they topped the hill, they pulled the horses around and held them in a loose circle, letting the packhorse loose, waiting for the attack of the *Unseleigh Sidhe.*

The beasts charged toward them. A green creature that looked like a man, but had a mouth filled with needle-sharp teeth and glittering sickly yellow eyes launched itself at Tom. He kicked his horse forward and swung his sword down, slicing through its spine. It tumbled to the ground as another Fey took its place, jumping and latching on to his horse's mane. Grey hair covered this one and its short vestigial wings beat at the head and neck of Tom's horse.

The horse reared and struck out with front hooves, breaking bones wherever they struck. Tom thrust forward with his sword, impaling the creature through the chest. He raised his leg and shoved it off the sword.

He signaled his horse to spin to the right. As it swung, he extended the sword and took the heads of three more Fey. His companions fought and killed as many and as quickly as he did.

He looked to the left and back to the right. All of the *Unseleigh Sidhe* that had followed them from the Forest lay dead. Jenni, Anne and Jeremy sat on their horses, panting from exertion. The four sheathed their swords. A dog-like creature had bitten Jeremy's leg. All of the horses bore wounds on their legs and sides.

"We don't have time to take care of these," he said, gesturing to the wounds. "The other monsters are getting closer. We need to go."

Without a word, they wheeled their tired horses and asked them to run again.

The black beasts slowly gained ground, seeming to run without effort, forcing the group to keep going, never giving them a chance to slow and rest. The leader of the pack of three drew even with the streaming tail of Tom's horse. The beast was huge, its back reaching as high as his horse's belly. Red eyes gleamed. Lips drawn back in a snarl revealed a mouth full of razor sharp teeth, ready to pull them down. A black tongue curled at the front of its mouth as it panted, running easily next to his laboring horse.

The two beasts behind the leader pulled even with Jeremy's horse. He reached for his sword as he kicked out with a shout of fury, catching the muzzle of the nearest with the hardened toe of his book. Blood flew from the blow, but the beast did not drop back. It sprang toward the side of Jeremy's horse and bit into its belly near the girth, disemboweling it.

The horse shrieked and kicked out, lost its footing and tumbled head over heels. Jeremy flew wide, away from the kicking, dying animal. He rolled as he landed, coming to his feet and jerked his sword from its scabbard, setting himself to battle the horrors bearing down on him. *I am BloodForged, come to battle the Demon Horde.* Something spoke in his mind as the sword ignited with flames.

Anne and Jenni pulled their horses into wide circles, one right and one left, racing back to rejoin the fight. They ripped their swords from scabbards.

Tom yanked back on his horse's reins, pulling it into a sliding stop and signaling it to whirl and face the leader of the pack. The sword in his hand burst into flame. He gave a shout of surprise and almost dropped the blade.

Deciding to ignore the flames, Tom kicked his horse toward the nightmare. He swung the burning blade in a wide arc, decapitating the beast. Blood sprayed from its neck and the head dropped to the ground as Tom continued his charge toward the other two.

As the women raced toward the battle, their swords ignited as well. Jenni gaped at the sword and its burning blade for half a second, then clenched her teeth and lowered it toward the monsters. Fire erupted from its tip, reaching toward the beasts.

Tom's horse caught up with the monsters racing toward Jeremy. Tom plunged his sword into the heart of the one on the right. The fire from Jenni's sword enveloped it. Tom swung his sword over the neck of his horse and sliced through the back of the one on the left, killing it instantly. Its momentum carried it within feet of Jeremy, snow fountaining from its slide. Tom's horse continued past Jeremy in a flurry of kicked up snow. He turned it back toward his wife and friends.

Jeremy stood as if rooted to the ground holding the flaming sword. *Who had spoken to him?* The women and their horses stopped at his back. Anne's horse danced away from Jenni, coming to a halt beside Jeremy.

Greetings, Lady Gobhlan. I am StormBringer. Anne jerked
in disbelief as she stared at the Sword she held.

Well come, Lord Tom Arach. We meet at last. The flames
from the blade in Tom's hand abruptly winked out. Tom
held the sword as if it was a snake about to strike him.
Everyone jerked in surprise as the Swords spoke in their
minds.

The fire twisting along Jenni's blade dimmed and
faded away. *I greet you, Lady Jenni Arach. I am FireGuard.*

Tom tried to drop the blade. His hand refused to
open.

"What are you? What do you want?" he barked with
angry intensity. He looked frantically at Jenni. Eyes
wide, mouth hanging open, she sat frozen on her horse,
arm holding the sword rigidly out in front of her. Anne
mirrored her expression.

*I am BattleSworn, oldest Sword of Light. I am here to kill
those who would bring the end of this world. You chose me
unknowing. You are* my *chosen in this time. We fight together
to end the Dark.*

"By the Three Gods," Tom exclaimed. "This is insane."

Chapter 21

The Search for Cameron

"Has anyone seen Cameron?" Breanna asked.

She and Marta sat on the steps leading up to the Duke's table in the great hall of Red Dragon's Keep, waiting for mid-meal. Breanna's red-gold hair had come loose from its braid. Marta looked as composed as always. They had been working with the new foals, teaching them to walk beside a human.

"I haven't seen him," Evan told Breanna. He sat at a table nearby, playing a game of fox and geese with one of the men-at-arms, as everyone waited for Thomas.

"I saw him earlier this morning," Marta volunteered. Thomas bounded down the stairs.

"Sorry I'm late. I was working with Gregory, searching for more facts like we found in the archives." His dark blond hair stood up in spikes and dust smeared the front of his tunic. He brushed at it with dust-covered fingers, trying to dislodge the smear. He gave up with a shrug and hurried up the stairs to take his place at the high table, unstrapping HellReaver and leaning the sword against its edge. Breanna pushed herself from the stairs to her feet and followed him.

Marta started to go to a lower table. "Join us here," Thomas motioned for her to sit next to him. He dipped his fingers into the fingerbowl on the table and dried his hands.

Marta frowned, her green eyes narrowing, obviously disturbed by this sign of preference. She relaxed the frown and walked up the stairs, sitting down next to Thomas. He sent her a grin. "Stop it," she whispered. "This isn't seemly." She leaned her own sword against the side of her chair.

"It's seemly if I say it is," Thomas teased her.

Evan didn't look up. He reached out and moved one of the pegs on the board. "Ha. I won again," he said, rubbing his hands together, his grin from ear to ear.

"That you did, squire. That you did," the man-at-arms told him, pushing away from the table and standing. "Thanks for the game."

"You're welcome. Maybe tomorrow?" he asked hopefully.

"I'd like that." The man moved toward the table where his friends sat.

Evan joined the others at the high table. The skullies started delivering trenchers filled with sliced beef, gravy, and vegetables to the tables.

"Where is Cameron?" Thomas asked. Silence greeted the question.

"No one knows where he is," Breanna told him.

Thomas frowned. He stopped eating and set his knife on the edge of his trencher. "That's not like him. HellReaver —"

Before the question was finished, HellReaver and all the Swords of Light sent jolts of surprise and consternation to their partners.

I no longer feel GhostWalker's presence, HellReaver told Thomas.

The humans sat back from the table, wide-eyed, as their Swords told them the same story.

What? Why can't you feel him? Do you know where he is? Thomas questioned.

Do any of you know where he went? HellReaver asked.

He was with Neulach, HellScream sent through their link. *I felt them beneath the Keep, but beyond it,* he said, puzzlement evident in his tone. *Then my sense of them vanished.*

"Neulach asked me if he could search the Keep with Cameron," Thomas said. "He thought he could feel Dragon magic and wanted to find where it had been used. They were going to search the undercroft and were supposed to be finished by mid-meal."

Breanna frowned. "How can a Sword of Light disappear?"

Magic, replied SunWalker.

"I need to get back to the Library," Thomas told those at the table, his face twisted in a scowl and reluctance in his voice.

"I'll meet you upstairs," he called to Gregory. He turned back to the others at the table. "I've got to figure out what we need to do next about ... you know," he said cryptically. The others nodded understanding. He turned to Breanna and Marta. "Can you two please see if you can find Cameron? Evan, maybe you can help them?"

Breanna's eyes widened with astonishment. "You want *us* to do it?" her voice squeaked.

Marta rolled her eyes and shook her head. "Of course, my lord. We'll start right away," she told Thomas. Evan just grinned and kept eating.

Thomas stood and picked up HellReaver, hooking the scabbard to the belt around his waist. He bounded up the stairs at side of the great hall, taking them two at a time. Gregory followed him more slowly.

Do you know where Cameron and Neulach disappeared? Breanna asked SunWalker.

I do, answered her Sword.

Marta looked at Breanna as SunWalker included her in the answer. "Show me where," Breanna demanded.

SunWalker projected a picture of a tunnel in the undercroft into her mind. Breanna shook her head. "I don't know where that is. Evan, have you ever seen this tunnel?" *SunWalker, can you show him?* she asked.

Of course. SunWalker sent the picture to Evan. He shook his head, blond hair flying. "No, never seen it. Should we go look for it?" His blue eyes sparkled with excitement.

Breanna pushed back her chair as she stood. "Yes, we need to go. Now."

Evan jumped up, grabbed his sword and whipped its belt around his body. Marta and Breanna were already strapping on their Swords.

The three walked to the passageway bordering the great hall opposite the stairway Thomas had taken. Beyond it were the kitchen and the stairs descending to the undercroft.

"Wait here. I'll get some waterskins we can fill in the well room." Breanna went to the kitchen and picked up three waterskins hanging on the wall.

She returned to Evan and Marta. They hesitated at the top of the stairway that turned in a spiral to the right. She'd been down there when the *Seleigh Soren* had been killed. Breanna took the first step down. The others followed her lead. Magelight glowed in brackets lining the wall on the left.

They came this way, HellScream told Marta. *The other stairs to the undercroft are blocked.*

Marta grabbed Breanna and Evan by their arms. "Wait," she said. *Tell them what you just told me, please.*

HellScream did as she asked.

"What other stairs?" Breanna demanded. "I've never seen or heard of any other way into the undercroft."

There is a set of stairs descending from the family quarters to the undercroft. I suspect it was an escape route in case the Keep should fall, Breanna's SunWalker remarked.

Breanna stopped on the stairs. "Why would they close it off?"

"Maybe to block the stairs to Demons." Marta's slow response to her question raised the hair on the other's necks.

"Or maybe it was blocked to keep them in when the Demons attacked," Evan said. "I'll bet it was that Jalyn who Thomas had to execute!"

Breanna turned to Marta, concern written all over her face. "Should we try to find Cameron or this blocked stairway?"

"My father always says to carry out orders first," Marta told her. "Let's look for Cameron. After we find him, we'll deal with the stairs."

Breanna nodded. "HellScream, lead us to the last place you felt Cameron and Neulach."

The trio started into the main room of the undercroft. Two corridors on each wall opened from the room. The corridor to the well room branched off on the left. Breanna turned into that passage. She and Evan both shuddered, remembering how Thomas, Aeden, and their Swords of Light killed the *Soleigh Soren* Demon imprisoned in that well room. They filled their waterskins and left as quickly as they could.

The undercroft held all manner of things used in the Keep. Wine and produce were stored on racks set in rows between the massive pillars supporting the weight of the castle above.

HellScream urged the three to cross the room and enter the opening directly across from the well room corridor. They each created a ball of magelight and sent it ahead to light the way. The trio hesitated at the entrance. Breanna put aside her reluctance and stepped forward onto the stone floor of the passage.

A quarter of a candlemark later, Evan looked back. He could not see the entrance to the corridor.

"The tunnel must have curved," he reported, a tremor in his voice.

They stopped and looked back. Darkness yawned behind them, their magelight failing within a few paces.

"Look," Evan exclaimed, pointing at the floor. "Boot prints in the dust." They turned back and quickened their pace, tracing the path Cameron and Neulach had taken.

The three passed several corridors opening on the right and left. "I didn't know there were this many tunnels down here," Breanna whispered.

The group walked slower and slower. With a start, Breanna realized the corridor held an embedded spell. It was hard to move forward, almost like pushing through mud, sapping her energy to the point she wanted to sit down and sleep.

"Do you feel that?" she asked.

"Yes," Marta and Evan responded.

"What is it?" Evan asked in a small voice.

"Someone embedded a spell to keep us from going this way," Marta said.

We must break this sleeping spell, SunWalker advised.

Agreed, HellScream responded.

Breanna stepped in front of the others and raised SunWalker. She began to chant.

> In this hour, on this day,
> I demand this spell clear the way.
> Loose us from its deadly sway.
> As I will, so shall it obey.

She felt the sleeping spell twist and latch on to her power. It began to pull energy from her body, through her arm and out through her Sword of Light. With a snap and crack of magic, SunWalker broke the connection. Breanna staggered and collapsed against the wall as the spell tried to send all of them deeper into exhaustion. The others fell to their knees.

Panting with effort, Breanna pushed herself away from the wall. With shaking arms, she raised SunWalker again.

> By the power of Light and power of Dark,
> This spell I command to depart.
> Return to your maker, with none the wiser.
> An heir to the Keep, this spell I sweep,
> From sight of men, beyond their ken,
> By the power of three, I banish thee.

She swept her sword from ceiling to floor and wall to wall.

Her magic, augmented with the power of the Swords, caught, held, and broke the spell around them. An audible boom shook the corridor, dust sifting down from the ceiling.

Breanna wilted to the floor of the tunnel. Alarmed, Evan reached out and grabbed her shoulder. "Are you all right?"

Breanna patted his hand. "I'm fine. Do you have any water? Mine is all gone."

Marta unhooked the waterskin from her belt, uncorking it. "Here," she said, pushing it into Breanna's hands.

Breanna took a small swallow, followed by several large ones.

"That was harder than I thought it would be," she mumbled. She cleared her throat and slowly rose to her feet. Evan and Marta pushed themselves to theirs. SunWalker sent her small bursts of energy through her grip on the Sword, replacing what she had spent. The Sword's power felt depleted.

"Aeden taught us that there is always a price for magic. She was right." She handed the waterskin back to Marta. "Let's go."

$ $ $

"It feels like we've been walking forever," Evan complained.

"It's been no more than three-quarters of a candlemark," Marta told him.

"How do you know?" he asked, looking at her with a frown.

We are getting very close to the last place I felt them, HellScream warned.

"I smell burning," began Breanna. "Look at the walls!" she exclaimed.

Magelight reflected on an outline of what looked like flames rising up the left wall, over the ceiling, and down the other side. It was red, gold, orange, and yellow, as if the stone trapped flame itself. Evan reached out and hesitantly touched the wall on his right.

"It's warm," he said as he snatched his hand away.

"Look ahead at the floor," Marta gasped.

Black covered the floor of the corridor in a shape none of them had ever seen. What looked like clawed arms reached toward them, yet nothing was there. Marta squatted down at the edge closest to them and with slow deliberation touched the floor.

"It's as if a shadow has been burned into the stone," she murmured to her companions.

This is where all trace of them ends, SunWalker said. *We are no longer under the Keep. There was a portal further along this passageway. It is gone now.*

"Then where are they?" Breanna was mad. She had been sure they could find her cousin and Lord Neulach.

We don't know, responded the Swords of Light.

§ § §

Thomas loitered next to the door of the kitchen on his way into the Tower after weapons practice. He unbuckled the sides and shrugged out of the thickly padded gambeson he wore to protect himself during training. He thrust the gauntlets he'd used through his belt.

A man dressed in a rough tunic and trousers, shod in mud-covered leather boots, made his way around the wall of the Tower and headed toward the door. As he approached, he glanced around, perhaps looking for any observers. He pulled the soft cap he wore from of his head and bowed to Thomas.

"Sir, the trader has been meeting for the past day with two men from Fearmhar. She's passed them a bag of money and received something in return." He twisted the cap in his hands, as if he was anxious. "We don't know what she got. The wise-woman will check her vardo tomorrow and try to find the bag. The trader also has homing pigeons in one of the wagons. She's sent two of them off."

Thomas continued removing his protective clothing. He straightened and waved his arm as if angry at the supposed villager. "Well done," he murmured. "Keep watch. Let me know about anything new." He turned with brisk purpose and entered the kitchen. The man hung his head and turned away, trudging back the way he had come.

Chapter 22

Prophecy Fulfilled

"I ain't never seen anythin' like it. We was chased through the forest by this flyin' horror that took one man after another." Revulsion filled the voice of the soldier who had accompanied Sir Mathin. His audience listened with rapt attention.

"We couldn't get away, no matter how hard we tried. Sir Mathin told us to scatter from the trail, hopin' some of us might get away. There was monsters out there that attacked and killed them that left the trail. The flyin' thing stung each one of us here and then spun a cocoon around us once we was all down." He looked with very real fear at the entrance of the lair. "It's dead, right? Can't come back?"

"It's dead. We killed it," Aeden reassured him.

"Nothin' left to tell until you got here. Thanks for saving us. Is Sir Mathin about?" the soldier asked.

Aeden shook her head and laid a gentle hand on his shoulder. "He didn't make it," she told him. His shoulders slumped. "There was nothing you could do," she reassured the young man.

Owen stood mute next to the bodies of Mathin's men, Navar standing next to him, listening to the story. He made his decision and dropped his arms, walking over to Aeden and the soldier. "How long were you on the trail before the Mymarida attacked?" he asked. The elves drifted over to listen.

The soldier's face scrunched in concentration. "I think maybe three, four weeks. We rode to the confluence and found where the Duke and his party put up a fight. We followed the signs to the north and cut across the Darkened Forest. The tracks skirted the Forest and we thought it was faster to ride through it. Ha," he told them, bitterness lacing his words.

Owen shook his head. He thought he was prepared, but he wasn't. Regret filled his thoughts. He felt like he'd let down his father and his brother, even though he knew Sir Mathin and the men died weeks before his band had even reached the Forest.

He raised his head, looking at the circle of men and allies with haunted eyes. As he glanced from man to creature to elf, his mouth firmed into a straight line, his face hardened. "The Rift must be closed. Even I can feel its power from here. We cannot allow these monsters into our world anymore."

His voice shook. "If the elves and Agni didn't contain them here, what would they do to the rest of Ard Ri? Those without magic or protection ..." he flinched and shook his head, lower lip caught in his teeth, as he imagined the resulting death and destruction. "I'm not sure how to do this. We can't leave these men behind. We can't wait for reinforcements. Lady Aeden, Saleth, are we enough? What should we do?"

Aeden looked around the circle, as if weighing and measuring the strengths each possessed. Saleth rested his hand on Samhanach's head as he looked between her and Owen.

"There is this," Saleth spoke with slow deliberation. "The Forest Lords have never sent more than twenty against the Rift. We have more here right now, especially with the magic in each of you." He looked at Owen and his companions. "I will stay with the men who survived the Mymarida. Samhanach and I will be of no help against the Rift."

Relief flooded through Owen. "Thank you," he said to the elf. Aeden nodded with satisfaction. "Let's eat and plan for tomorrow morning."

§ § §

After a restless night filled with nightmares and imagined battles, Owen rose as daylight filtered through the trees. Reality thinned and, as he looked between the trunks, he thought he saw Sir Mathin walking through the trees. The figure faded as the Rift's power pulsed through the Forest.

He'd spent the night outside the lair, not willing to be in a place that had been the death-site of his father's men. The others rose and joined him at the fire he'd built for a hurried first-meal. They made short work of eating and getting ready to ride.

The five and their elven and Agni companions moved through the Forest, shadowed by the Dark Fey. Hoots, snarls, and gibbering followed their progress until Aeden sent a wave of deadly magic toward the Fey tracking them. Screams and whimpers faded into the distance.

The trees grew closer together, forcing them to a single file. The smell of damp earth and rotting vegetation filled the air. The rustle of disturbed brush leaning over the path and thud of hooves marked their passage. Reality faded and returned, revealing shapes of fantastic beasts and the outlines of those who had died.

Owen tightened his shield, attempting to hold it steady. Something moved in his peripheral vision. He jerked his head to the left and saw nothing. His jaw clenched with frustration.

Aeden, riding point, raised her right hand, fingers clenched in the signal to halt. "It's about two hundred paces ahead," she murmured. "There are guards set in the trees and on the ground. I'd not anticipated this."

Owen started to dismount. *No*, Navar told him. *We move faster together than you can on the ground. Stay with me.*

Aeden waved everyone forward for instructions. The elves filtered forward through the trees to join her and Owen.

"Here's what we'll do. Pair up. Don't fight alone. We need to take these guards out before we attack the Rift. Be as quiet and stealthy as you can. Others might try to come through the portal. Owen, we'll stay back and let the elves take care of the *Unseleigh*. The rest of us will create a shield to keep the Dark from noticing them. Go." She waved her hand. Owen drew his Sword.

He felt Aeden through his shield. He thinned it a little. *Let me in*, he heard Aeden say. He let the shield fall and felt her mind surround his. She gathered his magic, as well as Navar's and the Swords of Light into a reservoir that filled her with power. She sent a glamor to strengthen each elf and cover them with the illusion of nothingness.

Owen sensed the first kill. And the second. The silent killing seemed to go on forever until a haunting scream echoed through the Forest. In the following moment of silence, Aeden released the power she held back to those sharing it. Movement exploded from every direction.

A creature with enormous leathery wings dropped from the trees and landed on Owen, partially covering Navar. Its neck bent nearly double as it tried to stab him with its long, pointed beak.

He shouted in disgust and thrust HeartStriker up into the body. Ichor flowed down the blade and covered his arm. He flipped the body to the ground. Navar didn't move a muscle. When it landed, he stepped sideways and crushed the horror's head with a huge hoof. Owen heard the crunch.

Elves and Agni fought side-by-side, elven bows sending arrow after arrow into the horde, hooves and magic destroyed the enemy as the *Seleigh* fought their way toward the Rift.

Navar called the wind. Owen grabbed for his mane as they were suddenly on the other side of Aeden. A green kobold, hunched and twisted with deformed muscles, launched its body at her, mouth filled with needle-sharp teeth opened wide. Navar reared and Owen swung HeartStriker down across its neck, sending the head flying. Its body crashed to the ground.

Navar swept to the aid of two elves trying to keep a black kobold from tearing them apart.

A humanoid figure in black armor and black helmet raced past that battle and thrust a black spear toward Owen's face. Owen smashed down his Sword, deflecting the blow, but not enough. The spearhead tore through his elven chain-mail armor and lodged in his shoulder. Owen screamed.

Navar took them abruptly back next to Aeden. She threw herself from her warhorse and raised the whirlwind with a shout. In moments, the Red Dragon stood in her place. Without pause, she drew breath and released it, searing the *Unseleigh Sidhe* from existence with Dragon fire. Elves and Agni threw themselves to the ground, giving her a clear field. She swung her massive maw from side to side, tail lashing, eliminating all that stood against them. Trees caught on fire. The ground burned.

HeartStriker, heal him, demanded Navar.

I cannot. Not while the weapon lodges in his shoulder, HeartStriker responded, desperation in his tone.

Owen clutched at Navar's mane. Blood trickled from the wound. He was fast losing consciousness. "Help me," he gasped as he lost his balance and fell from the saddle, landing next to Navar's hooves. The shaft of the spear swayed back and forth, moving deeper.

The giant WindRunner kicked out with his hind legs as an ogre ran forward to kill Owen. His hooves connected, crushing the ogre's ribcage and killing it instantly. More Dark Fey converged on them. Navar danced around and over Owen, killing anything that came within range.

The Dragon turned from the Rift, its deadly intent clear. The remaining *Unseleigh Sidhe* fled back into the forest.

The whirlwind hid the Dragon and lifted away. Aeden rushed to Owen. She grasped the shaft near his shoulder. Placing her booted foot on his chest, she yanked upward, pulling out the head of the spear. Blood gushed.

With desperate intensity, HeartStriker sent magic into the injury, slowing blood loss, knitting cells together, pulling muscle to muscle and fusing them until only a long scar remained. Owen did not regain consciousness.

Aeden laid her hand on the scar. She pulled magic from the Aether that filled the world and spiraled it into the wound, finding the residual dark magic that was pulling Owen's energy into the Rift, helping to power its existence. The Rift pulsed as if with a heartbeat.

She clenched her jaw, breaking the link that was sucking Owen dry. As it snapped, the recoil threw her backward against one of the trees surrounding them. Owen lay still.

She rolled to her knees, more slowly than usual, and crawled back to his side.

Owen's back arched as he gasped with a huge in-drawing of air. He exhaled and gasped again. His eyes opened and he looked at Navar and Aeden as they peered down at him. "Where am I?" he croaked.

You were injured. Navar protected you and HeartStriker healed you, Aeden told him. Her head snapped up as they both felt a massive drawing of power.

The remaining elves and Agni were weaving a shield of protection across the Rift. From side to side, the barrier grew, layered in a pattern very like the weaving of a tapestry.

It was too slow. Owen turned his head as he lay on the ground and saw the Dark Fey on the other side, launching bolts of energy at the elves and the shield. He felt Aeden reach out with her magic and catch the energy from the other side, funneling it into the weaving. The shield finally reached the top of the Rift. Four of the elves collapsed where they stood.

Energy swept up and down the weaving in blinding light as those on the other side poured more and more power against it.

Owen rolled to his side and pushed himself to his hands and knees, head hanging. He slowly and painfully rose to his feet, picking up HeartStriker resting on the ground next to him. He leaned heavily against Navar for support, raised the Sword that seemed to weigh a million pounds and pointed the tip in a wavering circle at the shield. Power flowed from Navar through him and into the Sword. Shimmering waves of magic swept from its point to the shield. Aeden raised OathKeeper and did the same. She raised her left hand and the power of a Dragon flowed to the growing web of magic.

Those elves that still stood added their magic. The edge of the Rift began to contract. Slowly, as if a rope was pulling a bag shut at the top, the view to the other side shrank. More and more power poured into the shield.

Owen raised his other hand and added his own magic to the flood. As it hit the weaving, a blinding burst of light flashed out from the opening. The concussion of the collapsing Rift surged outward from its center, shattering the spell making the Forest a prison.

The Rift that had existed for a millennium vanished.

The breaking of the Forest prison foretold by the Bell of Prophecy was complete.

$$\S \S \S$$

Owen sagged to the ground next to his WindRunner, utterly spent. Navar's head and neck lowered toward the ground, ears akimbo, legs splayed to keep him upright. Elves knelt or lay on the ground, exhausted. Only Aeden stood — even she was as pale as the moon. She made her way to Owen with slow and careful steps.

She sat down next to him. "Well done, both of you," she murmured, her voice a hoarse ghost of its normal volume.

$ $ $

Blue, white, and red flames of Magefire danced and tumbled over the bodies of seven elves and five Agni as two of their elven brothers completed the *Téigh Trí Thine* — The Last Burning. The remainder of the band stood in silent tribute to their courage. When the last flames had flickered away, those left behind walked to the clearing where the Rift had once stood.

With some difficulty, Owen channeled his magic to the logs he and Aeden had stacked before the elven ceremony. Wrapped packets of jerky and journey cake sat in piles next to the fire. Two elves set water to boil over the fire. The remaining elves, Owen and Aeden found places to sit. The WindRunner and five Agni stood in a second ring behind them.

Silence dominated as food passed from hand to hand around the circle.

Eyes stared into the fire, minds very far away, as they remembered.

Owen looked at Aeden. "I feel a calling from the northeast, as if something is waiting for me," he told her, his voice soft and filled with puzzlement. "It's plucking at my magic."

Aeden turned her head and looked at him, eyes narrow, a frown ridging her forehead. He watched her look toward the northeast and felt her send her magic questing, searching for the taste of Demon magic.

Her frown turned to surprise and bewilderment. "Yes, something calls you. I can feel it too. If it is this strong this far away, you need to answer. It feels like the amulet in the Dragon Tower."

"Navar and I will leave tomorrow morning," he told her. "Will you take the men back to the Citadel? They need to heal there."

"Of course," she responded. "We'll return to the fairyfly's lair and join up with Saleth and Samhanach. I'm not sure these elves and their depleted magic can protect themselves from the *Unseleigh Sidhe* still in the Forest, so I'll stay with them. I need to return to Red Dragon's Keep to tell Neulach and Thomas what has happened."

Owen rubbed his hands on his aching knees while he thought.

"I will set a spell that will call me if you need me," Aeden told him. "Do not hesitate to trigger it. The Demons are out there, searching for you and the amulet. I'll bring the elves and the men of Red Dragon's Keep to Aos Si to help fight them."

"Thank you," Owen said with simple sincerity.

Chapter 23

A Dream of Dragons

"Where is my brother?" Evan demanded.

He stomped into the Library, followed closely by Marta and Breanna. Mid-afternoon sun poured through the windows.

Thomas, Gregory, and Haloran sat at the table in the center of the room, surrounded by piles of books and scrolls. Notes on their search for the locations of the remaining amulets were scattered over its surface.

"What?" Thomas mumbled, looking up with bleary eyes at the trio.

"Cameron and Neulach are gone. Even our Swords of Light don't know where they are," exclaimed Evan. The girls nodded in mute concurrence.

Thomas frowned. "What?" he repeated. He leaned back and stretched his arms wide as he pushed against his chair. His yawn was huge.

Evan stamped his foot. "Didn't you hear me? Are you deaf?" he shouted. "Cameron and Neulach are gone!"

"Wait. What? Where would they go? Where could they go?" Thomas asked.

Gregory and Haloran looked over at Evan and the girls. "Tell us," Haloran requested.

Breanna started the tale of unknown corridors and shadows burned into the walls and floor. Evan filled in what she missed. By the end, the three stood close together, leaning on each other for support. Evan shuddered, finally realizing just how frightened he had been.

Thomas's eyes narrowed.

HellReaver? Thomas asked his Sword.

I don't know. We need more information, the Sword of Light responded. *I suspect Cameron is safe enough with Neulach. Not many would be willing to confront the Dragon King. Neulach might also have his own agenda.* HellReaver spoke to them all.

"Sit," Thomas told them, gesturing to the chairs along the wall.

Evan pulled a chair from the side of the room up to the table and sat down with a weary sigh. Breanna and Marta followed suit. Gregory went to the sideboard between two of the bookcases, poured three mugs of cider and brought them back to the table, handing one to each of the searchers.

"Thank you, Gregory." Evan drank half of his mug of cider.

Thomas put his elbows on the table and rested his chin on his fists. He looked at his sister, his cousin and his friend for a long moment. He lowered his arms and crossed them on the table as he gave a sharp nod.

"Here's what we know. The Dragons have always been friends to men. Neulach has Cameron," he told them. "There's nothing we can do until he brings him back. I don't think anything will happen to Cameron while he's with the Dragon King. We have to trust Neulach will take care of him, no matter how hard giving that trust is."

Evan's eyes went huge. He sat, unable to move. He couldn't draw a breath into his lungs. His lips trembled. He struggled not to cry. Tears welled anyway. Breanna put her hand on his shoulder.

"It's all right, Evan. He'll be safe."

"You don't know that. You don't know anything!" Evan jumped to his feet, knocking his chair on its side. Tears spilled down his face. He ran from the room, the sound of his sobs trailing after.

§ § §

Breanna started to rise. "Let him be," Gregory said, putting a restraining hand on her arm. "He needs to be alone for a while. I'll talk to him when we're finished."

Thomas shook his head, rubbed his forehead with his fingers. He let his hands drop to the table. He pushed himself up from his chair and looked out the window.

"What time is it?" he asked. "It looks to be close to last-meal."

"It is, my lord," Marta spoke for the first time. She gathered the empty mugs and returned them to the sideboard. "Have you found anything in all this?" She reached out and absently pushed aside a pile of books resting on a map of Ard An Tir. A drawing of Dragons caught her eye.

What she uncovered had her hastily picking up the stack of books and setting them at the edge of the table. A beautiful rendering of a stylized black dragon filled the corner of the map.

"Where did you get this?" she demanded, her words tight with urgency. "I've seen this Dragon before," her voice trailed off with uncertainty.

"What? Where?" Thomas snapped out.

Marta could feel the blood draining from her face. Her mouth went dry. She turned to her father, eyes huge. "Da..." She reached out toward him.

"What is it, Marta?" Haloran asked his only daughter. He raised his hand and clasped hers.

"In my dreams," she whispered.

The sound of indrawn breath around the table told her all she needed to know. She had never told anyone about her dreams, wanting to be normal like everyone else. She dropped her gaze to the table in misery, pulling her hand from his. She felt herself shrinking away from all of them.

"What have you seen?" her father asked, his voice as steady as it always was.

Marta covered her face. She wished she could find a closet to hide in or a blanket to hide under, anything to block the censure she knew she would see if she looked up.

She kept her eyes focused on the map. "I was in a very large room," she mumbled. "I knew the map hanging on the wall showed where all of the amulets were hidden.

Then I was right in front of the map. I only saw the dragons flying over a very high peak somewhere to the northwest of Ard An Tir. Gold, purple, and green dragons flew around a great black dragon. Blue and copper dragons, and a red dragon, rested on the ground at the base of the mountain. A cave half way up the mountain showed a symbol I knew stood for the amulet."

Breanna touched her arm. "Why didn't you tell us?" she asked. "You know I dream true. Maybe that's what you and I have to do to help find the pieces of the Talisman."

Marta risked raising her eyes to look at the others. She was shocked at what she saw. Haloran wore a half smile that crinkled the side of his face as his eyes twinkled at her. Gregory's eyebrows almost disappeared into what little hair he had, his eyes were so wide. Thomas's face wore a huge grin.

She frowned. "What?" she asked in a small voice.

"You've seen a map. If your dreams are like Breanna's, we now have something to look for," her father told her. "We can find the other amulets."

"I know you've been chafing at the lack of progress we've been making," Thomas said. "I've not been able to tell you until now. We have a second amulet."

"What?" she and Breanna burst out together as they jumped to their feet.

"How?" Breanna demanded.

"Who?" Marta asked.

"A trader from Fasach bought it as a protection against Demons," Thomas explained. "Someone from their Mages Enclave in Fasach sold it to her. I think it was sent deliberately, although I don't know why. She had it wrapped in silk in a carved wooden box. She had it in her vardo in the cabinets under her bed. She just gave it to me when I asked for it."

Both girls slowly sank back into their chairs. Wild thoughts tumbled through Marta's mind. *Why was he in her vardo?* "Did you scry to make sure it is what you think it is?" she asked.

"Neulach said it was an amulet. I think I trust him," Thomas mocked gently.

"I guess that's all right then," Breanna shot back.

"We've been keeping watch on her," Thomas told them. "She's been meeting with some very interesting people who have shown up at the village." He looked out the window again. "I'm wondering if she might be a source for those portals that let the Demons in before the first battle. I wonder when she was here last. I'll have someone search her vardo," he muttered. "Maybe our wise-woman. She'll be able to sense any magical protections that have been set."

Breanna and Marta nodded slowly. "That's a good idea," Breanna concurred.

"Breanna, you and I need to talk to my mother about how to dream together," Marta told her. "She told me about, well — dreaming — when we first arrived here."

"Let's do it now," Breanna ordered. "We'll see you at last-meal," she told her brother as she and Marta left the Library.

The men watched them go in silence.

$ $ $

Breanna and Marta found Marta's mother in the infirmary room. She was mixing herb oils into salves. Moirra, the Keep's wise-woman, worked at her side, preparing the herbs for extracting the oils.

Raina turned with a smile and pulled the girls into a warm hug. "Welcome, both of you. It's been an age since I've seen you." She turned back to her bowl and continued to stir the concoction she was creating. "I've got to make this while the oils are still fresh. Would you like to help?" Raina gestured to the piles of herbs awaiting attention. "Talk to me while I work."

Marta glanced at her companion. Breanna gave a tiny shake of her head. "We'd love to help but ... maybe tomorrow?" Marta told her mother. "Right now, we need to talk to you about something I ... saw."

Raina slowed her stirring as she frowned at Marta. She put her spoon on its rest and wiped her hands on the apron covering her dress. "Moirra, can you complete this while I talk to the girls?" she asked the wise-woman.

"Of course I can. Shoo, all of you," she smiled as she made flicking motions with her hand. "Go to the kitchen for some cider. I'll take care of it."

Raina headed for the door, her hands ushering the two girls from the room. They made their way to the kitchen, arriving as the cook pulled bread from the oven next to the fireplace. All three drew in deep breaths. The sweet smell of warm baked grain was heavenly.

"Might we have some of the bread?" Raina asked the cook.

The cook chuckled. "For you, yes. There's nothing like a snack before last-meal. Warmed cider's on the hearth, if you want some." She cut thick slices from one of the loaves and handed them to Raina.

"Thank you," she said, with a hug for the cook's shoulders. Raina put the bread on a wooden plate on the hearth and spooned jam from a pot onto the slices. She sat down at the small table in front of the window with a view of the kitchen garden. The girls filled three mugs with cider and joined her there.

Marta hesitated, unsure of where to start her tale. Breanna had no such problem.

"Marta had a dream. It was about the Dragons and the amulets. She saw a map on the Library table that sparked her memory."

It was her turn to hesitate. She squirmed in her seat. "I don't know if you know I can dream true. I see what other people are planning and it always happens," she said in a small voice, rubbing her hands nervously on the surface of the table.

Raina reached over and laid a comforting hand on Breanna's. "It's all right, Breanna. I know about dreaming. Marta told me about her dreams when we arrived here. My mother dreamed true. The gift seems to skip a generation in my family, because I don't have it."

She turned to her daughter. "When did you dream about the map?"

"I think it might have been a month ago? I'm not sure. It was after the Demon battle, though," Marta spoke slowly. "Do you think this is a true dream?"

"Well, you saw the map upstairs and it helped you remember. Seems to me that's a pretty true dream," Raina told her.

"Do you think if Marta and I try to sleep and dream at the same time, we might be able to figure this out?" Breanna asked.

Raina rubbed the fingertips of her right hand over her lips, gazing out at the winter-killed garden, obviously far away in her thoughts. With a quick nod of her head, she returned and looked at both of the girls. "I think it can't hurt to try and may possibly be a very good idea," she told them. "I have a potion that will help you sleep. You won't fall asleep if you're too excited." She grinned.

"Good," Marta said. "We can finish with the new foals. We'll do it tonight." Pushing back her chair, she leaned over and gave her mother a hug. "Thank you, Mother. We'll find you after last-meal."

$$\S \S \S$$

The girls decided to sleep in Breanna's room. They picked up the potion from Raina and walked down the family corridor toward her chambers. Globes of magelight sat in iron brackets along the hall, lighting their way. Their Swords of Light hung on their belts, a habit they had continued since the first Demon battle in the Keep.

Worry roiled Breanna's stomach. True Dreaming disturbed her. She could never tell if what she experienced in the dreams was the truth or not. Confirmation could take days, weeks, or one time, months. She *was* able to tell the difference between regular dreams and True Dreams. The True Dreams were vivid, colors brighter. She felt like she was participating in them, not just watching.

A few times she dreamed with such clarity she knew she entered other's minds, spying on their thoughts, privy to their deepest desires and darkest fantasies. It happened spontaneously as she crossed the border from thought to sleep. Those dreams scared her.

This was the first time she would deliberately try to follow another into their dreams.

"If you don't want to do this, it's all right," Marta told her.

"No, I want to try," Breanna said. "Maybe I can learn to control the dreams I see. Maybe I can see things that will really help find the amulets. I won't know if I don't try."

She pushed the door open to her room and held it for Marta. The door swung closed as she moved aside and set the small sack holding Marta's sleep clothes and some bread and cheese from the kitchen on the trunk at the foot of her bed.

Breanna removed SunWalker from her belt and placed it on the sword-stand in the corner of the room closest to the door. A folding screen next to the fireplace blocked the opposite corner. She went behind the screen and changed into her bed shift. She undid her braid as she walk from behind the screen.

Suddenly shy, she looked at Marta. "I've never had anyone sleep in my room before. Have you?

Marta gave her a gentle smile. "My great-granma slept in my room with me before she died." HellScream joined Breanna's Sword on the sword-stand. She pulled her linen shift from her bag and walked behind the screen to change her clothes.

Breanna pulled a trundle bed out from under her bedframe. It was low to the ground and supported a thin mattress covered with sheets and a wool blanket. Marta would sleep there. Breanna climbed on her bed and sat brushing her hair.

Marta came from behind the screen and sat down on the trundle. "Better than the ground," she approved. She undid her braid and waited for Breanna to finish so she could brush her own hair. Breanna tossed her the hairbrush.

"Mother said to mix the potion with water," Marta reminded her. "I've got two mugs. Is there water?"

"We can use the water from the ewer on the commode." Breanna gestured at the chest on the other side of the bed. "It's fresh every night. Where are the mugs?" Marta pulled them from her pack.

Breanna poured water into the mugs. She took the vial holding the potion and tipped half of it into each cup. She swirled the mixture around in the cups and handed one to Marta.

Both of them sat on their beds and looked at the mugs with doubt in their minds. They looked at each other. Both started to smile, then to laugh. Breanna drank hers down and grinned. Marta followed suit. Marta handed her mug to Breanna. She set them on the trunk. "I guess now we wait for it to work," she said.

§ § §

A path of crushed red stone stretched into the forest in front of Marta. She was walking toward a round white tower with mullioned windows trimmed in blue that she could see in the distance. She knew she had been here before. She walked up the path to the tower and entered the front door.

A spiral staircase in the center of the room rose to the floors above. White furniture sat against the walls of the tower. A vase striped in red and yellow bands sat on a table under a window. It was the only color in the room.

Marta knew she had to climb the stairs. Instead, she walked over to the vase and looked inside. She saw a black dragon and Cameron swimming in water in a lake at the bottom of the vase. She had found Cameron.

She walked to the stairs and started to climb. Breanna was standing on the fifth stair, waiting for her. Marta smiled at her.

"What did you see in the vase?" Breanna asked.

"Cameron and a black dragon swimming in a lake," Marta told her.

"Good," Breanna said.

The two young women started climbing the stairs again. Marta knew she was looking for a map and she knew it was in the room at the top of the tower. A feeling of dread began to build in her chest. She slowed down. She did not want to go farther.

Something dark lurked somewhere in the tower. She wanted to turn around and run down the stairs.

She looked at Breanna climbing beside her. Her friend put a hand on Marta's arm and urged her to continue. Marta took one slow step after another. They reached the top floor of the tower.

A door stood partway open across from the stairs. She and Breanna walked to the door and Marta pushed it open.

The map she sought hung on the wall of a white room over a white desk and a white chair. White bookcases stood on either side of the room. The map was a drawing of Ard An Tir showing every country, every river, every mountain and every kind of inhabitant living there.

Bright yellow dots spread across the map. There were two in Fasach, five in Ard Ri, one in Fearmhar, and another two in Talahm.

There were dark blue dots on the map as well. One at Red Dragon's Keep, another in Fasach, one on the Windward Range, one at Falcon's Spire and the last in the far northwest corner of the map.

Marta looked at that corner. Dragons flew over a very high mountain somewhere to the northwest of Ard An Tir. There were gold, purple, and green dragons flying around a great black dragon. There were blue and copper dragons, and a red dragon resting on the ground at the base of the mountain. The blue dot floated halfway up the mountain.

She wanted to take the map. She went around the desk to try to pry it off, but she discovered it was painted on the wall.

Something dark and dangerous was coming up the stairs. She had nowhere to hide.

The room faded away.

Amulet

The WindRunner used his magic to capture the wind and raced across the land. The landscape blurred with speed as he ran. The cold wind of his passage fled past Owen's face, chilling cheeks, nose, and hands. His thoughts centered on the certainty in his mind that evil lurked in the limestone caverns and tunnels that remained after men quarried building blocks for Aos Si's fortified manor.

They had left the Darkened Forest just after dawn. The sun tracked their progress as it approached mid-day. At least the snow had stopped. Most of it on the ground had already melted.

Navar, could you slow down. I need to rest. Owen sent the hesitant thought to his companion. *I need to warm up.*

Navar loosed the wind and settled into a slow canter, then trot, and finally a walk. He stopped, blowing lightly. Owen slid from the saddle, weariness evident in every line of his body. He had ridden away from the Rift as soon as Aeden had left with the elves and his father's two soldiers to return to the Citadel. He was sure it was too soon. He knew he needed more time to recover from the spear thrust that almost killed him.

He leaned against Navar's warm side. *Can you light a fire?* he asked.

Navar snorted with contempt. *No. WindRunners have no need of fire. There is a herder's dwelling over this rise. Can you walk that far?*

I think so. I'll hold on to the stirrup. Maybe walking will warm me up.

They set off at a slow pace. Owen was very weak. The soup he'd eaten before leaving hadn't made up for his use of magic or the healing still taking place in his body.

I can make fire, HeartStriker said in a small voice.

Owen's answering chuckle was weak. *I'd forgotten,* he told his Sword of Light. *Not thinking very clearly.*

They topped the rise and looked down on a circular tent surrounded by a herd of sheep and goats. A small fire burned in front of the opening to the tent, tended by a man weathered by sun and wind to the color of dark bronze. His clothing looked worn, the top layer showing holes on elbows, collar and waist. Two long-coated herding dogs started to bark as Navar and Owen made their way down the gentle slope, scattering sheep as they went. The dogs wagged their tails but kept barking as they backed away.

The man stood. He bowed deeply. "Welcome *Gaothsiuloir*, rider. You honor my home. How may I serve?"

Navar raised his head high, looking down his long black nose at the man. He nodded his head once. *My companion would do well with a meal if you have enough to give. He needs your fire for warmth. He is Owen Arach, second son of the Duke of Red Dragon's Keep.*

The man stood mute, eyes wide. After some moments to recover from his shock at hearing the WindRunner in his mind, he bowed to Owen. "I am Taine, herder for Aos Si. You are welcome at my fire."

Owen took a step toward the warmth of the fire and almost fell. Taine hurried to him and took his arm, slinging it over his broad shoulders. Owen winced as the muscle over his wound stretched.

They hobbled forward and Taine helped him sit on the rug covering the ground beside the cheerfully crackling flames. Owen sighed with relief as the warmth began to thaw his frozen face, hands and feet. He huddled closer to the fire, holding his hands out and rubbing them together.

Navar, shall I have him remove your saddle? He twisted to look at the WindRunner. Taine had already loosening the girth and pulled the equipment from the back of the very tall creature. "Thank you, Taine. We'll only stay a short time. Navar needs to graze," he told the older man.

You need to warm up and eat, the WindRunner added as he dropped his head and began to nibble the short grass the sheep had left close to the tent and fire. Taine took his place opposite Owen and picked up a wooden bowl and spoon sitting next to the fire. He ladled mutton stew from the pot hanging over the fire into the bowl and handed it across to Owen.

His guest took it with a grateful nod and held the dish in his hands, savoring its warmth. He scooped up a spoonful of the stew and blew across the hot food. He put the spoon in his mouth and tasted mutton and onions. He blew out hastily, cooling his mouth. "Hot," he exclaimed. He traced its warmth all the way to his stomach as he swallowed. The headache he had not been aware of receded as he ate.

"I really needed this," he remarked. "Have you seen anything, well, weird, Taine? Did you know the magic imprisoning the Fey in the Darkened Forest has been broken? Has anything made it this far?"

The herder's eyes widened and he looked up at the top of the hill. "No, I've seen nothing. I've heard howls in the distance, but they just sound like coyotes. I did see some black things running on top of the ridge to the east day before yesterday, but they didn't come close."

Owen blanched. "How many?" he questioned.

"Looked like a big herd of 'em. I've never seen that outline before. High at the withers and sloping to the back legs. Think it was something from the forest?"

"No," Owen muttered, staring into the fire. "Have you heard about Demons?" He looked up at the older man.

"If you haven't, you will soon. I think we're at the beginning of a new Demon War. What you saw is a pack. I think they're headed for Aos Si. It's east of here, right?" Taine nodded.

"Is there somewhere safe you can go? They'd make short work of you and your charges." He gestured with his bowl toward the goats, and beyond them, the sheep grazing on the hillside.

Taine's alarm was clear. His eyes widened even further and his hands clenched. He straightened his back and his breath came faster as he considered the implications. He slumped as all the tension left his body. "There's a holding south of here I can make for with pretty sturdy walls. Nothing I can do if the Demons decide to attack."

"Do you have any weapons at all?" Owen asked, appalled for the defenseless man who sat across from him.

"Just this," Taine held up the knife he was using to eat, "and I've got a bow and some arrows over there," he said and gestured to the side of his tent.

An illusion stone, HeartStriker spoke to all of them. Taine jerked as if stuck with the knife.

"What was that," he exclaimed.

"That was HeartStriker, my Sword of Light." He lightly touched the scabbard laying on the ground to his left.

You can create an illusion spell that will hide him from the Demons. Ask if he has any stones you can use.

Owen looked at Taine. "Do you?"

Taine sat in thought. He rose with a grunt and went into his tent. He returned holding a small geode of amethyst. He held it out. "Will this do?"

"Yes. Good. An amethyst is protective in its own right." Owen responded. Taine dropped it into his outstretched hand.

HeartStriker, I know the basics. I'll need your help.

Owen cradled the geode in his hands. He calmed his mind and slowed his breathing. A tendril of power from HeartStriker pooled in the cup of his hands around the geode. He began to chant:

"Light pass through, then around, none will see.
Light pass through, then around, none will see."

He felt the power flow from his hands into the stone. He knew it could only hold a small amount of magic. When it felt full, he finished the spell.

"By the power, three by three,
With harm to none, so let it be."

He sat for some moments, feeling the spell fill the crystals within the geode. When it settled, he handed the rock back to Taine. "This should work as you travel. Keep it next to you as much as possible, maybe in a sling on your hip. If something comes, leave your flock. Remember, whomever you try to hide from, they can still hear you." He rose to his feet.

"We need to go. Thank you for your hospitality and your information. Watch for strange things, things out of the ordinary. They're probably from the Darkened Forest and aren't your friends."

Taine automatically rose with him. He bowed to Owen. "Thank you, lord. I'll help you saddle your WindRunner."

He swung the saddle up on the back of the WindRunner and tugged the girth tight. He held out his hands, fingers interlaced. Owen slipped his foot into Taine's hands and he lifted Owen high enough to set his foot in the stirrup. Owen looked down at the man who had shared his food and fire.

"Stay safe," he said and leaning forward, raised a barrier around himself against the cold. Navar jumped into a gallop, called the wind and they were gone.

§ § §

The gale whispered away as the WindRunner released it and dropped into a walk. A thin layer of clouds spread from horizon to horizon, dimming the bright light of mid-afternoon. They were close to the canyon filled with limestone caverns north of Aos Si. Owen's magic tingled, sending a warning crawling up his spine and straight to his mind. He could feel Demons like insects skittering in the depths of the earth.

Navar walked into the canyon. A small screen of budding shrubs, birch, and aspen trees bordered the banks with a trickle of stream flowing along its bottom. Wind, weather, and man had created a landscape of caverns, fallen spires of stone and shallow caves along both sides of the canyon. The WindRunner strode down the center beside the stream.

All three extended their magic into their surroundings, searching for the closest manifestation of what they sought.

Reality pulsed.

Owen shuddered in response. Goosebumps rose on his body.

Navar, do you feel that?

I do, Navar responded. *Evil walks in the dark. Another Rift brings forth its spawn. It does not open to the same world that feeds the Darkened Forest.*

You cannot go into the caverns. I played here as a boy, Owen told him. *They are too small for you.*

Then I shall stand guard at the openings along the canyon and send you my power as needed, the WindRunner told him. He snorted. *I can smell them from here.* He turned to the left and faced the cliff. The opening to a cavern beckoned on its wall, across the stream. Navar launched himself and his rider over the expanse of water. Owen unconsciously gripped the sides of his mount with his legs as Navar took off. They landed lightly on the other side.

Owen shuddered again. Gritting his teeth, he threw his leg over Navar's withers and slid to the ground. He turned to the WindRunner. *Should I take the saddle and headstall off?* he asked.

No. We might need to leave in a hurry, Navar said with slow deliberation. He tossed his head. *You need to go now.*

Owen pulled HeartStriker from its scabbard, unhooked the scabbard from his belt and hung it on the side of the saddle. He faced the yawning opening that gaped black beyond the flat light filling the canyon.

Hesitating for only a moment, he strode toward the cavern. He entered its mouth.

The floor of the cavern was flat, worn smooth by the boots and tools of men over the ages. Rough-hewn walls showed the care used by the hands that had created and extended them. Wooden columns braced beams every six to eight feet to support the roof. Darkened by age, the wood looked very dry. Dust on the floor held the tracks of something huge and vaguely dog like.

Demons, observed HeartStriker.

Owen agreed. He found these same tracks in the corridors of Red Dragon's Keep after the first battle. His stomach tightened and his breathing hitched. He created a small, dim globe of magelight and set it to hover in front of him at waist height. It lit the tunnel stretching before him for a short distance. *No sense in announcing I'm here with a bright light.*

Owen put his back to the right side of the tunnel. Sword extended in front of him, he moved carefully deeper into the tunnel system. He stopped abruptly. *I should use the cloaking spell now.*

He lowered the tip of his sword to the ground and tried to quiet his mind. He emptied it of all thought, slowing his breathing. As he did, his heartbeat slowed as well. His mind calmed. He centered himself, sending his *ki* deep into the earth, drawing strength and purpose into his body.

He began to chant with quiet intensity.

"Light pass through, then around, none will see.
Light pass through, then around, none will see.

By the power, three by three,
With harm to none, so let it be."

He felt the magic settle around his body. He hoped it would be enough to hide him from whatever he faced in the depths.

The pull of the amulet was to the right and down. He stepped toe to heel, feeling his way, gliding along the passage. He weakened his mental shields to better feel any threat before it arrived.

Openings to other tunnels yawned to his right and left. He paused at each, searching with his mind for a way down to the amulet.

The tunnel ended at a blank wall. *Well, I guess I'd better explore some of those side tunnels.*

He turned around and made his way back to the first opening, on his left now. The pull of the amulet was much stronger. He could hear something moving in the tunnel. Echoes distorted its location. Was it from this corridor? Or another, back toward the opening to the outside world?

Owen decided to explore the closest and turned into the tunnel. He noticed the tracks in the dust on the floor. They entered but did not leave. The Demons were here.

The salty smell of cold stone filled his nose, as well as the coppery undertone of old blood. Despite his magelight, he stumbled over small rocks fallen from the walls. The ceiling dropped lower, and he had to half-crouch as he moved forward.

A truncated oval of dim light beckoned up ahead. He banished his magelight and stood still, waiting for his eyes to adjust. In the darkness, his hearing sharpened. He heard the scuff of footsteps and the short, rasping sound of breathing. A growl echoed toward him. Another joined it. The snap of teeth and a yelp followed. Owen shrank against the wall.

Maybe I should just leave and wait until Aeden gets here. I don't want to meet this in the dark. He shook his head. He began to sweat. His breathing increased. He wrestled with his fear and his duty.

I am here, HeartStriker reminded him. *As am I.* Navar's voice was fainter, but just as reassuring.

Owen slowly straightened, letting the fear go. *Thank you*, he told them.

He moved toward the light. When he reached the opening, he clung to the side of the tunnel. He pushed his head past its edge until one eye was clear.

Stalactites hung from the ceiling, stalagmites grew from the floor. The light came from narrow holes in the roof of the cavern many feet above the floor. Massive columns of quartz refracted the light in a coruscating rainbow of color around the cavern. He didn't see any of the Demons he knew were there.

He wanted to scuttle out of the tunnel and hide behind one of the columns close to the wall to his left. Instead, he slid along the wall toward it. Not sure how well his spell was working, he moved as slowly as he could to prevent detection. Something dark pushed its head past a column on the far side of the cavern.

Owen froze, blanking thought from his mind. He watched as wide nostrils flared, searching for a scent. Blood-red eyes squinted in the light. With a snort, the head withdrew.

He slid faster along the wall. He swung behind the column and crouched down. Sweat trickled down his face. His shirt stuck to the sweat tracing its way down his back. His breathing quickened as his heart pounded. He opened his mouth and panted with shallow breaths to quiet the noise. Fear slowly abated.

He put his hand on the column for balance. It was damp and felt somehow greasy from the water running down its sides. He pulled his hand away with a grimace and wiped it on his pants. He risked sliding halfway around the column, looking for any place in the cavern where the amulet might be hidden. Across from him, the mouth of another tunnel gaped. The amulet was that way.

He began to slide along the wall, using columns as cover. Almost to his goal, he halted again and ducked down as three Demons made their way into the cavern from a tunnel to the right of his target. Their black coats seemed to drink the light, somehow dimming it within the cave.

Owen's heart hammered. The three Demons separated and began to search the cavern, looking behind columns and gradually making their way to the wall. Owen made himself as small and quiet as he possibly could.

The Demon nearest to his hiding place came closer and closer. Owen's throat tightened, his lungs threatened to stop drawing in air. His knuckles whitened as his grip on HeartStriker tightened. He set his feet.

The Demon sniffed the ground, as if following Owen's tracks. It paused five feet from where he crouched. It jerked up its head and looked right at him. Owen launched himself toward the beast, his sword arm fully extended.

Owen made no sound. Teeth bared, nostrils flaring, he drove HeartStriker up through the bottom of the jaw and into the Demon's brain. It dropped like a stone, dead before it hit the ground.

The two remaining Demons whirled toward him when they heard the thud as their pack member fell. Owen's illusion spell collapsed. They charged with an explosive burst of speed, snarling as they came.

Owen set himself. Time seemed to slow. He waited. The first Demon leapt toward him. He stepped aside and swung HeartStriker across its throat as it passed. Ichor flew wide as its head was almost detached from its body. The body fell and began to dissolve as the power fueling it failed.

The third beast veered wide as Owen killed the second. It tried to swing past and come at him from his back. Using the column to protect himself, Owen crouched and waited. The Demon's lips writhed back from teeth that would rend and tear his body to pieces should he fail.

Head down, it took slow step after slow step toward him. Owen locked eyes with it and saw his death within them. It leapt. Owen danced to the left and drove

HeartStriker into its side, piercing its heart. It slid past him, taking HeartStriker with it.

He fell to his knees, his breathing as deep and swift as a bellows as he panted from exertion and fear. He pushed himself back to his feet and lurched to the last dead Demon. He grasped HeartStriker and pulled him from its side. A gush of bubbling blood followed the withdrawal. He backed away from the bodies and watched as they dissolved before his eyes.

When the bodies vanished, he ripped a piece of fabric from his shirt and wiped HeartStriker's blade clean. He made his way to the opening where he could still feel the amulet's pull. He braced his back against the wall and slowly slid down to sit on a larger flat-topped boulder that had fallen from the wall eons in the past. Setting the sword's point on the floor, he rested his hands on the crosspiece of the pommel. He let his head fall forward onto his arms, slowing his breathing and heart as he rested.

You have done an amazing thing, HeartStriker told him. *Sent here by some power unknown, these Demons would kill you and any who call themselves your family. They failed.* Approval flowed from the Sword to Owen, sending him strength along their bond. Navar added his support as well. Owen absorbed that praise as if he was a dry desert thirsting for the drops of rain that fell so infrequently.

He raised his head and watched light flash around the chamber, mesmerized by its beauty. He stood with a groan. He cast his magic into the tunnel system men had created. He felt no other Demon presence.

Reality pulsed, just as it had in the Darkened Forest. Another open Rift was located in these tunnels, or very close by.

Owen debated with himself. Should he find the Rift and try to destroy it, or go after the amulet? It had taken eighteen magic-wielders to close the Rift in the Darkened Forest. He decided to go after the amulet. He could return with reinforcements to close the Rift later.

With a flick of his hand, magelight gleamed clear and bright in the mouth of the tunnel before him. Magelight moving before him, he walked forward, sword held ready. Fifty paces in, the tunnel jogged to the right. He took the turn and halted as another cavern opened up before him.

Towers of limestone blocks covered the floor in cascading piles, as if they had fallen from the roof far above. He sent a surge of power into the cavern. It reflected back from an object set between two blocks about halfway up a pile straight ahead of him.

A smile lit his face. He carefully laid HeartStriker on the ground and climbed up the pile arranged as if it were a staircase. When he reached the third level, he stopped and admired the piece of the Talisman he had found. He picked it up.

Even covered in dust and small enough to rest in the palms of his two hands, he felt the enormous power locked within it. He took his shirt and gently wiped the dust from the face of the Aos Si Amulet. Rubies, sapphires and diamonds set in a triangular matrix of copper and gold flashed in the light. His nostrils flared as he drew in a very deep breath.

Tucking the amulet in the crook of his left arm, he hopped down the staircase of stone and landed on the floor of the cavern. He picked up HeartStriker and left the cavern. His magelight guided him through the tunnels until at last he stood at the entrance.

Navar, HeartStriker, if I feel the amulet's power now, so will every magic wielder on the Windward Range. Do you know a way to shield it?

We will create a covering of magic, impervious to all, Navar told them. *Stay within the tunnel. Set the amulet on the ground.* Owen reluctantly placed his find on the ground.

Let we three join now. Navar reached out with his magic to HeartStriker. Owen reached out to both of them. This joining was much deeper than any other they had attempted. Owen felt Navar's heart beating and HeartStriker's essence bound to the metal of the Sword. Each knew the thoughts and desires of the others.

With his mind augmented by power willingly shared, Owen began to weave an ethereal covering over and around the amulet with careful precision. The blaze of power the amulet radiated dimmed as layer upon layer of magic covered it. Finally, it lay hidden from his awareness. Owen let the joining fall away.

He walked over and carefully picked it up. He left the tunnel, raising his arm to block the light from his eyes made sensitive by his time underground. He went to Navar who stood by the stream, ears rigidly erect and eyes shining. He held the amulet out in both hands. The WindRunner nosed it gently. Owen slid HeartStriker into the scabbard hanging on the saddle and pulled a shirt from his saddlebag. He wrapped the shirt around the amulet and placed it carefully on top of the clothing in the bottom of the bag. He covered it with the remainder of his supplies. He buckled the flap closed and gave it a final pat.

He swung up onto Navar's back. "Let's go find my aunt and uncle."

§ § §

Scott and Debra stood on the parapet running along the walls of Aos Si. Just above man-height, they could watch the approaching line of darkness they knew was the Demon horde. Scott pulled his wife close.

"I love you. No matter what happens, remember I love you," he told her with quiet intensity.

She hugged him back, her face a mask of stone although tears glittered in the corner of her eyes. "I love you, too. I always have."

The thunder of hundreds of feet began to shake the earth. A great swelling sound as of a smith's bellows resolved into the panting of approaching death.

"They'll be here within half a candlemark. Get everyone up on the parapet. We need to keep them out as long as possible," she said.

Scott relayed the order.

Chapter 25

Tapestry

Dust motes floated in the beams of sunlight falling through the cracks in the shutters covering the windows of Breanna's room. They fell across Breanna's bed, shining on her face. She stretched and yawned. Sitting up, she swung her legs over the side of her bed and yipped in surprise. She'd forgotten Marta was asleep on her trundle. Breanna remembered the dream.

Excitement quickened her breathing. She reached down and shook Marta's shoulder. Her friend awoke, aware and ready between one moment and the next. She looked at Breanna. "Do you remember?"

Breanna gave her a happy grin, a sparkle in her eyes. "Yes, I do. Let's get dressed and go tell Thomas!"

"I remember everything," Marta said, elation filling her voice. "I know where the amulets are and I think the yellow dots are Rifts." She pulled her clothes on and pushed her feet into her boots. Breanna dressed behind the screen, stepped from behind it and grabbed SunWalker as she passed the stand, strapping the scabbard to her side. Marta did the same with HellScream. They swung out the door and walked down the corridor toward Thomas's room.

Marta looked at the tapestries hanging on the walls. The women of the Keep spent years weaving them. The huge fabric representations of major historical happenings were hung to block the stone walls from taking heat from the Keep. Tapestries worn beyond other use were laid on the floor of the corridors for the same reason.

Marta halted, her eyes caught by the Dragons flying in the background. She reached out and grabbed the back of Breanna's tunic, pulling her to a stop.

"Look," she gasped, eyes wide, pointing at the wall.

Breanna turned back to her. "What?" she demanded.

"Look at the pictures," Marta exclaimed. She shook Breanna's shoulder. "What battle is this? Where is it? See the Dragons? They've got riders! I haven't seen another tapestry with Dragon riders."

Breanna gaped at the faded weaving hanging on the wall. "I've never really looked before," she admitted.

Dragons of every color belched fire from their mouths onto Demons battling with men. Men sat on the backs of some of the Dragons, flaming swords held aloft. Very thin creatures with pointed ears mounted on strange looking beasts battled beside them. They had to be elves. The army fought in front of a red wall curving around a manor house of grey and black stone.

What looked like the face of a large mirror floated in the background to the left of the battle. Demons seemed to pour from the mirror. Bolts of lightning filled the sky around the Dragons.

Marta stepped closer, her hand outstretched, finally resting it against the cloth. A vibration pushed its way up her arm and from there through her body. She gasped and tried to rip her hand away, grabbing it to still the vibration. HellScream sent a bolt of power against the attack, breaking her contact with the weaving. The vibration in her body slowly faded.

Breanna reached out toward the wall.

Marta knocked her hand away. "No," she growled. "I felt a presence trying to come through. I felt it," she insisted. "We need to tell Thomas."

Still holding Breanna by the shoulder, she propelled her through the rest of the hallway to Thomas's door. She knocked hard.

"Who is it? Hold on ..."

The door opened. Thomas stood there in a long robe, obviously getting ready for the day. Open shutters let in early morning light, although candles flickered on the mantle of the fireplace and on the table next to the chair where his clothes were laid out.

"What is it?" he asked, voice sharp, brows lowered as he noted Breanna's agitation and Marta's white face.

Marta clenched her teeth, lips thinned in irritation at his brusqueness. "We may have found another piece of the puzzle." She turned and marched back toward the tapestry, anger stiffening her back.

"There are men riding Dragons in the tapestry on the wall down the corridor," Breanna told her brother. "Marta says something tried to come through when she touched it." Marta slowed her footsteps.

"Wait," Thomas ordered as he hurried back into the room and pulled on his clothes. He grabbed HellReaver from its stand and pulled the door closed as he joined Breanna in the hallway.

"Dragon riders?" he muttered.

"Yes. Marta saw them in the tapestry. We dreamed last night and found the map she told us about," Breanna chattered on, oblivious to Thomas's incredulous expression.

"Marta's mother said you should try this? Raina actually said it was possible?" Thomas asked, his tone skeptical.

"Of course it's possible. We did it last night," Breanna shot back. "You know I dream true. So can Marta."

"I remember. I was there," Thomas reminded her.

The two joined Marta, standing in front of the faded wall hanging.

In the forefront, Demons and humans slaughtered each other. Winged Demons, the *smachtmaistir* of legend, flew over the battle, directing their minions. Dragons attacked the *smachtmaistirs* with flame. Burning Demons fell from the sky. Men shot arrows and threw spears, killing the Demons as they attacked the human army.

"Look," Marta exclaimed. "Isn't that an amulet in the wall? See there, in the foreground?" She pointed toward the bottom of the tapestry. "Where was this battle?"

"I think it's the wall of the Aos Si manor before they finished it," Thomas said, bending forward to look more closely. "I was there once with Mother and Father." He reached toward the tapestry.

"Wait," Marta said urgently, grabbing his arm. "I really did feel a presence trying to come through. HellReaver, SunWalker, HellScream. Could you please make a shield, just in case?"

Of course, HellScream responded. The three Swords answered her request. A faint shimmer in the air and a layer of magic enclosed the tapestry.

"You shouldn't do this, Thomas. You're the heir." Marta reached out and pressed her hand against it.

A circle into another place expanded from her touch. She snatched her hand away from the weaving as the threads started to disappear. It grew until the entire tapestry held only darkness. Demons writhed on the other side.

All three jumped back from the portal.

Nothing can come through HellScream told them all. *We have bound it.*

Thomas held up his hand, palm facing the weaving. A burst of light blasted out from his hand to join the magic of the shield. An explosion of every color bulged against the shield, pushing it out toward them. The blast sucked back into the disk. It shrank to the size of a hand. The circle disappeared with a bright flash of light.

Nothing marked the tapestry as a portal to the Demon world.

Thomas turned to the young women, as white as they were. "It's sealed," he said. Breanna and Marta clutched each other for support. Marta drew a shuddering breath. They let each other go.

"Why did this tapestry become a portal?" Thomas mused. "Why hasn't it turned into a portal before?" He reached out and ran his right hand over the weaving.

He stopped as he felt a bump behind the tapestry. He clenched his teeth. "Marta, Breanna, can you hold the tapestry away from the wall? There's something behind it." He pulled the right side of the weaving away from the wall.

"Breanna, take that corner and we'll pull it out," Marta directed. Breanna reached down and gripped the bottom of the weaving. They lifted up as they backed away from the wall. Thomas slid behind the tapestry.

A translucent disk, little thicker than a piece of parchment, was stuck to the stone. Thomas ran his hand over the slick surface. He pulled his belt knife from its sheath and inserted its tip behind the disk. He gave the knife a twist and the disk popped off the wall, falling into his hand. He back out from behind the wall hanging.

"This, this is a portal." Teeth clenched, lips narrow, eyes filled with fury, Thomas looked at the girls as they let the tapestry fall back to the wall. "There's still a traitor, or traitors, here. No one but people we've known forever has access to these halls."

Breanna took a step back. "We need to talk to Gregory and Haloran about this," she told him, a tiny bit of fear in her voice.

Marta had never seen Thomas this angry, not even when the Demons first attacked the Keep. She raised her hand and rested it on his arm.

"Now we know. Now we can do something about it," she told him. He snorted.

"Let's get first-meal and then find a map." Ever practical, Breanna had already shaken off the experience. "Marta and I need to mark where the amulets and Rifts are that we saw last night. Thomas, you go tell Gregory and Haloran," she said as she organized their day to her liking. She hooked her arms through Marta's and her brother's. "Let's go talk about men riding Dragons."

§ § §

Maaike swung the drab brown cloak around her shoulders. The fire had gone out in her stove and the vardo was chilly. She added charcoal to its belly and used a long match to light the tinder below it. The wood caught. She sat back on her heels to watch it burn. She had hopes for the meeting this morning with a man who hinted he had information to sell. Her patient wait might be rewarded.

Once dressed in the faded brown and green dress she carried for meetings like this, Maaike left her wagon, making sure the door locked behind her. She lifted the shawl from her shoulders and covered her hair, wrapping the ends around her neck. She nodded at her men who listened at the inn and the various shops for any information she could use. She walked away from the caravanserai toward the town and the tannery where she was to meet her informant.

People were already hurrying through the streets, even at this early hour. She set her pace to a brisk walk, doing nothing to draw unwanted attention. The tannery wasn't open yet. The smell of fresh bread and meat pies filled the air, making her mouth water. She slowed her pace and glanced around for anyone watching her. No one even looked her way. She entered the bakery on her right.

A table stretched across the width of the shop. Loaves of bread fresh from the oven rose in fragrant stacks. Mounds of small hand-pies filled with meat and vegetables sat next to the bread. Juices bubbled from slits in the crust.

The baker, a thin old woman stood behind the table, her cheeks a rosy red from the heat in the room. "How can I help you?" she asked.

Maaike looked with longing at the pies, knowing the price would be dear. "How much for a pie?"

"Five copper farthings," the old woman told her. "Two for eight."

Surprised by the low cost, Maaike smiled. "I'll take two," she said. She dug into the fabric pouch hanging from her belt and sorted eight coins into her palm. She handed them to the woman and chose her two pies.

"Thank you," she told the woman as she turned and exited onto the road. Small black eyes watched her as she strode away. A man unremarkable in every way stepped through the door. "She bought two pies," the old woman told him. With a nod, he slipped back out of the bakery.

Maaike made her way toward her meeting, eating the pies as she walked. They were good!

The tannery was set well away from the rest of the town. The smell reached her long before it was in sight. Walking closer, she could see the hides stretched on frames and watched as fumes rose from barrels where others were soaking. She stopped on the side of the road and finished eating.

Curious, she looked around at the buildings surrounding the tannery. They were rickety shacks made of whatever was available to the poor people who lived in them. Children dressed in rags played listlessly in front of doors that were just fabric draped over the openings.

Maaike sniffed with disdain. In her land, the poor received modest housing as decreed by her faith—much more humane than what she saw here. She turned slightly to check her back trail. No one watched her. She looked back at the tannery and saw a man in a dark cloak standing at the side of the steaming barrels. When he saw she had noticed him, he turned and glided toward the trees to the right of the tannery.

Maaike followed when he reached the trees. Twice she checked behind and saw nothing.

An old man dressed in rags stepped out from behind one of the hovels and limped toward the trees. He held an axe in one hand and a strip of fabric over his shoulder. Maaike watched him totter to a thin tree at the very edge of the grove. He leaned against the tree, then straightened and began to chop it down. She turned back toward her own quarry. The cloaked figure stood just within the trees. The sounds of chopping stopped and she heard the tree fall.

She dismissed the woodcutter from her thoughts. Fallen leaves squelched under her feet. Joining her informant within the trees, she asked, "What do you have for me?"

The man pushed back his hood, revealing the short haircut of a soldier. "The heir is looking for the *Cumhacht ar Draigoini*, the Dragon Talisman. He has found one of the five amulets. His brother searches for the second at Aos Si."

The news sent her heart hammering. The *Cumhacht ar Draigoini*. The Power of Dragons. She knew the search for its shards was decades, if not centuries, old. Legends said its breaking had opened Rifts into other realms across Ard An Tir. Demons came from those Rifts.

"Do you know what it looks like or where it is," she asked, urgency sharpening her voice as she stepped closer and laid a hand on her informant's arm.

He answered with a curt "No", shaking off her hand and stepping away. "You owe me a gold piece."

She reached into the bag at her waist and pulled out a gold coin. She handed it to him and he turned and hurried away through the trees.

She did not see the woodcutter returning to his fallen tree as she made her way back to the caravanserai.

§ § §

"Lord Thomas, wait for a moment please," Gregory called to him as he walked down the corridor toward the kitchen. Thomas turned and paused at the arch through which flowed the enticing smells of roasting pork and fresh biscuits.

Gregory caught up with him and they continued down the hall. "I've received a report from the woodcutter, my lord. The trader met with one of the soldiers we set up as a lure. She took the bait."

Thomas stopped. "I want Moirra to search her wagon tomorrow morning," he told Gregory. "Regardless of what she finds, I want the trader brought in quietly by tomorrow afternoon. There are many questions she needs to answer. Moirra should give her something that will make her confused so she won't remember what happens. I don't want to make her suspicious if at all possible. She can remain an unwitting spy that we can use."

"Yes, my lord," Gregory replied.

§ § §

"My lord, I found these in a box under the trader's bed, spelled to keep anyone without magic away," Moirra told Thomas the next morning, handing him the disks that she had found. "No one saw me enter and no one saw me leave," she said. "I left a compulsion on her cup to drink the potion that will muddle her thinking by this afternoon."

"Thank you, Moirra," Thomas told her with grave courtesy. "Please, have some cider or some water." He gestured at the table set at the side of his father's desk.

"My thanks, Lord Thomas. I've not had first-meal yet," Moirra said as she poured a mug of cider.

"I'll need you and perhaps Raina to do one more thing," Thomas said to the Keep's wise-woman. "We must find the traitors that still lurk in this Tower. Would you speak with her and come up with some kind of test that we can use?"

"Yes, my lord. I'll talk to her now," Moirra told him as she finished the cider. She put the mug back on the table and hurried away to find Marta's mother.

"Sergeant Timmons," Thomas called to one of the guards standing watch at his door. "Please find Master Sergeant Haloran and have him meet me here."

"Yes, lord," the guard responded.

Haloran knocked on the doorframe a quarter candlemark later. "Come," said Thomas, not looking up from the papers on the desk.

"I'm here, Lord Thomas," Haloran said.

Thomas looked up at his advisor and friend. "Sorry, Faolan," he said with wry humor. "I forgot I sent for you. How did my father do all of this work?" he asked, waving at the papers spread over the top of the desk, not expecting an answer.

Haloran shook his head. "I don't know, my lord. I do know that he would pass things on to me and to Gregory to handle when I was still at the Keep. He didn't try to do it all himself."

"Never mind," Thomas said. "Sit." He waved at a chair in front of the desk. Haloran poured two mugs of cider and handed one to Thomas as he took his seat.

"I sent Moirra to search the trader's vardo this morning," Thomas told his seneschal. "She found the portal disks hidden under the trader's bed. I checked the gate guard records from just before the first Demon battle and a caravan arrived from Fasach two months before it began. That would give anyone time to access the Tower and distribute the portals throughout the Keep."

Haloran held his mug forgotten in his hand, listening hard.

"Moirra left a potion that Trader Maaike will drink this afternoon," Thomas continued. "Please have her picked up from her vardo by guards in regular cloths so no one knows who has her. Have them take her to the second corridor cells in the undercroft. You, Gregory, and I will question her there and then return her to her vardo. I want her to remain a valuable spy for Fasach."

"Yes, my lord," Haloran told Thomas as he placed his empty mug on the side table. "I'll see to it and let you know when she's ready." He turned at the door. "It's a very good plan," he told Thomas with a huge smile. He left to carry out his orders.

$ $ $

"Well done, my lord," Sergeant Haloran complimented Thomas. "The trader's information is vital."

"I agree," Gregory said. "The question is how do we use it?"

Thomas put his elbows on the table in his father's office and rested his chin on the back of his hands. His eyes drooped with fatigue. The questioning of Trader Maaike had lasted for hours.

The three men had taken turns asking her questions about her family and who she reported to in Fasach. Her answers to questions about her mission and the information she was sent to gather shocked all of them.

"I'm still stunned about the amulet," Thomas croaked on a dry throat. He took a sip of water from the cup on his right. "I didn't even think to check for a spell set to trigger when the amulets are reunited. I'm going to wait until Aeden returns to remove that magic."

"I'm not surprised she's a spy for Fasach," Haloran mused. "I *am* surprised that the Minister of Spies is her direct contact. He must have a lot of faith in her."

"Why would she want to know how many people are here?" Gregory added. "And the information she gathered about supplies and resources is worrisome. It sounds like Fasach may be preparing for war." Haloran shook his head, his face grim.

Thomas pushed back his chair and stood up with a groan. "There's nothing more we can do tonight. She did get back to her vardo without problems?" he asked Gregory.

"I've had no report of anything untoward," Gregory told them. "She'll wake up with a massive headache and no memory of our questioning. Thank goodness for Moirra and her potions."

"Good. Then let's get some rest," Thomas said.

Thomas pulled the door closed as the three left the office.

Hell's Spawn

Owen scanned the area around them with his magic as the three raced south across the snow. He felt a great gathering of the Dark to the southwest, near the Darkened Forest, another to the southeast where he very much feared his aunt and uncle were under attack. He triggered the seeking spell Aeden had placed on him.

Navar, we need to stop. I have to eat and so do you. We need to plan what we're going to do. I'm not sure which group of evil we should find first.

Agreed. Navar released the wind, slowed his run, dropping to a canter, a trot, and finally a walk.

Owen noted the edge of the Darkened Forest. He looked for trees marking a stream or some other place they could safely stop. He saw a group of standing stones not far from the trees of the Forest.

There, he pointed. He felt amusement from both his sword and his WindRunner.

Well chosen, HeartStriker remarked.

Why, he asked, curiosity catching his attention.

Let's find out, HeartStriker responded.

Navar broke into a canter. He stopped at the eastern entrance to the circle. Owen slid from his back. He felt a welcoming and sense of peace from this place. He walked in.

Spring enfolded him. Warmth, the smell of new grass, and a sprinkling of flowers among the green greeted him. Navar paced into the circle, dropped his head and began to graze. Owen sighed with relief as the tension he'd been carrying bled away.

A crude fire pit lay near a tumble of boulders and rocks filling the spaces between the standing stones. Owen went to Navar, slung the saddlebags over his shoulder, loosened the girth and pulled the saddle from the WindRunner's back. Navar grunted with relief.

Owen settled the saddle on the ground and draped the bridle and saddlebags carefully over the seat. He searched the circle for deadfall. Finding none, he left the stones and quickly gathered a large armful of wood littering the ground between the Forest and the edge of the circle. He lit a fire. Rummaging through the saddlebags, he found the jerky and journey cake he'd been eating since the Citadel. *I am so tired of this. Maybe I should do some hunting, get some fresh meat.*

He scanned the plains stretching away from the circle. *No time.* He noticed the growth inside and saw the tops of spring onions and dandelions. He started a pot of water heating over the fire and gathering his find, dumped everything in the hot water except the journey cake. Gnawing on the tough bread that could survive just about anything, Owen sat on the ground and waited for his food to cook.

His gaze wandered the ground as he thought about what had happened in the caverns. Questions filled his mind. Where had the Demons come from? Where was the Rift in the caverns? Who had hidden the amulet there?

He stiffened as his eyes caught sight of the hilt of a knife buried under the grass, a hilt he'd seen his entire life. He reached out and laid his fingertips on the blue stone topping the pommel. He carefully grasped the dagger and pulled it from under the grass. It was his mother's.

His breathing stopped. Shock raced up and down his body. Hope flared madly.

Navar! he shouted. Navar threw his head up, startled. *This is Mother's dagger. She's been here!*

He jumped to his feet and looked wildly around the circle. He began to scuff through the grass around the fire, looking for any other signs she and his father had been here. This was the first inkling he'd had that his parents, or at least his mother, might be alive.

This is good news. Calm now. We can do nothing in this moment. We'll search for them tomorrow, HeartStriker told him.

You're right. Owen sat back down by the fire, cradling the knife in his hands. He pulled the pot from the fire to cool so he could eat.

Tomorrow was soon enough.

§ § §

Sunrise found him standing at the opening to the circle, arms crossed, looking beyond it for traces of his parents passage. No tracks remained on the ground. He sniffed at the air, searching for some scent of them or for anything that might show him the direction to follow.

He turned back to the fire, his mood morose. Navar stood hipshot, one hoof cocked, head hung low as he rested.

Owen heard something drifting on the wind. He looked toward the west.

It sounded like the booming of thunder in the distance. It stopped. The sound repeated. It was getting louder. Navar awakened and raised his head, shook himself, and faced to the west. Owen grabbed the saddle and swung it onto Navar, cinching it tight. He slipped the headstall over the WindRunner's ears. He tied the saddlebags behind the cantle.

He quickly kicked dirt over the ashes long since cold. He knelt and placed his hand on the ground. *Thank you for your welcome.* He sent a wave of peace into the circle. Standing, he turned to his WindRunner, leapt and got a toe in the stirrup. He swung aboard and rode out of the circle.

They faced west. Owen drew HeartStriker.

They waited.

Out of the brightening sky appeared the outstretched wings of a Dragon gliding through the air. Thunder reverberated as it flapped those wings, arrowing toward them. Owen gave a half-laugh. *I should have known.* He sheathed his Sword.

The flyer glided across the standing stones and swept across Navar and Owen. It turned in the air on a wingtip and came to land in front of them.

"Thomas!" Owen shouted with joy. He threw himself from the saddle and raced toward his brother perched on the neck of the great creature.

Thomas slid down the Red Dragon's leg, landing hard on the ground with both feet. Owen grabbed Thomas in the tightest hug he'd ever given. The Dragon called the whirlwind. Aeden appeared as it lifted away.

"I can't believe you're here," he exclaimed, holding Thomas out at arm's length. He turned and gave a shallow bow to Aeden. "Thank you for coming so fast. I didn't expect you until tomorrow or the next day. Since when are men allowed to ride Dragons?"

Before Thomas could answer, Owen remembered the dagger sheathed on his belt. "Look. Look what I found in the circle." He pulled the knife from his belt. Thomas stared at what he held, his mouth hanging open.

"It's Mother's," Thomas whispered. "It's Mother's!" he shouted. He reached for the blade. Owen handed it to him. Thomas ran his fingers over the hilt and blade. He handed it back.

"I found the Aos Si Amulet," Owen told his brother.

The day grew still and silent as Aeden and Thomas simply stared at him. Neither seemed to breathe.

"You're kidding," Thomas whispered, eyes going huge, eyebrows rising toward his hairline.

Owen shook his head. "No. It's in the saddlebag. We wove a protection spell around it to hide it. I guess it's working if you can't feel it."

As if released from a spell, Aeden and Thomas moved toward the saddlebags. "Show me," Thomas demanded.

Owen lifted the bags from the saddle and set them on the ground. He pulled the flap open and dug to the middle, grabbed the amulet wrapped in his shirt and pulled it out. He flipped the shirt open and held the amulet out to them on his palm.

They bent in close to look. "Oh," murmured Thomas.

Aeden reached out and held her hand over it. "Very well-done spell," she said. Owen smiled.

He re-wrapped it and shoved it back in the bag. "Have you eaten?" he asked. "I've got journey cake."

Thomas made a face. "No I haven't and I'm starving. I'll take some of that cake. We left before daybreak."

Owen handed him a small bag of the journey cake, taking some out for himself. He offered another bag to Aeden, who shook her head.

"There is a pack of the Dark to the southeast and another to the southwest," Owen told them. "I think the one to the southwest is probably the *Unseleigh Sidhe* who've escaped from the Darkened Forest. I'm not sure what's to the southeast, but I expect it's Demons," he told them. "On their way to Aos Si. They may already be there."

Aeden scanned the surrounding prairie. "The elves from the Citadel are coming, as well as the men you left there." She looked at Owen. "They will be here in a day."

"I've got three companies coming from the Keep," Thomas said. "That's sixty more men. They'll be picking up volunteers on the way."

"How did you know?" Owen frowned. "I just fought the Demons in the caverns a day ago, I think," he faltered, trying to remember.

"Breanna and Marta dreamed you closed the Rift in the Darkened Forest and left to find the Aos Si amulet," Thomas told him. "As soon as they told me, I had Haloran organize the companies and sent them out. Good thing I did," he said with quiet satisfaction.

"We've got another amulet; I think it's from Fasach," he continued. "A trader thought it was holding a spell against Demon raids on her caravan. It seems we might have friends in the Fasach Mages Enclave." A smile lit his face. "I hid it in the passage behind the great hall mural. Then again, it's got a spell on it set to trigger when the amulets are finally rejoined." His face lost its smile.

Owen absorbed the information. He shrugged.

"So, should we wait for the elves and our men? Which group should we go after first?" Owen asked. "I don't think leaving enemies at our back is a good idea."

Thomas looked to the southwest. He crossed his arms, left hand supporting his right elbow as he pursed his lips and rubbed his chin. He looked at Aeden.

"Enemies at your back are never wise," she said, a hint of laughter coloring her remark.

"Guess we need to go southwest, then," Owen said.

§ § §

The elves and Agni are a few miles west of the main body of Unseleigh Sidhe, the Dragon reported.

She tipped her wing and flew wide of the main body of elves, tilting so Thomas could see the advancing army. Sun glinted off the silver armor and helmets the elves wore. Spears held upright by stirrup and gauntlet looked like row after row of saplings topped with wickedly barbed heads.

Knuckles white, Thomas gripped the thick strap of leather encircling the Dragon's neck with both fists. Straps ran from the leather belt he wore and hooked on to the leather strap so he couldn't fall off and plunge to his death. He'd shown Aeden the tapestry depicting men riding Dragons when she'd arrived to tell him about the Darkened Forest Rift. With no time to create a harness, this was the best idea they had devised. He wished he had never shown it to her.

The unfeeling coldness of the Dragon's voice disturbed Thomas on many levels. It sent a shiver down his spine and reminded him forcefully that he rode the most powerful creature in Ard An Tir. Its words didn't even sound like Aeden.

They scouted the pack of *Unseleigh Sidhe* as they searched for the elves. It seemed every Dark Fey in the Forest had decided to make for Aos Si and the battle in the making.

A thought crossed his mind. *Who sent them out of the Forest to a battle they should know nothing about?*

Navar raced across the prairie, snow and mud flying as his hooves slashed at the ground. His mane snapped and whipped in the wind of his passage. Owen held tight to the coarse hair. He'd wrapped a wool scarf over his head and around his face until just a slit for his eyes remained.

They followed the Dragon as she flew toward the elven army. Owen was amazed Navar could run almost as fast as she could fly.

Why are you surprised? Navar asked. *Magic created both of us.*

True, Owen admitted. *It's just that, well, the ground has more obstacles, like snow and mud.*

Yes, Navar responded. *But the power of the wind lifts us and helps move us.*

Owen watched as the Dragon spiraled down and landed next to the front ranks of the army. Within moments, he and Navar had reached them. The elven King, riding at the front of his troops, guided his Agni toward the Dragon and WindRunner. Two guards flanked him. The remainder of his troops kept moving. The Dragon called the whirlwind and emerged as Aeden.

The companions faced the King and bowed. Alberick nodded.

"Sire, this is my brother, Lord Thomas Arach, heir to Red Dragon's Keep." Pride rang in Owen's voice as he introduced Thomas. Thomas gave him a sharp glance.

"Well met, Lord Thomas. We march to join you in the battle against the Dark," Alberick greeted him. "We've brought your men with us," he told Owen.

"Thank you, Sire," Thomas said. "We welcome any aid you can give. The horde is two or three miles ahead. I have three companies, a hundred and fifty men, a candlemark behind you. Perhaps your Swords could stop and wait until they arrive?" Thomas suggested.

"My soldiers are not as well armed as yours," Thomas continued. "I'd like to divide them and send them out to the right and left flanks. They will take out stragglers as they go and attack on your command." Thomas looked at the elven King. "If we can turn the flanks, the Dark Fey will be driven in on themselves and back into your troops."

"That is a well thought-out plan," Alberick approved. "I'll keep back a quarter of the Swords as a reserve. *Gaothsiuloir* — Navar — and Lord Owen, I ask that you ride at the front of my Swords with me. Lady, if you would help direct the humans, we will synchronize our attack."

"Lord Thomas and I will be happy to do so," Aeden responded. She glanced at Thomas, a sparkle in her eyes. "He so enjoys flying."

Thomas rolled his eyes.

Alberick turned to his guards. "Alert the Sword Seconds. We'll stop here until the humans arrive."

§ § §

Owen rode Navar beside Alberick at the head of two hundred Elven Swords. The glittering coats of their

Agni mounts flashed in the sun. One company of humans rode on the right flank, commanded by Master Sergeant Haloran, the other on the left commanded by Sergeant Jory. Baggage wagons followed to the rear.

"I see you have mastered riding a WindRunner," the King said.

"Just recently," Owen responded. "It took some pretty hard lessons."

The King looked at him, amethyst eyes gleaming. "You have the amulet."

Owen's head whipped to the right. His eyes widened as he looked into those eyes.

"How do you know?"

"Your spell of concealment is well made, but magic is our very essence," he told Owen with a small smile, in a kind voice. "It flows through us and in us. I can feel the *Power of Dragons* in that small piece of it."

"Do you know where the other amulets are hidden?"

The King shook his head with regret. "No. They lie far apart so that nothing can control the Dragons. That Demons are searching for them tells us nothing good."

"Aeden thinks Dragon magic is creating the Rifts and chaos that follows. Have you felt any of that yourself?" Owen asked.

"No. We are as blind to that great power as you are," Alberick shook his head with regret.

The horde marches a thousand yards ahead. The Dragon's voice echoed in both of their minds.

Alberick's nostrils flared in surprise. Owen shuddered. *Cold. That voice is so cold.*

At her alert, the humans kicked their mounts into a run, racing at oblique angles to left and right, following Haloran and Jory, separating them from the main battlefront.

Owen drew HeartStriker. Alberick flinched away.

"Your blade holds such magic as I have not felt for eons. It is well he journeys with us," the King murmured, awe in his voice.

The King signaled his Agni into a canter, then a gallop. Navar flowed across the ground beside them as they made their way to the side of the charge. The Swords following urged their Agni into a gallop. The thunder of pounding hooves shook the ground and rumbled through the air.

A dark line stretched across their charge. The *Unseleigh Sidhe* turned to face advancing death.

The flanks attack. The Dragon's voice rolled through their minds.

The human companies turned into the horde and charged. Ogres on the left turned to face them, raising stone axes and spears tipped with flint points. They bellowed defiance, lumbering into a run. Winged fliers, beaks filled with serrated teeth, lifted higher into the air. They dived toward the oncoming charge of the Swords, followed on the ground by the main body of the Fey. The humans on the left faced a ragged line of red-eyed wolves and saber-waving misshapen orcs.

The lines of battle met with a crash of weapon on weapon. Shrieks, screams, and thuds filled the air. The spears of the elven Swords impaled those on the front line, and the second, and the third. Silver swords hissed from sheaths. Death ruled.

Navar crashed into the muscle-bound ogre in front of him with a shriek of rage. It swung its axe at Navar's head. The WindRunner ducked to the left, grabbing its shoulder with his teeth, leaving Owen open to swing HeartStriker across its throat. The axe continued to fall, the tip slicing down Owen's right cheek from eye to chin, narrowly missing the eye itself, as the creature's head rolled off its shoulders. The axe fell to the ground.

White-hot agony ignited along the cut. HeartStriker spared a trickle of magic to dampen the pain. Owen used the momentum of his sword-strike to swing down, then back up and over Navar's neck, taking the hand of a goblin thrusting a tri-tipped spear at Navar's side.

Owen panted with shallow breaths, struggling to keep his hand clenched around HeartStriker's hilt. Navar whirled and kicked out with both hind hooves, crushing the chests of a green-toothed ogre and a short boggle swinging a war-hammer.

HeartStriker sent another stream of magic to the injury, deadening the pain.

The human companies came thundering in from the right and left flanks, turning the horde in on itself. The *Unseleigh Sidhe* turned to face all sides and fought desperately, swinging scythe, sword, and hammer, thrusting with spears, attacking with teeth and claws. The flyers dove and landed on heads, backs and shoulders.

The elven Swords fought, silent and grim. The Dark Fey surged against them, killing line after line of elves and Agni. The tide of battle turned.

The elven King signaled his guards. *Retreat!* The elven horns sounded.

Owen stood up in his stirrups and thrust HeartStriker into the air, screaming in fury. He and Navar fought on, never faltering.

The shadow of the Dragon rippled over the heaving, battling bodies below. She came in at a shallow angle. Flame erupted from her maw, igniting all in her path along the leading edge of the battle between elves and Dark Fey. She wheeled in the air at the end of the run and spiraled in for another attack.

The Swords pulled back from the Fey as she began her second run. A line of fire crept across the ground toward Owen. Their paths crossed. With a scream of agony, Navar reared and leapt through the Dragon fire, back toward the elves. Owen could smell his hair burning and feel Navar's pain. They landed on the other side of the barrier the Red Dragon had created.

He panted with pain, not feeling the fire engulfing the material of his trousers. Sword magic enfolded his legs and extinguished the flames.

Pressed from behind by the ingathering Dark Fey, the mass of dark beasts were forced through the fire. With mindless viciousness, they continued to battle the elves and humans. Bellowing with fury, Owen thrust HeartStriker into the air and attacked. The elves fought on even as they pulled back.

Navar surged forward, shouldering the hobgoblins and grundles throwing large rocks aside to reach the orcs and ogres behind. Owen and HeartStriker made short work of the smaller and lighter Fey. An orc reached toward Owen and met a whirling edge of steel, removing hands and head. The ogre next to it died on the blade that pierced its heart.

Alberick watched as Owen advanced into the teeth of the horde. Resolve replaced fear. He could do no less than the human and WindRunner.

Charge! he roared at his troops.

The battle cry swept from one end of the remaining Swords to the other. Determination replaced defeat. One step forward became two, then ten and the army was in full stride. They hit the line of Fey with devastating effect.

Bodies were broken, smashed beyond recognition. Fey died on that tide.

They broke through to the far side of the horde. The Agni wheeled, prepared to charge again.

Owen and Navar slid to a stop.

Slaughtered Fey surrounded them. Not one beast survived.

Chapter 27

WindRunners and Demons

Humans, elves, and Agni met in council to the east of the battlefield once all had regrouped. Recovered bodies of the slain human, elf and Agni, lay in long rows, guarded by their compatriots. The carrion birds had already gathered, squabbling over their feasting on the dead Fey. Weary warriors sat on the ground or squatted next to their mounts, waiting for the baggage wagons to arrive and set up camp.

The leaders of the armies and Aeden sat slightly removed from the troops, chewing slowly on the rations they carried in their saddlebags and sipping from waterskins. Navar and the King's Agni grazed close by them. Owen's cheek had stopped bleeding by the end of the battle. Aeden ran her finger down the wound, closing and healing it, leaving a faint scar.

"We need to rest tonight before we move on to Aos Si and the Demons," Owen said into the silence.

"Agreed," Thomas and Alberick replied at the same time. A tired smile crossed Thomas's face.

"As time permits, I would look at the amulet," Alberick requested.

"Why not now, Sire? Aeden, could you shield us, please?" he asked.

"Of course," Aeden nodded, creating a shimmering barrier around the four. Owen pulled his saddlebags into his lap and unfastened the buckles. He pushed his clothing cushioning the precious cargo aside and pulled out the wrapped amulet, carefully handing it to the King. Alberick took it from his hand, slowly unwrapping its covering. He looked at it for long moments.

"This amulet has been touched by Dragon magic." He raised his eyes from their study and met Owen's frown and Navar's piercing gaze. "I have felt this same magic for half my life coming from the Rift." He re-wrapped the amulet and handed it back to Owen. "Keep it safe."

Aeden looked at the King, speculation in her eyes. "Why do you think a Dragon touched the amulet?"

Owen shoved the amulet back into the saddlebag, adjusting the contents to protect it, and fastened the flap shut. Aeden let the shield fall.

The King pondered Aeden's question. "A Dragon opened the Rift at the breaking of the Talisman in the waning days of the first Demon war. The Rift and the amulet bear that same feel overlaid by something else, something twisted and dark. They are the same. Rift magic haunts us always. We sought to close it for almost a millennium and could not do so. We are not weak. Only the joining of all of our magic," he gestured at every creature, "could seal the Rift and send it away."

Sergeant Jory and Master Sergeant Haloran walked toward the group, deep in discussion. The four broke off their conversation as they arrived at the circle.

Haloran nodded to all of them. "Sire, my lords, our men are settled. The Swords have asked about sharing their supplies with us. I'd like to share ours with them. Would that be acceptable?"

Alberick glanced at Owen and Thomas. He looked back to Haloran. "Of course. I would warn you the Swords know little of humans. Ask one of the Seconds to stand watch, by my command."

"Aye, Sire."

"Master Sergeant, how many men did we lose?" asked Owen.

Haloran looked at him, his face expressionless. "We lost a third, my lord, fifty-three men. Eighty-five elven Swords and sixty Agni. We've gathered the bodies to the south of the horde."

Thomas jerked as if from a blow. The elven King sat silent and unmoving, showing no emotion. Owen felt tears start in his eyes and looked up at the sky to keep them from falling. He knew most of the men Thomas brought to the battle. He puffed out shallow breaths. Once in control, he looked at Thomas.

"We'll bury them here," Thomas growled in a hoarse voice.

"There might be a better way," Owen told him. He looked at Alberick. "Magefire?" he suggested.

"Aye," Alberick approved.

Owen frowned. "Magefire burns quick and clean, but leaves nothing behind. Perhaps we can raise a monument to this battle and all of the warriors lost when this war is over."

Thomas agreed reluctantly, sadness evident in squinting eyes and clamped lips.

Haloran and Jory stood in silence behind Owen and Thomas.

"What of the Fey, and your own?" Aeden asked Alberick.

Alberick took a deep breath. Nodded.

Aeden stood and walked west toward the battlefield, sending a powerful surge of magic toward the carrion feeders to frighten them away. They scattered as she approached.

The Swords gathered to the left of the battlefield rose as she walked. The human soldiers beyond them started to their feet as they saw the Swords rise.

Move away, OathKeeper spoke to the warriors standing guard over their dead. They hastily rejoined their comrades.

Aeden stood at the edge of the slaughter. Owen felt her pull magic from the earth and air, from every living thing. She raised her arms. The Swords and the King channeled their magic to her. Magefire flashed from her hands to the bodies of the slain. The bodies burned with a fierce blue-white flame and were gone.

A sigh from every throat rolled across the plains.

§ § §

A small cloud of dust marred the horizon to the north. Troops turned to face the threat. Four galloping horses emerged from the dust. As they drew closer, Thomas reached out and grabbed Owen's shoulder, unconsciously gripping hard. Owen looked at him wide-eyed and looked back at the figures astride those horses.

"It's them," he whispered. "It's them," he shouted. With whoops of pure joy, he and Thomas raced toward the approaching riders. Two of the riders dismounted as they pulled their horses to sliding stops.

Owen and Thomas shouted in jubilation as Lord Tom and Lady Jenni raced to their sons and grabbed them in triumph and delight.

§ § §

Jenni held Owen out at arm's length and pulled Thomas to her. "I still can't believe you're here. And saved the day with your heroics." She gave each of them a small shake. Reaching out, she traced the scar that rode his cheek. Tears glittered in her eyes, but did not fall. "Honorably earned," she told him.

He has done well. Navar's voice echoed in everyone's mind.

Jenni's eyes widened and his father took a step forward to stand next to his wife. Anne ranged herself next to Jenni. Jeremy joined his wife, his hand dropping to the hilt of his sword.

"Who is that?" Tom demanded, frowning.

Navar, WindRunner of the Windward Range. Owen is my rider. The second son is mine.

Tom's frown deepened. Jenni bristled.

"He's not the most diplomatic person, Father, Mother. He came to the Dragon Tower, demanding I go with him. I went," Owen said with a resigned shrug.

§ § §

The army headed for Aos Si, the reunited family and Alberick riding at its front. The Arachs and Gobhlans shared the story of their capture and escape from North Meall. The tale of the awakening of their Swords of Light and the healing of their wounds on the ride to join the army silenced any questions from Thomas and Owen.

Thomas rode a warhorse recaptured after the battle. The King's Own elven guards followed them. Dust billowed into the air, raised by the army's marching feet.

The Red Dragon flew toward them, skimming low to the ground. Alberick raised his hand, signaling a halt. He removed his silver helmet and cradled it with his left arm.

Orders flashed back through the ranks. The army slowed and halted.

The Dragon landed. The whirlwind hid her form. As it dissipated, Aeden walked toward them.

"Lady, how far ahead are they?" Owen asked.

"Three candlemarks," she told them. "You've made good time."

"How many do we face?" Thomas asked.

"At least five hundred," Aeden's answer was grim.

The silence that met this news was deafening.

A shout from the Swords behind them caused everyone to swing toward the columns of elves and men.

"Can you see what it is?" Thomas asked urgently.

Unable to see over the army, Owen pushed himself up on Navar's back and stood on the seat of the saddle, looking southwest. He shaded his eyes with his hand. Navar stood stock-still.

"It's Saleth and Samhanach," he exclaimed. "They've brought more Swords! And a host of Agni!"

He dropped back into Navar's saddle, a huge smile spread across his face.

"Good news, then," Alberick said. "We'll wait until he reports."

Saleth, Samhanach running easily at his side, joined them in a quarter-candlemark. "Sire, I've brought all of the warriors," he said, the curve of his bow rising above his head, the shafts of deadly elven arrows extending from the quiver slung over his shoulder. "The Bell of Prophecy tolled for four days straight. We had to come. Most of the adult Agni insisted on joining us."

"Well come, Saleth. How many?" asked the King.

"Seventy-five Swords and one hundred Agni," he reported.

"Excellent," the Forest King said. "We at least have a chance now."

Owen gestured to his family. "Saleth, Samhanach, this is my father, Lord Tom Arach, Duke of Red Dragon's Keep. My mother, Lady Jenni Arach. My uncle, Lord Jeremy Gobhlan, Duke of Falcon's Spire. My aunt, Lady Anne."

Saleth gave a sweeping bow to the humans. "You honor us with your presence," he told them.

"And this, this is my brother, Lord Thomas Arach, heir to Red Dragon's Keep," Owen held out his hand toward Thomas, introducing him to two he counted as friends.

Saleth bowed to Thomas, a slight smile lifting the corner of his mouth. Samhanach, panting lightly, sat and looked at Thomas. He cocked his head to the side, as if measuring him. He stood and gave a long stretch, front legs extended, then pushing forward and stretching rear legs one at a time, seeming to bow.

Thomas nodded his head to both of them. "Well met, indeed," he said.

"The plan is to come at the Demons from the rear, just as we did with the Dark Fey," the King told Saleth. "The humans will split their forces and circle wide to the left and right, coming in on the flanks to turn them and drive them into us. Have your Swords and Agni deploy with the humans, half to each side. Return here when you are done. I want you by my side."

"Aye, Sire," Saleth responded. "I'll see to it now."

Owen watched him glide away.

"In two candlemarks, the flankers should separate," Thomas said, a thoughtful note in his voice, his look far away. "Send half of each flanking group at two candlemarks and the second half at one candlemark. Two waves on both sides will re-enforce the maneuver," he suggested.

"Good idea, Thomas," Alberick agreed. He looked at the young men's family. "Will you ride with me?" he asked them.

Lord Tom gave him a grave nod, joined by Lady Jenni. The Lord and Lady of Falcon's Spire echoed him. "We will."

HellReaver, please give the sergeants their new orders. Thomas sent the request to his Sword of Light.

"Should each of us take command of one of the wings?" Owen asked. He looked at Thomas and glanced at Alberick.

"Yes," Thomas said in simple response.

"Yes," responded Alberick.

Owen jerked his head in a tight nod. "I'll take the left flank," he told them.

"I'll take the right," Thomas said. "In a candlemark, then."

Owen wheeled Navar to the left as Thomas wheeled to the right. Owen rode back along the lines of the Swords as the King gave the signal to advance. The army resumed its march.

$$\S \, \S \, \S$$

The candlemark seemed to pass quickly. The first wave of flankers split off left to the northeast and right to the southeast from the main body of the army.

Owen thought about the coming battle as they traveled. *This is the third time I've faced Demons and the evil they have brought. HeartStriker, does the fear ever stop?* he asked his Sword of Light.

The fear is always there, HeartStriker told him. Remember this. Without fear, there can be no courage. Face the fear and know it for what it is: doubt within yourself. Pass it by.

You have gained in strength and skill, Navar added. We are together. We will do our best.

Yes, he thought to himself as he straightened in the saddle. *Yes, we will.*

§ § §

At the second candlemark, using the sun shining intermittently through the cloud cover as a guide, Owen signaled for the turn to the south. Those following wheeled their warhorses and Agni, trotting toward the body of the Demon pack they knew swarmed ahead.

A dark line appeared on the horizon in front of them. The line grew in size and definition as they accelerated into a canter. The walls of Aos Si rose small in the distance to the left, intersecting the darkness. The line resolved into the shapes of individual Demons as Navar began to run. The outer ranks of Demons turned toward the flanks of their pack.

Arrowing out of the northeast a line of racing black shapes swept toward the humans and Swords. A great herd of WindRunners drove forward, gleaming eyes, whipping manes and tails streaming with their speed, their hooves hammering the ground. Thunder rumbled.

Join my mind, Navar cried out to him. Owen dropped his mental shields and reached for Navar's thoughts. In an instant, he was overwhelmed with the essence of creatures great and small within range of the WindRunner's magic. He felt fear, pain, hunger, thirst, and the need — There it was. The reason he'd been searching for: the *need* to protect all life against evil — to beat back the Dark.

He felt the power of the wind rushing through the creature he rode. His heart and mind rejoiced in the magic he held within himself. He drew HeartStriker from his scabbard and roared a challenge to the creatures of evil racing toward him. The Sword of Light burst into a gleaming blade of white fire.

Lightning arced and struck from the Sword of Light, etching burning Demons in brilliant bursts as they danced in death. Navar raced forward, opening a way toward Aos Si, leading the flood of WindRunners, elves, and Agni following them. Sword and staff, hooves and teeth decimated the hordes of Demons as they slammed into the mass. More of the Dark rushed forward to take the place of those destroyed. The shadow of a great flying creature rippled over those below. Owen glanced up and saw dragon-fire erupt from the mouth of the Red Dragon, flame igniting the Demons to either side of Owen's charging column. Fire exploded high into the air along with screams and shrieks of the dying. Owen roared again with battle fury. The column pounded on, turning the flank of the attack, coming to the rescue of the WindWalkers and all they held dear.

§ § §

The defenders manning the walls battled with desperate intensity. Scott and Debra fought side by side, protecting each other's backs as the Demons climbed the walls and sought to kill all those within.

Flyers dropped down and attacked humans that fought Demons within the walls. Blood fountained and splashed to the ground as men and Demons died. Trained for battle, warhorses without riders attacked Demons and killed them by the dozens before the monsters dragged them down. WindRunners who called Aos Si home during the winter battled beside man and warhorse alike, pounding Demons into pulp with hooves and teeth.

Men fought Demons on the walls, thrusting spears and swords, throwing the dead Demons over the walls, knocking off those who climbed. War hammers smashed heads and bodies as the humans fought back. Desperation lent power and speed to the defenders. Slowly the tide of battle turned. The flood of Demons became a river, then a trickle.

Scott thrust his sword through the chest of a Demon and kicked it off his blade. The weapon broke at the cross-guard. Nicked and cut on face and arms, the shirt on his left side flapping from a graze by powerful Demon claws, he panted for breath. He looked for a new sword and the next enemy and found none. Debra, equally as battered, stood in her blood soaked shirt and trousers at the edge of the wall. She watched the battle between Demons and an army of shining figures raging in front of the walls of Aos Si, the spear that replaced her shattered sword leaning against the wall.

Those standing on the parapet stood silent, weapons forgotten. They watched with building elation as the Demons attacking them turned to counter the assault of the army on the right led by a night-dark WindRunner. The rider held a Sword aloft, a Sword that sent ropes of lightning into the Demons, destroying them on contact.

Elves drove into the Demons from the rear, killing them as they tried to flood past the Swords. A dire wolf plunged into the Demons time after time, teeth slashing, ripping and killing. An elf armed only with a longbow protected the shining figure fighting next to him. Four more figures, two to the left and two to the right of the shining figure, held Swords lashing brilliant whips of light down on the Demons attacking the elves.

The warriors on the left charged into the flank of the horde, their leader holding his flaming blade aloft, driving almost halfway across the Demon lines.

Shouts of incredulity erupted from the defenders on the walls as a red Dragon descended from the clouds and lit the sky with fire. Winged *smachtmaistirs* fell, burning.

The Demons turned away from the army with shrieks of fear and pain. Those in the rear turned and ran to the north and south. As more Demons fled, those attacking the flankers thinned and finally broke, following their kindred. The column of elves and men split and thundered after the Demons, running them down and finishing the slaughter.

The WindRunner raced toward the wall, his rider holding his Sword of Light aloft. The stallion slid to a stop and reared, screaming a battle cry after the retreating Demons.

Scott and Debra stood stunned. Debra grabbed Scott's arm and staggered to the very edge of the wall.

"That's Owen!" she shouted, pointing. "And Thomas!"

The Dragon flew in at ground level, racing toward the walls of Aos Si. The watchers gasped as it reached that barrier, shooting straight up the wall and into the sky, spiraling as it gained altitude. They ducked away as the wind of its passage buffeted them.

They rushed back to the edge of the wall, watching in stunned silence as the Dragon spun on a wingtip and flew back down to land beside Owen and the WindRunner. Thomas galloped in from the left to join the three. He pulled his horse to a stop next to the massive WindRunner. The watchers on the wall looked on, struck dumb, as a whirlwind veiled the Dragon's form and lifted away to reveal a warrior woman.

"Lady Debra, Lord Scott, I've brought the elves," Owen shouted, throwing his arms wide, then raised his Sword of Light high. "And a Dragon!"

Debra raised her arm and pumped it in exaltation. "Welcome, WindRunner and Owen...and Dragon Lady? Thomas! Most welcome, indeed." Twisting around toward the gates to the left, she gestured broadly. "Open the gates for our rescuers!"

Chapter 28

Aos Si

Owen rode Navar through the gates of Aos Si that hung drunkenly from twisted hinges barely keeping them upright. The Demons had rammed against them repeatedly, trying to gain entry. They had almost succeeded. His brother rode beside him. Lady Aeden glided on his other side.

Blood and bodies littered the ground. Dead Demons were steaming and bubbling. The smell of acid mingled with the smells of death and dying. Owen wrinkled his nose in distaste.

The surviving Aos Si WindRunners streamed past the group to join their kindred gathering outside the gates.

Debra and Scott hurried down the stairs from the parapet to the ground. They slowed to a stop as the four halted in front of them. Owen swung down from Navar. Thomas followed suit from his warhorse.

Debra rushed forward and threw her arms around Owen. "Thank you, thank you for saving us. We thought we were dead," she mumbled into his shoulder, tears leaking down her face. Owen held on tight, hugging her back.

Scott reached out and grabbed Thomas's hand and arm. "Never a more timely entrance than you just gave," he said. He shook his head. "I can't believe this."

Owen kept one arm around Debra as he turned to Aeden and motioned her forward.

"This is Lady Aeden, the Red Dragon of Red Dragon's Keep," he said, introducing the creature of legend to his aunt and uncle. Humor crinkled his face and gleamed from his eyes as he bowed to Aeden. She shot him a glare.

"Just Aeden will do," she told the suddenly quiet Lord and Lady of Aos Si.

Movement at the gates caught the corner of Scott's eye. He looked over. His jaw dropped as silver armored forms made their way through the uprights. Debra stepped back from Owen, smoothing her hair away from her face. She stepped forward to stand next to Scott.

Owen walked over to the figure at the head of the shining Swords and glittering Agni.

"Sire, may I present Lord Scott WindWalker and Lady Debra WindWalker, my aunt and uncle. Lord Scott and Lady Debra, the King of the Forest Lords, Alberick.

Alberick removed his silver helm. His white hair cascaded down his back as his amethyst eyes glanced across the scene of such carnage.

"Welcome to Aos Si, Highness." Scott bowed with deep respect. Debra bowed just as deeply beside him.

Alberick nodded with grave calmness.

"Thank you for saving us, Your Majesty," Debra told him with simple directness. "What can we do for you and yours?"

A slow smile crossed Alberick's face. "I believe the question is 'what can we do for each other'." A broad gesture encompassed the entirety of Aos Si. "Let us help set this to rights and then we will talk."

"As you say, Sire." Scott's reply was soft and low as he bowed again.

Debra gasped as her sisters and their husbands rode through the gates. She turned white and crumpled to the ground.

§ § §

Debra roused long moments after she fainted, her head pillowed in Scott's lap. She watched as the body of the army set up camp outside the walls of her manor. She finally sat up and let Scott pull her to her feet. Anne and Jenni hurried over to her when they noticed her standing. They enfolded each other in a tight embrace, tears flowing freely.

Elves and men worked together to gather the bodies of the dead, laying them in the center of the courtyard in front of the manor, a space large enough to hold four hundred men. The corpses filled over half of the space. The army's baggage wagons sat outside the gates of Aos Si, ranged in ordered rows.

All of the battle comrades lined the walls and filled the remainder of the courtyard. WindRunners filtered through the gates and stood in a line across the courtyard behind the host of defenders. The sighing of the wind and twitter of birds were the only sounds. The sun hung low on the western horizon.

Aeden, OathKeeper riding her hip in his scabbard, stood on the ground in front of the stairs of the manor. The Forest Lord King, Owen, Navar, and Thomas stood on the highest step. Scott and Debra stood on the step immediately below them and to the side. Tom, Jenni, Anne, and Jeremy stood on the other side of that stair. Owen and Thomas drew HeartStriker and HellReaver.

Aeden raised her arms with solemn dignity. Magic rushed to her from the earth, sky, and those gathered. Magefire burst from her hands, flowing over the bodies of the honored dead. Owen, Thomas, and their Swords of Light added their energy. Tom, Jenni, Anne, and Jeremy drew their Swords and joined them in the rush of power.

Blue flame mixed with white as the bodies faded away. No smoke rose from that fire.

"It is done," Aeden intoned as she lowered her arms.

Those gathered stood in silence, remembering.

§ § §

The mourners broke into small groups, talking quietly about the battle. Owen's family stood together, retelling stories about the journeys that had brought them together. Six of the WindRunners watching the gathering shouldered their way through elves and Agni, coming to stand behind Owen and Navar.

We have come for the choosing one of them spoke in every mind in the deepest voice Owen had ever heard. He turned on his heels to face them.

The members of Owen's family turned in alarm to face the WindRunners. The others gathered in the courtyard, on the stairs, and standing on the porch faced the impending confrontation.

The rulers of Aos Si, Red Dragon's Keep and Falcon's Spire are chosen.

As one, the six stepped forward to stand in front of Owen's family. He and Thomas watched, mouths hanging open. Aeden crossed her arms over her chest, a tiny smiling lifting the corners of her mouth.

Why are you surprised? Navar asked Owen. *They are the pivot on which this war hinges, as are you. Thomas has a Dragon. They need us to help them survive.*

Anne locked eyes with the WindRunner facing her. She reached out and laid her hand on its muzzle. *I am Gaoth* the WindRunner told her.

Scott's face went white when the enormous WindRunner facing him stepped forward and lowered its head. He started to back away. The WindRunner followed with implacable intent. The WindRunner pressed its nose to Scott's heart. *I am Cridhe.*

Tom slowly raised his arm and rested his hand on the jaw of the black creature in front of him. At his touch, the WindRunner stepped forward and rested his chin on the human's shoulder. *I am Anial.* A small whisper of wind pushed against the pair.

Debra looked at the WindRunner before her. It winked at her. A crooked smile crossed her face. She barely kept a laugh from bursting out. The WindRunner flipped it nose at her and she reached out to cup its chin. *Ajillech.*

Jeremy hesitated. He wasn't sure what was expected of him. With a snort and a shake of its head-sending forelock and mane flying, his WindRunner pushed its head against Jeremy's chest and shoved. Jeremy staggered back. *You are mine* the creature of wind and magic told him. *I am Siomh.*

Jenni stood, still and silent. The WindRunner mirrored her. Magic swirled between the two. Oblivious to the rest of the world, they stared into each other's eyes, each other's souls. *I am Lubach* he told her.

The WindRunners swung to face the rest of those watching in stunned silence.

We have chosen.

Aeden uncrossed her arms and nodded.

You honor us all she told the newly chosen pairs.

$ $ $

Dawn light filtered through the shutters covering the windows of Owen's room. The arrival of his parents and the battle had drained his emotions. The long night of returning Aos Si to some semblance of order drained his body. The night finally ended when Owen and the others wearily stumbled to the bathing chambers and then to their rooms, falling into exhausted sleep.

Every muscle in his body rebelled when he rolled to his back and started to stretch. He groaned aloud. A mumble from the floor met the sound.

"Go back to sleep," it said. Owen recognized Thomas's voice.

"I can't. I hurt too much. Maybe someone here has something for the pain," he told his brother. He threw back the covering on his bed and swung his legs over the side. He groaned again.

Elbows on knees, he rested his head in his hands. After a few deep breaths, he raised his head and pushed himself to his feet. He shuffled to the chest where he had thrown his clothes. He pulled on the blood-encrusted shirt and charred trousers. He wondered when they had been burned.

Thomas sat up with a moan. "Why? Why do you have to get up now?"

"I told you. I also want to see Mother and Father, and everyone else. Don't you?" Owen queried.

"I forgot," Thomas answered as he flipped off the blanket he'd used and sat up. He still wore the clothes he'd worn the day before. He pulled on his boots.

The brothers made their way to the dining room, hoping for food and water. Maybe some willow bark in the water for the pain.

Elves and humans filled the room. A buffet table stood along the wall closest to the kitchen, filled with food. Anne, Debra, and Jenni stood close together, laughing at a comment one of them had made. Owen made straight for his mother. He grabbed her around the waist and hugged hard. His father turned from his discussion with Alberick and grinned at him.

"I've got something for you," Owen told her. He pulled the sheathed dagger from his belt and handed it to his mother. "I found this in a circle of standing stones and knew it was yours. It gave me hope," he told her as he tightened his arm around her waist.

Jenni lifted the dagger from his hand. "I thought it was gone forever," she said in wonder. "We stopped in the circle to take care of my leg. This dagger was a gift from your grandfather when your father and I were married.

He has done well. Navar's voice echoed in everyone's mind. *After he became my rider.*

§ § §

"After he almost got killed by a wild boar and I was sending him on a mission to get more warhorses and wardogs from Aos Si," Thomas added. "He was supposed to look for you and Father and Sir Mathin on the way. Sir Mathin went off with twenty-five men to search for you after you disappeared. He never returned.

A fairyfly in the Darkened Forest captured and killed all but two of his men. Owen here," he waved at his brother, "rode in with twenty more soldiers, recruited help from the elves and Agni, killed the fairyfly, then closed the Rift that allowed the Dark Fey into the Darkened Forest. Aeden and I found him at the standing stones. He'd already recovered," Thomas hesitated for a brief moment, "something we desperately need. I'll tell you about that later," he told his parents.

Owen's face turned red with embarrassment. "It wasn't just me," he protested. "The elves and Lady Aeden did most of the work and I had help from Navar and HeartStriker."

Those standing close enough to hear looked at Owen with new respect. Jenni shook her head in amazement.

He has done well, repeated Navar.

"He has," both Jenni and Tom admitted at the same time. Standing behind them, Alberick smiled.

"Lady Aeden filled us in about the first Demon battle," Tom said, looking at his oldest son. "You've done well too, Thomas."

"Let's finish our meal and meet in the greeting room afterward," Thomas suggested. "Mother, do you have any white willow bark? Owen and I could really use some," he asked in a plaintive voice.

"Debra, do you have any?" Jenni asked her sister. "I'm a little light on supplies at the moment," she said.

Debra stroked her chin and looked up at the ceiling as if in thought. "I think there's some in the still room," she told her nephews with a smile. "Let's go see."

Jenni placed a hand on each of her son's shoulders and guided them from the room.

You know, we could take that pain away if we were asked, the Swords of Light spoke in unison.

Everyone met in the greeting room in two candle-marks. Aeden stood silent and still in the corner of the room. Owen and Thomas entered the room soon after. Thomas sent for Haloran to join them. Alberick was the last to arrive. The two guards who followed him took up their stations on either side of the door that he closed behind him.

Open the window, Navar demanded from beyond the shining panes of glass. The other WindRunners crowded close behind him.

Owen unlatched the frames and pushed them open. The WindRunner stuck his head through the opening as the cool morning air cascaded into the room.

Thomas began.

"Cameron found information in the old records at Red Dragon's Keep about a Talisman, the *Cumhacht ar Draigoini* — the Power of Dragons. It gives the bearer power to call the Dragons. Through it, the Dragons are required to do whatever the bearer desires. It has the power to kill all the Dragons and all at once if he so desires.

The record said that after the first war with the *Ciardha* Demon, the *Cumhacht ar Draigoini* was broken by the *Rune of Getal* into five pieces that are hidden in five strongholds throughout Ard Ri. The mages did this to protect humans as well as Dragons, removing temptation. All five pieces have to be united with an incantation we still need to find if we are to call the Dragons."

"Where do you think the incantation is located?" Tom asked his son.

A knock at the door. Haloran entered.

"I'm not sure, Father. We're still looking through the records," Thomas answered. Tom waved his hand for Thomas to continue.

"We've found three of the broken pieces – the amulets – so far. One at Red Dragon's Keep, another sent from the Mages Enclave in Fasach. We don't know why it was there or who sent it. Owen found the third in the Aos Si limestone caverns after fighting and killing three Demons in its depths. I think one is hidden in Fearmhar or Talamh, not in Ard Ri. Or it could be at Falcon's Spire or Cathair Ri. We're pretty sure the Dragons hold the fifth amulet."

"Why?" Lord Tom interrupted again. "Why do you think the Dragons have one?"

"Neulach, the Dragon King, arrived just before Owen left on his mission. He suspects a renegade Dragon, or Dragons, have been helping the Demons try to take over Ard An Tir."

Owen's father shook his head in disbelief.

"When he made the King's messenger disappear, I asked him straight out and he wouldn't answer," Thomas continued. "Plus, Breanna and Marta 'dreamed'," Thomas raised his hands and curved his fingers into quote marks at the word, "of a map with the locations of all of the amulets and every Rift in every country."

Lord Tom's eyes widened as he nodded his head in understanding.

"Neulach and Cameron went after some kind of Dragon magic in the undercroft." Anne and Jeremy leaned forward in their chairs, tension in every line of their bodies.

"The Dragon King has our son?" Anne blurted out. Thomas nodded.

"Evan, Breanna and Marta tried to find Cameron and discovered where they disappeared in a tunnel no one knew about under the Keep." An uneasy murmur circled the room. "Neulach told us that there's a Rift in southwestern Fasach where the Demons have been entering our world. We think their goal is to kill the Dragons using the Talisman and take over Ard An Tir, turning it to their own use."

"So you think we," Lord Tom gestured at those in the room, "need to find the amulets, unite them and then what? Use them to call the Dragons and get them to help us close the Rifts?"

"Basically, yes," Thomas responded with a shrug and a grimace.

Owen cleared his throat. "Navar insists an amulet is hidden in Fearmhar. He also insists he and I travel there and recover it."

"Father, we think the King may be part of the problem," Thomas continued. "You and the others were on your way to help him plan for the war. Maybe you can continue that mission and find out if he has betrayed us?" Thomas asked.

Lord Tom sat quietly, a thoughtful frown marring his brow, staring out the window past the WindRunner's shapes blocking much of the light.

"That's a good plan." He turned to Jeremy, Anne, and Jenni. "What do you think? Can we pull this off?" he asked. "Ride for the capital and convince the King we've escaped and come straight to him?"

Anne spoke first. "It could be the best option. We'll be in a position to find out what's going on and either help him or find a way to stop him." Jeremy and Jenni murmured their agreement.

"What about the WindRunners?" Owen asked.

"Would the King know that they are WindRunners?" Thomas said into the silence that followed Owen's question.

"Possibly not," Alberick responded. "But any other magical being would know exactly what they are. Could you disguise them with a spell?" The elven King looked at Aeden.

Aeden looked around the room. "Yes," she answered. "It will hide their essence, but they will need to stay out of Cathair Ri itself, and away from the Mages Enclave. Best not to tempt fate and make it easy for magic wielders to see through the spell. I suggest you take warhorses to ride in and around Cathair Ri. You can meet regularly with the WindRunners. Make sure you are at least a mile from the capital."

"Good. It's settled then." Tom listed the decisions they'd made. "Thomas, you'll return to Red Dragon's Keep with Master Sergeant Haloran, taking as many warhorses and wardogs as Aos Si can spare to replace those we've lost. You're to raise more men for the war." Lord Tom spared a quick smile for Haloran, his longest confidant. Thomas frowned.

"Let Breanna know we love her and we'll see her as soon as we're done at Cathair Ri," he continued. "Find out where Cameron has gone."

"Owen, you'll go with Navar to Fearmhar and find the amulet hidden there."

"I would send Saleth and Samhanach with Lord Owen," Alberick's quiet voice filled the room. "There are verses of the Prophecy speaking of a hero's journey with elf and dire wolf as fell companions."

Silence greeted his words, which were not so much a request as a command.

"Owen?" the King asked. Lord Tom looked at his son.

"Yes. I'll have them as companions. They are most welcome," Owen answered quickly. The relief on his face told his father that he wanted the elf and dire wolf with him.

I will be with you, as will HeartStriker, Navar said in Owen's.

I know, but it's better to be with company than without. They will be assets, both of them, Owen responded.

The Duke of Red Dragon's Keep pushed himself from his chair, ready to begin.

Thomas stood as well. "Father, I'll be returning to the Keep with Lady Aeden. She brought me here on her back and she'll take me home. I should take the Aos Si Amulet as well. Perhaps Master Sergeant Haloran can return to the Keep with the wardogs and warhorses."

"Good. I'll go get it," Owen jogged from the room to retrieve his saddlebags.

Incredulity widened Tom's eyes, his jaw dropped as he looked at his son and then to Lady Aeden. She nodded once with slow deliberation. Indrawn breath from around the room signaled everyone's astonishment.

"Well then, let's see you off," Lord Tom said. "We have a few more details to work out among ourselves, particularly with Master Sergeant Haloran. We'll finish up as soon as you've gone."

"Yes sir," his son responded. He and Aeden left the room together. The others followed them out to the courtyard.

Aeden opened herself to power and called the whirlwind. It drifted around her in spinning loops, hiding her from sight. It swirled into nothingness and the Red Dragon stood in her place. She shook herself and stretched her wings wide.

The collar Thomas used for safety still encircled her neck. She stretched out the leg closest to Thomas and lowered her shoulder. He sprinted toward her and ran up her leg, sliding into his place on her neck between the spines rising from her backbone.

He clipped the straps hanging from the collar to the leather belt that he wore. He waved to those on the ground and saluted his father.

Owen raced out of the manor and tossed his saddlebags to Thomas. Thomas snagged them out of the air and wrapped one of the straps around the bags to secure them.

Aeden deepened her crouch and pushed off with her powerful hindquarters. The downstroke of her wings sent dust and debris flying into the air. Those on the ground turned away to protect their faces.

She was already several lengths into the air when they turned back.

"To fly," Alberick murmured.

"Indeed," Tom concurred, both their faces lifted to watch.

§ § §

The story continues in

**The Dragon's Children
Book Three**

DreamWalker

Acknowledgements

Many people helped make this book possible.

My girls, Anne, Debbie and Jenni, helped me over the rough spots and said, "Yes, you can."

Their husbands, Jeremy, Scott and Tom, listened while I talked and gave me some good ideas.

My grandsons, Thomas, Owen, Cameron and Evan and my granddaughter Breanna – well, without them this story would not even have been a gleam in my eye.

Many thanks to Susan Hicks and Nikki Gullette for keeping me grounded.

To the Rocky Mountain Fiction Writers Aurora Critique Group: John, Jenni, Karen, Aimee, and Mary. Wow. They helped immeasurably with their critiques; they made WindRunner much, much better.

To those who I haven't named — you know who you are — thank you.

Characters

Agni – ancient magical creatures resembling a cross between a horse and goat. They carry the Forest Lords during the great hunt

Alberick – High King of the Forest Lords

Aos Si – manor house of the WindWalkers

Duke Sir Tom Arach

Duchess Lady Jennifer Arach

Thomas Arach

Owen Arach

Breanna Arach

Lord John Arach – grandfather of Tom Arach

Lady Eirin Arach – grandmother of Tom Arach

Duke Sir Jeremy Gobhlan

Duchess Lady Anne Gobhlan

Cameron Gobhlan

Evan Gobhlan

Duke Sir Scott WindWalker

Duchess Lady Debra WindWalker

Captain Braden - appointed captain of the guard after Captain Mathin leaves

Captain Mathin - captain of the guard

Cathair Ri - The King's City - Capital of Ard An Tir

Ciardha Demon - Demons of the Dark

Claiomh Solas - Swords of Light
    BattleSworn - Lord Tom Arach's sword
    FireGuard – Lady Jenni's sword
    BloodForged - Lord Jeremy's sword
    StormBringer -Lady Anne's sword
    HellReaver - chooses Thomas
    HeartStriker- chooses Owen
    SunWalker - chooses Breanna
    GhostWalker - chooses Cameron
    ShadowSworn - chooses Evan
    HellScream - chooses Marta
    OathKeeper - Aeden's sword

Falcon's Spire - home of the Gobhlan's

Garan Tilden - squire, son of Earl Tildon of North Meall
Gregory Anur– Red Dragon's Keep seneschal

Faolan Haloran - Steader, former Master Sergeant
Jaiman Haloran – oldest son of Faolan
Kevin Haloran – youngest son of Faolan
Marta Haloran – daughter of Faolan
Raina Haloran - Faolan's wife
Rand Haloran - grandfather of Marta

Jago – Gregory's clerk
Jalyn – head cook
Jory Quinn – sergeant in the Keep's army

Lady Aeden - Dragon/Mage/Sword Mistress

Maaike Soth Lahri – Fasach trader/spy sent to watch
and sabotage the Arachs

Centak Soth Lahri – trader, deceased father of Maaike
Maccon - squire – friend
Mannan - High Draiolc - evil high wizard suborned by
the Ciardha Demon
Moirra - the Keep wise-woman/healer

Neulach – King of the Dragons, Aeden's Father
North Meall - northern mounds – badlands – held by
Earl Tilden and his son, Garan

Red Dragon's Keep - home of the Arachs

Saleth – scout for the Tua Dé
Samhanach – dire wolf companion to Saleth
Sayathia Khan Maruk – King of Fasach – Sayathia
means King
Seleigh Soren - Demon created by the High Draiolc to
attack and kill those that are its designated prey
Sharley – (Shar – lay) the Sorceress's apprentice
Simon - chamberlain
Stefan - squire – friend
Siubhan – (Su - van) the King's Sorceress

Tiarna Geal - Lords of Light
Tua Dé – Lords of the Trees. Elves

WindRunners
Ajillech – Debra's WindRunner
Anial – Tom's WindRunner

Cridhe – Scott's WindRunner
Gaoth – Anne's WindRunner
Lubach – Jenni's WindRunner
Navar – Owen's WindRunner
Siomh – Jeremy's WindRunner

Windward Range – Lands of the WindWalkers

Dictionary

Aeden - Fire
Arach - Dragon
Arach Ri – Dragon King
Ard An Tir - The Shining Lands
Ard Ri - King's Land
An bhaile – (ahn wail) townsmen
Aos Si – (ā ōs see) ancient lands of the WindWalkers,
    the Windward Range

Bolscaire bhaile – (bols care wail) town crier

Cailleach – (cal yish) - witch
Ciardha - (Kay r da) - the Dark - source of all Demons
Claiomh Solas - (Klay m So las) - Swords of Light
    BattleSworn - Lord Tom Arach's sword
    FireGuard – Lady Jenni's sword
    BloodForged - Lord Jeremy's sword
    StormBringer -Lady Anne's sword
    HellReaver - chooses Thomas
    HeartStriker- chooses Owen
    SunWalker - chooses Breanna
    GhostWalker - chooses Cameron
    ShadowSworn - chooses Evan
    HellScream - chooses Marta
    OathKeeper - Aeden's sword
Coimeadai – (ko mi dye) - Guardian

Cosain Morroin - (ko sane Mo ro in) - Shield Lands
Crionna baen - (kron a bay en) – wise-woman
Cumhacht ar Draigoini – (come act ar drago in i) -
  Power of Dragons

Demon – (dee man) – Demon
Demon Marfoir – (dee man mar fo ear) – Demon
Killer
Dorcha Dubh – (dorka dew) - Deepest Black
Draiochta - (dray ok ta) - magic
Draiolc - (Dray olc) - dark wizard

Foraois - Forest
Fuil - blood
Fuilba - (Fool ba) - dark bay color
Fanai – (fan eye) – Nomads

Gaothsiuloir (Gwaysilor) – WindRunner
Gharda Machaire (Garda Makeda) Guardian
Mountains

Hold - small farm held by a holder
Holder - either indentured serf or small landholder
  beholden to a Steading

Ki - spiritual essence

Lands of Ard An Tir
    Ard Ri - King's Land

Fearmhar (fear m har) - grasslands of the Horse
Lords
Talamh (Ta lem) - farmland Freeholders
Fasach (Fa sash) - desert kingdom south of Ard Ri

Midach - (Mi dak) – doctor
Mymarida - (My mar i du)(plural - ae (aye)) Fairyfly
wasp - huge flying Fey that paralyses its victim,
wraps it in an egg case and holds it to eat or lay its
eggs in the victim

Ri - (Ree) - King
Rivers
        Banuisk
        Caladen
        Samphir

Sabhdan – (Say dan) – sultan, ruler
Salle - (Sal) - weapons training hall
Seleigh Soren - (Su lay so ren) - carnivorous Demon
compelled by magic to devour flesh and soul
Slieve Geal – (Sleeve Ga el) - Shining Mountain
Smachtmaistir – (Smawk t May stir) master Demon
controller
Steading - large land holding granted by the Lord to a
freeholder
Suibhan - (Su - van) - High King's Mage
Sword of Light - sword created by the first mages,
imbued with their own personality, blades

tempered by Dragon fire. Created to battle beasts
and monsters from other realms

Téigh Trí Thine - The Last Burning – elven ceremony
for the dead
Tiarna Geal - (Tee ar na Ga el) - Lords of Light
Tua Dé – Lords of the Forest

Vanner – small, solidly-built horse of cob
conformation similar to a small Shire. It is often,
but not always, piebald or skewbald
Vardo – colorful wagons owned by traders and used
as traveling homes

About the Author

Natli fell in love with science fiction when she 'borrowed' her father's copy of *Sixth Column* by Robert Heinlein. She was twelve. She was soon reading every science fiction book she could find.

She was always the hero in the stories she wrote for herself. She thought she might be a veterinarian, a chemical engineer, or an astronaut.

She joined the Navy instead, and became a meteorologist and anti-submarine warfare specialist. Natli designs websites, shows Shetland Sheepdogs and writes fantasy and science fiction. She has three girls, four grandsons and one granddaughter. Natli is a native Coloradan and lives in Aurora, Colorado.

She would love to have a Dragon for a friend. She enjoys quilting, target practice, riding, and jumping out of perfectly good airplanes. Next is learning how to sword fight.

(She still has that paperback copy of *Sixth Column*)

Other Titles by Natli VanDerWerken

The Dragon's Children: Red Dragon's Keep
(Book 1 - 2017)

The Dragon's Children: WindRunner
(Book 2 - 2019)

The Dragon's Children: DreamWalker
(Book 3 forthcoming)

The Dragon's Children: Falcon's Spire
(Book 4 forthcoming)

The Dragon's Children: Talisman
(Book 5 forthcoming)

Connect with Natli VanDerWerken

Thanks for reading my books. I enjoy hearing from all of you. Check out my website at
https://www.natlivanderwerken.com
for news about upcoming books, new short fiction and thoughts about writing in general.

You can also find me on Facebook at
facebook.com/Natli VanDerWerken-Author

Email me at natli@natlivanderwerken.com

Reviews are the lifeblood of authors. Tell me what you think about my books. Please leave a review if you like them. Every review is important, both for placement and to help me improve my writing. I read every one of them.

If you know anyone who loves fantasy, tell them about The Dragon's Children and WindRunner.

Find all my books on Amazon or Barnes and Noble.
Ask for them wherever books are sold.

www.ingramcontent.com/pod-product-compliance
Lightning Source LLC
Chambersburg PA
CBHW031131120726
47905CB00006B/1645